Praise for

THE COUNCIL TRILOGY

"Her knowledge of the fantasy genre is evident, as she skillfully weaves fantastical elements with politics, society, and history. The result is a love letter to San Francisco and fantasy—a city where the culture thrives and hides a darker and more mysterious underbelly. . . . Evette Davis's *The Others* showcases her deep passion for story-telling and the enchanting world of the supernatural."

—INDIEREADER

"A rollicking supernatural jaunt through time that leaps out of the famous San Francisco fog and right onto our latest news pages. Davis combines her inside knowledge of Bay Area politics with a gripping tale of vampires and shape-shifters that leaves us never quite looking at the city the same way again."

—DAVID CALLAWAY, former editor-in-chief, *USA Today*

". . . a paranormal romance and thriller for the intelligent reader. It has it all: political issues, social issues, family issues, witches, vam-pires, demons, time-walkers, fairies, werewolves, empaths, romance, violence, danger, and espionage. Davis does a laudable job by weav-ing an intricate storyline around a well-developed, blossoming ro-mance. She ties storylines together and introduces backstories to explain complicated characters. Moreover, the protagonist is ex-tremely likable and easy to relate to. This may have been a paranor-mal book, but I found her story to be motivational. Who hasn't want-ed to turn their back on the world and throw in the towel? When Olivia begins her training sessions to get her life back on track, the book becomes nearly therapeutic."

—REBECCA SKANE, book reviewer at Seacoastonline.com

"Let me begin by first saying, WOW. I loved this book from start to finish. Evette Davis's book truly packs a punch and has plenty to offer, including the supernatural, romance, fantasy, politics, and more. This is a beautifully written book with an exceptionally strong plot."

—A.C. HAURY, Bibliophile Book Reviews

"Davis brings all the quirkiness of San Francisco to life like never before, seamlessly weaving together the modern and mystical. Depicting a secretive society in our midst, comprised of witches and fairies, demons and vampires, *The Others* is a delicious adventure, unconventional romance, and compelling parable for our politically wrought time."

—MIKE TRIGG, author of *Bit Flip* and *Burner*

"Politics, romance, and a compelling protagonist power this series starter. The San Francisco setting enriches the fantasy subject with vivid detail and a charming blend of fact and fantasy—the Bay Area's fog is both spookily atmospheric and a clever element of the worldbuilding. This book is ideal for readers with modern values rooted in anti-fascism. Richly engaging characters and a deft blend of the magical and deeply human populate this enthralling world."

—EDITOR'S PICK, *BOOKLIFE, PUBLISHER'S WEEKLY*

THE GIFT

THE
GIFT

BOOK TWO
IN
THE COUNCIL TRILOGY

By

EVETTE DAVIS

Published 2025
Printed in the United States of America
Print ISBN: 978-1-68463-296-1
E-ISBN: 978-1-68463-297-8
Library of Congress Control Number: 2024922326

For information, address:
She Writes Press
1569 Solano Ave #546
Berkeley, CA 94707

Interior design by Stacey Aaronson

She Writes Press is a division of SparkPoint Studio, LLC.

To Robin, my sister and best friend.
I can't wait for our next adventure.

Madame Sosostris, famous clairvoyante,
Had a bad cold, nevertheless
Is known to be the wisest woman in Europe,
With a wicked pack of cards. Here, said she,
Is your card, the drowned Phoenician Sailor,
(Those are pearls that were his eyes. Look!)
Here is Belladonna, the Lady of the Rocks,
The lady of situations.
Here is the man with three staves, and here the Wheel,
And here is the one-eyed merchant, and this card,
Which is blank, is something he carries on his back,
Which I am forbidden to see. I do not find
The Hanged Man. Fear death by water.
I see crowds of people, walking round in a ring.
Thank you. If you see dear Mrs. Equitone,
Tell her I bring the horoscope myself:
One must be so careful these days.

—*The Waste Land*, T. S. Eliot

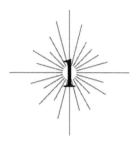

1

THE FORTUNE-TELLER LIT A STICK OF INCENSE AND PLACED it in a small holder before she spoke, her long, creased fingers steady and sure as she turned the tarot cards one by one.

"You have an enemy," she said, not a trace of surprise in her voice. "Death. The Tower. Five of Swords. Nine of Wands. Queen of Swords . . . shall I draw a sixth card for emphasis?"

"*Da*," I said, nodding. It was the same price regardless. Ten euros, or what amounted to about ten dollars for a basic reading.

I was passing time on a sunny January afternoon in Budva, a medieval city perched on the coast of Montenegro. Everything about this tiny country near the border of Croatia pulsed with mysticism. I'd never had my tarot cards read before, but it seemed perfectly normal amid Budva's incense-filled Orthodox churches and colorful, crowded streets. I'd been exploring the ancient city when I'd come upon the woman, her small table with its bright floral cloth and two chairs set up adjacent to a church built in the ninth century.

Having recently recovered the empathic skills that were my birthright, I could tell she believed what she was telling me. Whether the cards could really predict the future was an entirely different story.

"Four of Swords, reversed," she said, turning over the sixth and final card and placing it upside down in front of me. It showed a woman lying on some kind of pedestal, three swords dangling above her head, one sword lying flat beneath her. The fortune-teller, whose long black hair, streaked with gray, was pulled tightly into a braid, eyed me suspiciously.

As I gazed back, I felt a shock of recognition pierce my chest. How had I not recognized her? We'd met before but in San Francisco. She'd performed a spell on me to embed a map of magic locations on my arm. Nadia was her name, and she'd been introduced to me by my friend and mentor, Elsa. After everything that had happened, it felt like a lifetime ago.

Now, as then, her expression was stern. She clearly had little interest in talking about old times.

"The energy around you is strong. Too strong," she said. "You should have told me of all your powers, *chuvihani.*"

I looked up, startled to hear the word. Josef, the brooding vampire brother of my lover, William, occasionally used the term to describe the types of supernatural beings that held sway in Eastern Europe, where he was born. If I'd understood him correctly, the word meant "witch" or "wise one" in Romani.

Was it possible she knew that I wasn't exactly human?

"I'm not sure what you mean," I said, drawing another skeptical look.

"Tell me, *chuvihani*, why didn't you know? You should have sensed it."

A flash of anger quickened my pulse and pushed me to be honest, regardless of the risk. "I was lied to," I said, instinctively turning my head to scan the area before continuing. "Nobody told me until just recently that my father was a powerful witch."

"Things are changing," she said, clearly unruffled by my response. "The cards say as much. See here: Death. It usually means a break with your old life—leaving your past behind. But look, for your present, the Tower. It tells me you have suffered a great shock or surprise."

"Yes," I said, pushing down the anger that again surged through me. "To learn I had a father? That was a surprise indeed." And the reason I'd come to Montenegro.

I paused, feeling that I shouldn't say more. My father, Gabriel Laurent, came from a long line of ancient and powerful witches. He was also the head of the Council, a shadowy organization that plays a major role in the fate of humans and Others. Regardless of my grievances, I'd sworn to keep the Council's existence a secret.

"*Chuvihani*, you must assume your responsibilities," Nadia implored. "A witch is wise. She protects her village. She's the keeper of the seasons and the spirits."

Wise? Hardly. I'd been born with supernatural empathic skills, the ability to read the emotions and intentions of others. But I'd spent most of my life shunning those talents.

"A witch must embrace her strength," she continued. "She reads the minds of the living and the dead and leads her people to their destiny."

"I think you've got the wrong *chuvihani*," I said, the sarcasm slipping out against my will. I hardly qualified as a clear-sighted leader. I'd been blindsided, kept in the dark, and manipulated by the people I loved. My mother, through omission, had lied to me my whole life, never uttering a word about my paternity. My father had recruited me for the Council but hadn't had the courage to tell me the truth about who he was—until my mother spilled the beans.

"I understand you've struggled," Nadia said, finally bestowing a bit of empathy. "But that time is over." She looked into my eyes. "The cards tell the story."

"Go on," I said, pointing at the third card in the line of six.

"Five of Swords," she said, showing me the card.

It depicted a young man holding a sword in his hand and looking off into the distance. Two more swords were lashed across his back, and another two were lodged in the ground in front of him.

"You have an enemy, one who is very dangerous. A saboteur. He may be more than you can handle."

※

She placed her hand on the card and closed her eyes. "You are taking on great evil," she murmured.

I didn't need the fortune-teller to explain. I knew exactly what "great evil" she was referring to: Nikola Pajovic, a thousand-year-old vampire. The world's financial elite knew him as a wealthy Serbian hotelier and casino owner, but I was certain he was something else: a murderer who'd recently orchestrated the bombing of my colleagues after our holiday party at the Academy of Sciences in Golden Gate Park, in San Francisco, killing my colleague Aidan Burke in the process. And it just so happened that I'd pushed Aidan to investigate possible ties between Nikola and a syndicate of former Balkan war criminals in the days before the attack. Unable to stay and grieve for Aidan, I'd had to flee to Paris to avoid the inevitable police investigation—and any further entanglements with Nikola.

"Go on," I said. "I was momentarily distracted. What do these cards mean?"

"The Queen of Swords," she said, pointing at a card with an image of a woman standing alone on a bluff, holding a sword in her hands. "You are entering a time when you will have to stand up for yourself, perhaps alone."

I nodded. I certainly *felt* alone. After the encounter with my mother in Paris, where she'd revealed that Gabriel Laurent was my father, my trust in her had been destroyed. Thankfully, William had helped me pick up the pieces and escape to Montenegro to think. His love was one of the few things that I knew I could trust. Late at night, when I tried to picture my future, it was the feel of his body next to mine that kept me from falling into despair. No matter what happened, we would be together—sometimes I imagined we might even marry—and we would find a way to get on with our lives.

Once again, the card reader's words pulled me back to the moment: "Beware, though, because the card is not certain. It could also mean that soon you will be dealing with a solitary female who has known great sadness—a widow, perhaps."

Elsa. The raven-haired time-walker and spirit guide who'd helped me access my supernatural abilities. She'd helped save my life when Stoner Halbert, a conservative political consultant and my professional nemesis, had dabbled in black magic and summoned a demon whose dark powers wreaked havoc on my once-peaceful life in San Francisco. It was Elsa who awakened my sixth sense and trained me to fight supernatural evil before the demon could destroy me. Then, after the car bombing, it had been my turn to see her life fall apart. She'd been Aidan's lover, and his death had undone her. After the explosion, she disappeared. I suspected she had jumped back in time to somewhere none of us could find her.

"And this card?" I asked.

"Yes, the Four of Swords reversed. Normally it means a time for rest," she said. "But for you, upside-down like this, it means the opposite. It means no rest. You must start work immediately. It means troubles are coming to you."

I would have laughed aloud, but I didn't want to offend her. Trouble coming? I tried to imagine what that might be. Before I'd arrived in Montenegro, I'd encountered a criminal gang of Others in San Francisco, and their supernatural powers had nearly blinded me. Then there was the car bombing. My own injuries after the blast had been serious enough that William had reluctantly shared his vampire blood to heal me. A risky gesture. All that was left to bind our lives together, at least according to my supernatural friends, would be for him to drink my blood.

"Troubles are coming," I said, repeating her phrase like an idiot.

"Well, I guess I had better get ready, then." I wasn't exactly sure how to close our transaction. Saying thank you seemed like a bit of a non sequitur.

"What will you do?" she asked, scrutinizing me as she folded my dollars and stuffed them into a small cloth change purse in her lap.

"Go home," I said, not knowing what else to say. For the moment, "home" was not my cozy 1930s house in San Francisco, but a restored fifteenth-century stone cottage on an island fortress in the Adriatic. In the summer, wealthy travelers paid a handsome sum to stay in the place we'd selected. But in late December, the place had not been difficult to book. I was traveling with William and his brother, Josef: two ancient and powerful vampires who'd lived through wars and had trained me to fight. We had Josef to thank for finding our small home in Sveti Stefan, the fortress-turned-luxury resort just slightly south of Budva.

Before becoming a vampire during World War II, Josef had lived in what was then Czechoslovakia and had traveled across Eastern and Central Europe; the cottage in Sveti Stefan had lodged in his memory as a welcome place to retreat. It turned out to be the perfect hideaway for the three of us. We were biding our time, hiding out, avoiding my family and Nikola, unsure of who to trust or how to proceed. Now though, according to Nadia, that was all about to change.

"You cannot hide from what is coming," she said, her eyes dark with foreboding.

"I need to think," I said as I gathered up my things. I didn't say it out loud, but my first impulse was to board a plane for somewhere else. Turn and run. It was becoming my habit, for better or for worse. If Elsa were here, she'd no doubt scold me for the thought. She wouldn't have wanted me to turn my back on my parents like I had in Paris. And she'd expect me to rise to the occasion now. After all, she'd picked me up off the floor where Stoner Halbert's demon had laid me out, then trained me to use my instincts and fight.

I missed her.

"You don't have much time," Nadia said. "Your fate will outrun you, if you're not careful."

"What do you suggest?"

"Assemble your allies," she said, rummaging around in a bag next to the leg of her chair. "You need to bring your people to your side and prepare."

"You make it sound like war," I replied.

"Perhaps not war, but a battle nonetheless," she said. "Now go. You'll be late if you don't leave now."

"Late for what?" I asked. I used my empathic skills to probe her feelings and sensed her certainty growing stronger as if she were being influenced by an outside force. I looked up, but there was no one else in the square.

"Just go, *chuvihani*. It's time to accept your destiny."

AFTER LEAVING NADIA, I FOUND MY DRIVER SITTING IN HIS USUAL place, at a table in a café in the main town square, a single espresso and his phone in front of him. He nodded as I approached and rose from the table to take me home.

I settled into the backseat, trying not to obsess about how Nadia had sensed all of my abilities. Everyone seemed to know more about my powers than I did. At least now I understood that beyond the empathy I'd had since I was a child, I was slowly learning to communicate telepathically. My sixth sense applied to those alive and *undead*, but that was a fact I didn't share with many people. I also seemed to have the ability to disappear—to become invisible—in times of danger. But I didn't understand how that skill worked at all. Since fleeing Paris, I'd remained just as much in the dark about my powers, including about whether I might have other skills—and this was a condition that felt perfectly agreeable.

"Any other stops?" the driver asked.

"No, thank you," I said. "Straight home."

I wanted to laugh as I said it because few routes in this part of the world were straight. Although the travel time from Budva to Sveti Stefan was marked in travel guides as ten minutes, that was merely an estimate, a best-case scenario: if there was no traffic, or road construction, or car accidents—if no truck had overturned its contents. On a couple of trips, we'd been stopped by a policeman stepping out of the brush with a small handheld stop sign. His job was apparently to conduct spur-of-the-moment checks on the licenses and registration of the taxis that traveled up and down the coast. I saw a small amount of bills pushed through the window to settle the matter and realized that the checkpoint had caused cars to queue in both directions for miles. This short trip had once taken us more than ninety minutes. Josef, familiar with these complications, had hired this local man to escort me around town.

As I glanced outside, I noticed a massive fog bank moving across the bay toward us. In all the time we'd been staying in the area, I'd seen little more than a morning mist on the water, so this set off alarm bells.

"Is there usually fog this time of year?" I asked my driver, who, while polite, was not much of a conversationalist.

"*Ne*," he said, using the local word for no. "Only when the Others come."

At first, I thought I'd misheard him.

"Who?"

"The Others," he repeated. "You know—magic."

I did know, but I wasn't sure how he did. "How can you be sure?" I asked.

"We are an ancient civilization," he said. "We have lived with many types of people. Romans, Turks—Others."

I thought that over for a minute. Although William and Josef, as vampires, never slept, they preferred to stay inside the thick stone walls of our guesthouse until dusk. In the evening, we roamed the region together. We often availed ourselves of the massive car ferries crossing the Bay of Kotor to visit Dubrovnik, in Croatia, for a few hours. The ancient city, founded sometime in the seventh century, lay inside an enormous stone wall. The brothers had shown me how to climb the back stairs and alleyways to reach the top of the wall. Leaning over the massive stone ramparts, we'd gotten a glimpse of what it

must have been like to gaze out to sea a thousand years ago, searching for invaders.

It had also given me the shivers. The mysticism in this part of
the world ran deep. Even when we spent the darkening hours just
sitting on our deck, admiring the glint of the brilliant blue-green
waters of the Adriatic, it was impossible to ignore the sense of ancient
magic that pervaded the region—especially with two magnetic
vampires at my side.

"You believe in magic, then?" I asked.

"Of course," he replied. "I'd be foolish not to."

Foolish indeed. The great gray miasma caught up with us, en-
gulfing the peninsula. As we crossed into the wet, clammy mess, I felt
a presence, creeping ever closer. So, there was little surprise on my
part when I spied my father standing in the doorway of the cottage as
the car pulled into the driveway. I could hear his voice inside my
head the moment I met his eyes.

"Your mother," he said. "Your mother . . . she's dead."

I let out a cry like a wounded animal and doubled over in my
seat. When my lunch from the afternoon threatened to return, I
opened the car door, thinking I'd be ill. I hadn't spoken to my mother
for weeks, but I always assumed we would reconcile. My last words to
her had been far from *I love you*. I leaned on the door for support.

When I glanced up, Gabriel and the brothers were approaching.

I sent a message back to my father, silently asking. "How?"

"All in good time, daughter," he replied privately.

I must have stayed in the car a minute too long. The driver
turned to face me.

"I should have known you were one of them," he said, scrutinizing
my features. "You heard him speak before he opened his mouth."

"That's impossible," I replied. So much for being inconspicuous.

I must have looked alarmed because he spoke again, this time in
a reassuring voice. "Don't worry." Then he pulled up his sleeve to

reveal a tattoo that looked suspiciously like a fountain in San Francisco. The Guardian, we called it. The image, an enormous cat fighting off a serpent held between his mighty paws, is unforgettable. It's also a portal, a way to move through time and space.

"The Guardian?" I asked.

"*Da, da,*" the man said, nodding furiously.

I stepped out of the car, and the driver also emerged to greet all three men. William handed him a few euros. "*Hvala,*" he said, thanking him.

Our banter seemed like wasted time once I turned towards Gabriel and read the grief etched across his face. I felt his pain deep inside, a mirror of my own suffering. All these weeks, I'd not felt a shred of guilt for walking away from my mother in Paris before she could explain herself. Time seemed infinite, long enough for me to stew and then devise a plan for explanations and reconciliation. The shame of what I now recognized as reckless impulsiveness burned deep in my chest.

"Let's go inside," I said, my voice sounding strained even to my own ears. "I need to know what happened."

Maybe it was the weight of the news, but as we walked into our little cottage, our accommodations began to feel too small. I shook off a shudder as we took our seats in the living room. Once we were settled, Gabriel began to speak.

"Your mother's body was found by the French police yesterday," he said. "They told me it was suicide, that she jumped out of the window of her hotel. But there is no note. They would like you to come and identify the body."

"I can't believe she killed herself," I said.

"I don't know what to believe, either," Gabriel said. "We continued to see each other after you left. She was *très désolé*—very sorry—for what she did, for causing a scene and surprising you. She had the best intentions. She truly thought you and I were about to become lovers. She was desperate to stop us."

For a moment, I allowed myself to imagine how things must have looked to my mother: the idea of my father unknowingly wooing me to be his paramour must have horrified her. No wonder, I understood now, that she'd been so distraught that night at the bar.

"Go on," I said.

"Of course, I had my own part in this, hiding my identity as your father," he continued. "We both felt responsible for hurting our child."

Tears welled up in my eyes. *I have parents,* I thought. *A mother and a father. Or at least I did.*

"Do you believe she killed herself?" William asked, his tone grave.

"*Je ne pense pas,*" Gabriel replied. "I don't think so, but then there are moments when I am not *certain.* India was distraught about your disappearance," he said to me, "but she held out hope that you would be reunited. Do I think she would jump out the window of her suite at the Ritz? It seems"—he paused, and then in French—"*impossible.*"

Josef, who'd been silent until now, spoke up. "Gabriel," he said. "Do you happen to know if Nikola was in Paris recently?"

Gabriel nodded. "Yes, he is there. Well, he was. I met with him," he said. "Why do you ask?"

"As part of your investigation?" Josef asked.

Gabriel frowned. "Unfortunately, no. Nikola is positioned to be the next deputy director of the Council. You may recall that the leadership of the Council rotates every five years. Central and Eastern Europe are next in line."

"After the car bombing?" I said, horrified at the direction this conversation was heading.

"There's no proof he did it," Gabriel said gently. "Since you left Paris, our investigation has stalled. Nothing has surfaced that would discredit him. Without hard evidence, we have no grounds to cancel the transition. Normally it would have been Aidan handling this type of discussion for the Council, but since his death . . . well, it falls to me."

"The transition doesn't happen until the fall. Why do you have to meet now?" I asked.

"It's up to the incoming director to decide how much time is needed for the change of administration. Some directors, such as myself, make few changes in operations," he said. "Other directors replace staff, shuffle personnel, even remodel offices. It is not unusual to begin discussions early. Nikola wants to start things as early as possible, in no small part, I'm sure, to annoy me."

"So, Nikola was in Paris in the last few days," Josef said, nudging the conversation back on topic.

It took Gabriel a few seconds, but then he understood. "You think he killed India?"

"I do," Josef replied. "Her death flushes us out of hiding and it directly attacks Olivia, whom he views as a threat to his criminal empire. It also keeps you from continuing your investigation into his misdeeds."

"Does Nikola know she's your daughter?" William asked.

"He might, although I haven't told him," Gabriel said. "He did ask where Olivia was. I told him she had requested a leave of absence after Aidan died. I don't mind telling you, our first meeting was awkward." He threw his hand in the air. "I met with the man I think killed my dearest friend and frittered away time discussing routine logistics. But as I already mentioned, without proof, I cannot stop the transition."

"We're going to get proof," I replied, rising from my chair abruptly. "We need to pack. I want to be in Paris as soon as possible. I take it you didn't arrive by plane," I said, addressing my father, who seemed to be able to conjure the weather on command and transport himself through thin air.

"*Non,*" he replied. "I will explain everything, at some point."

"I've heard that before," I replied, but my heart wasn't up for a fight. He was my father—and the only family I had left.

"The airport is in Podgorica," William said, coming to take my hand. "It's five o'clock, and we're about forty miles away. I'll check if there is a flight out tonight."

The last flight to Paris from Montenegro had already departed, and we had to wait until the next morning to travel. Gabriel called the police precinct in Paris and informed them that as next of kin, I'd arrive the next day to identify my mother's body.

I decided to pack, craving something mundane to focus on. But even that proved difficult when I came across a pair of leather gloves that my mother had given me. I'd almost forgotten they'd once belonged to her. Now, tears spilled down my cheeks as I held them, remembering her. Suddenly I wished for a time machine, a way to go back and tell my mother I loved her. Instead, I was left with the real possibility she'd died not knowing.

I could not process the enormity of the situation: the last member of my immediate family was dead. I had Gabriel, of course, but I'd been raised without a father. All I'd had was my mother. And despite her drinking and mental health issues, she'd raised me as best she could. In her own way, she'd loved me. She'd brought me to Europe—more importantly, to France. My whole being was tied to her and to our experiences together.

Yet as I stuffed my belongings into my luggage, I realized that even absent, Gabriel had been a part of my life too. My mother's focus on all things French took on added meaning now. She'd clearly decided that she would honor Gabriel's heritage and make it a part of my upbringing, even as she hid the fact that I had a father. She'd created a link between the two of us without either knowing the other existed. My heart sank, but I couldn't stop to grieve for her or my misdeeds. Trouble was coming.

THE FIRST FLIGHT OUT WAS AT 6:00 A.M., WHICH WAS FINE FOR all of us. Sleep seemed only the remotest of possibilities to me, and as vampires, William and Josef never needed to sleep at all. We sat stone-faced on the plane, too wrapped up in the task ahead to speak. In Paris, the National Police dealt with unusual deaths. If my mother had simply died in her sleep, a doctor could have signed the death certificate and the mayor of Paris would have issued a burial permit. But my mother had not died in her sleep, and so we were on our way to a very different kind of appointment.

Once our plane arrived at Charles de Gaulle, we charted a course straight to the police station in the First Arrondissement, near the Ritz Hotel, where my mother had been staying as a long-term guest. As our private car sped toward the city, I turned to William and took his hand to soothe myself.

"My mother came here to find happiness," I said, thinking of her success as a landscape artist, her paintings sought after by a small but persistent client base. "She loved living in Paris, putting on exhibitions at the galleries. Instead, the city became a death trap."

"Shhh, Olivia," William said softly. "Don't think that way. Your mother couldn't have known what was coming. Until that last moment, she *was* living her dream. Try to remember that."

I shook my head. "Paris may be the City of Light, but I'm not sure I'll ever be able to feel comfortable here again."

"Give it time, Olivia," William said. "Maybe we could revisit our plans to be married. Honor your mother with our vows."

"No." I spat the word, surprising myself. "I don't see a place in my life for happy memories, at least not for a while."

"That's too bad," William said, a chill in his voice.

I lapsed into silence again. My sense of time was distorted, blocked by the monolithic fact that my mother was dead. There was no getting around it, no going over it, and no passing through it. I felt myself present only in alternating moments, like a trauma patient coming in and out of consciousness. Time whirred by, though, and suddenly we were parked at the curb of the station. William exited the car, waving off our driver to open the door himself. I remained inside, staring at him through the window as he stood on the side-walk. He met my gaze, standing motionless, understanding too well that I had no wish to take the next few steps into the building.

No child could imagine being asked to complete the task I was charged with; most parents spend their entire lives hoping to avoid such a fate. Yet here I was. One more sudden death, another loved one ripped from the world too early. Was I to blame? I heard the voice of the tarot card reader once more: *You have an enemy, one who is very dangerous. . . . He may be more than you can handle.*

As we walked inside the majestic sixteenth-century stone building and waited in line, I wondered how we might phrase things. Gabriel and I hadn't discussed what we would tell the police, but it seemed certain we would not be sharing our theory that a one-thousand-year-old vampire had killed my mother. My primary goal was to bring my mother home, so to speak, and scatter her ashes across her beloved farm in Bolinas, where she'd lived and painted. That meant confirming her death as a suicide with the police.

Finally, it was our turn, and Gabriel approached to speak with the officer. William, Josef, and I remained a few steps behind.

"*Comment vous appelez-vous?*" the officer asked.

Gabriel gave his name but explained that he was here to identify a body under the name of India Shepherd, the mother of his child. And then he pointed at me. "*C'est ma fille,*" he said, telling them I was his daughter. Listening to Gabriel acknowledge me as his child nearly buckled me at the knees. I'd gained a father even as I'd lost a mother. But there was little time to reflect. In short order, we were led down a long hallway to a room with a metal door. The officer knocked once, and the door opened, held by an older woman I presumed was a coroner or some kind of technician.

"This is the deceased's daughter," the officer said in French.

The woman regarded me with a look of such profound pity that I gasped involuntarily. William grasped my hand and held tight. Josef, assuming his regular place as of late, came to stand on my other side, his hand resting upon my arm. My father was inside my head.

"Olivia, my daughter, my dearest. This is my fault. I will spend my lifetime trying to make it up to you."

I replied silently, gazing at my mother; her head was turned to one side to face me on the gurney. "No, *Papa*," I replied. "The fault lies with Nikola."

"Yes, that's her," I said, my voice cracking slightly as I spoke. "But why is her head turned to the side?"

The technician hesitated but then replied in perfect English. "When she jumped and fell to the pavement, she landed on the other side of her face. It is heavily damaged."

Another gasp, and little air left in my lungs. Yet I wanted to scream aloud. *My mother didn't jump. She was murdered!*

I looked at her body lying on the gurney and resolved to re-member this day for as long as I lived. A reprisal was in store for Nikola. Only then would I erase the image of my mother's broken body from my mind. For the moment, however, there was nothing I could say. I let the technician think my grief had rendered me mute.

In the end, when I did give a brief statement, I found it wasn't as difficult to lie as I'd expected. Explanations rolled right off my tongue. Yes, I told the officer, my mother, while alive, had been an eccentric artist, an unpredictable person prone to bouts of alcohol and drug use. He'd nodded gravely.

A few phone calls by the police to local art dealers in Paris had backed up these facts. Her death made sense on paper. I assumed Nikola must have known as much. How easy it had been for him to orchestrate her death and make it look like suicide.

Gabriel played the overprotective father, asking the officers to spare me additional questions once I'd completed my main statement. The police never once questioned his authority, or his role in helping close out this sorry chapter of my mother's life. We were at the station for little more than an hour, and we left with the proper permits to have my mother's body cremated so we could take her ashes back to San Francisco. It had taken no more time to complete these tasks than it would to hold a marriage ceremony at City Hall.

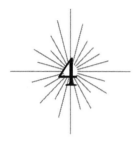

ACCORDING TO THE POLICE, IT WOULD TAKE A FEW DAYS FOR my mother to be cremated. In the meantime, we would wait in Paris. As much as I wanted to speak with my father, to spend time with him, I asked him to return to California ahead of us to help with arrangements to honor my mother and deal with her estate.

With time on my hands, I also began to plan. There were calls to make to my mother's friends and colleagues. A few relatives on my grandfather's side still ran the family's dairy farms in Marin County. With great difficulty, I delivered the news that my mother had passed away in Paris, her favorite of cities, the place where she felt most at home.

Because she was an artist of some note, it seemed unfair to let her passing go unnoticed, so I drafted a press release highlighting her accomplishments and her death for the arts and culture press. I'd closed my own business, Olivia Shepherd Consulting, a few days after leaving Paris, and I'd helped my few remaining employees find jobs elsewhere. So, it was oddly comforting to dust off my professional skills as a communications consultant to ensure that my mother would be remembered properly for her talents.

I also placed a call to Jason Rawley, India's representative in San Francisco and proprietor of the Rawley Gallery, which had been a fixture in the city for decades.

"Have you drafted a press release?" was his first question, throwing me off-balance.

"Yes," I said. "Can you send it out for us?"

"Of course," he replied. "I apologize if I sound too businesslike, but we want to try to manage the stories around your mother's death and maintain the value of her art."

Agreeing on a strategy, we made plans to meet once I returned to San Francisco. I also asked him to contact the gallery in Paris where her works were currently being exhibited, to help with arrangements to close the exhibit down.

"Leave it to me," he said. "I will manage everything. Your mother has told me so much about you. I am only sorry to be meeting you for the first time under such tragic circumstances."

"Thank you, Mr. Rawley," I replied. His voice was strangely comforting. "I'll be in touch when I return."

"Mr. Rawley was my father," he said quickly. "I'm Jason."

"I appreciate your time, Jason," I said.

"I'm sorry for your loss," he replied. "Your mother was an extraordinary woman. She was one of my favorite clients, despite her inexplicable indifference to baseball."

I found myself laughing in spite of my grief. "You *did* know her well," I said. "I'm afraid she left rooting for the Giants to my grandfather and me."

"Good to know," he replied. "In the meantime, let me take care of things for you. I'll make sure your mother's legacy is protected."

I found myself smiling as I hung up the phone. I turned to find William standing in the corner of our bedroom watching me. He and Josef both had been silently monitoring my behavior since we'd left the morgue. William's scrutiny made me feel foolish for bantering with Jason, then a surge of irritation washed over me. William couldn't possibly understand, but for a moment, on the phone, talking with Jason had made me feel *normal*, maybe even *human*. I returned

William's look with a wary one of my own. I wanted William's love and support, but as usual they seemed to come with pain and complications. And things were only going to get worse because I was about to plot my next move. With preparations for my mother's service underway and her agent managing the media, it was time to focus on Nikola, to uncover his secrets, and, with any luck, to make him pay.

Gazing down at my hands, I cleared my throat. "I want to visit Nikola and see what the people around him are thinking and feeling," I said. "Is there a bar or café he frequents? He must have an entourage. Men like him always do."

William snorted. "I told Josef it wouldn't be long before you were ready to re-enter the world."

"I need to do something besides sitting around the apartment sulking," I replied. "I'll always regret the way I left things with my mother, but I can't go back in time and change it. For now, the best way for me to make amends is to find Nikola and make him pay."

"Or you could try fencing," remarked Josef, as he strolled into our bedroom. Vampires have very sharp hearing, so I wasn't surprised he'd overheard and decided to join our conversation. "It's been several days since we've sparred," Josef said. "You're going to get soft if you don't train."

I stared him down. "I'll train if you tell me where Nikola is," I said, certain he knew exactly where to find him.

Josef paused, a look in his eyes telling me he was contemplating his reply. "Nikola is well-known for a party he hosts when he's in Paris. It's called Bal des Vampires, the Vampire's Ball," Josef said. "It's a joke, of course, because it's not really a ball, and no one knows he is a vampire. They think of him as a wealthy developer with a taste for wild bacchanals. He hosts it at Club Rasputin near the Champs-Élysées. It attracts fashion models, artists, actors—people who like to live in the fast lane."

"Perfect," I replied. "How do we get an invitation?"

"We don't," Josef said. "It's too dangerous."

"I wasn't asking permission," I said. "It's not up to you. We're going. As you are fond of reminding me, I'm heir to the powerful Laurent family. Gabriel will never uncover Nikola's plans. He's too wrapped up in the bureaucracy of the Council to be effective. We have to act."

William regarded Josef with a knowing smile, as if he'd warned his brother ahead of time this would happen. "We will discuss the ground rules later," William said, still smiling. "You will need a dress. The party is formal. Vampire couture, to be specific."

"Shopping?" I said. "Are you joining me?"

"No, I have a few errands of my own. I will meet you here," he said, before kissing me on the lips and slipping several large de-nomination euro notes into my hands. I tucked them into my wallet, having already decided to use my own money. I appreciated his gesture, but I wasn't ready to live off his resources—not yet, anyway. Maybe if a judge pronounced us husband and wife, I'd feel better about spending his money.

It took a few hours and several visits to Paris's better *fripperies*—what we call consignment or secondhand stores—but there, finally, in the window of a small shop near the Jardin du Palais-Royal, the per-fect outfit appeared. Bidding the lone sales clerk a *bon après-midi*, I asked to try on the *robe*. She was more than happy to oblige, and I soon found myself gazing in the mirror approvingly. The dress, a deep crimson, was sleeveless on one side. The right side of the gown featured a high collar that cloaked my throat in the rich silk material and then cascaded into one sleeve ending at my wrist. I gazed at my left side, at my shoulder and the portion of my neck that would be left bare, admiring how the color gave my skin a pale glow.

"*Bon*," I said to the saleswoman, who'd been standing quietly in the corner.

"*C'est très elegant,*" she said. "You'll be the belle of the ball."

I laughed. "Yes, but barefoot, if we don't find suitable shoes."

"*Oui, bien sûr!*" she replied, slipping back into French. She disappeared into the far corner of the boutique and reappeared minutes later with a pair of scarlet heels.

It was near sunset when I slipped the key into the lock of our apartment near the Canal Saint-Martin, my prize slung over my shoulder in a garment bag. Past the soaring entry hall, I strolled through the sitting room, its grand windows shrouded in heavy, expensive drapery. I was still somewhat awed by the place. William's father had purchased the apartment in 1930, and since his death during World War II, William had maintained the apartment beautifully. It was my home now too.

I found William and Josef, as usual, outside on the terrace—vampires are immune to winter's bite—a bottle of Jack Daniel's, their usual poison, on the table beside them.

"*Bonsoir,*" I said. "You'll be pleased to know I've returned victorious."

"Excellent," William replied playfully. "But don't show us. We want to be surprised."

"OK," I said. "I'm famished. I'll be back in a minute."

Although I lived with vampires, I knew fresh produce, meats, and cheeses would be awaiting me in the kitchen. Thanks to William, the concierge had replenished our supplies before we arrived. This was his usual way. It helped keep his identity a secret and happily ensured I wouldn't go hungry, though I spent my days with two men who never thought about food.

I rejoined them on the terrace, a small salad of Roquefort and beets in my hands along with a glass of rosé. For some, rosé is strictly a summer wine, but for my palate it suits all year long. William allowed me a few bites of my dinner before he spoke.

"We need to establish a few ground rules," he said. "Josef and I are taking you to this ball with the understanding that you will not confront Nikola."

"Why not?" I asked. "What can he do to me that he hasn't already done?"

"A great deal, I assure you," Josef said. "We'll make him pay for his treachery, but you must be patient."

"And if it had been your mother lying on the slab in the city morgue?" I asked. "Would you feel patient?"

"Don't be so human," Josef snapped. "It bores me. He's expecting you, Olivia. He knows you want revenge. He's counting on it."

"So, how are we planning on getting in?" I asked, ignoring Josef's remarks.

"We walk in," William said. "Nikola cannot refuse real vampires entry. That is the rule."

"And me?"

"Josef is right," William said. "We're certain Nikola is expecting you to appear."

"Why?" I asked.

"Because you're predictable," Josef spat out.

"Enough, Josef," William said.

"So if it were you, you wouldn't go to the ball?"

"No," Josef said. "I would stay away and let him wonder. Then, when he least expected it, I would strike."

"And would you kill him?" I asked. "For what he's done?"

Josef's face grew serious. "As a vampire, I am forbidden to kill one of my own," he said. "But yes, he deserves to die."

"Is that true?" I asked, turning to face William.

"I am afraid so," he said.

"Can you at least help?"

Two shrugs met my question.

"It will depend on the circumstances," Josef said.

I jumped up from my chair. "First, you tell me that I'll have my revenge, then you say you can't help me?" I asked, my indignation growing.

"Olivia, we are not your only allies in this," William replied. "You have other weapons at your disposal."

"Besides," Josef remarked before I could respond. "Our job is to keep you alive, and that, madame, is a full-time occupation."

"Oh, I promise your work has only begun," I said, feeling aggrieved.

"*Calme-toi, ma chérie,*" William said as he came to stand at my side. His hands massaged my arms as he spoke. "Do not chase death, Olivia. He is only too happy to slow down and oblige."

My anger peaked and then collapsed into sadness. "I'm not chasing death," I said, taking William's hand in mine. "He's following me."

William led me away from the terrace and ran a bath for us. I slumped miserably against the marble sink, burying my face in my hands while he lit the chamber's candles. When their flames illuminated the room, he came to me.

"Olivia," he said, putting his forehead against mine. "Let me in."

I pulled back a bit and met his gaze, feeling my pulse quicken as I sensed his deep desire for me. I slid my hands beneath his shirt and pulled him closer, my palms flat against the cool muscle of his lower back. As my fingers climbed his spine, I thought about the large angel tattoo on his back. William was my angel, always nearby to pull me out of my despair.

As usual, our attraction for one another quickly overshadowed any other emotions. His gaze began to smolder as he moved back, enough to lift my shirt over my head and tug down my bra straps. Within moments, we were both undressed, exposed, our bodies pressed together. Urgency overtook us. He lifted me to the counter and thrust into me as he gently nipped at the skin around my collarbone with his teeth. My head tilted back, a scream of pleasure upon my lips before I remembered Josef's sharp hearing and thought better of it.

Afterward, we slid into the bath, and he washed my limbs and gently rubbed my neck and shoulders in the golden glow. I emerged feeling better, languid and relaxed.

But by the time I'd toweled off, my mind was back to Nikola's *soirée*.

"You're not going to try to persuade me not to go, are you?" I asked.

"You should know me better than that by now," he said. "Now let me help you dress."

Wrapped in robes, we walked into the bedroom, where William approached the eighteenth-century chest of drawers that held his clothing. "I thought you might need a few things for this evening," he said, pulling out a small package of tissue paper wrapped in a pink bow.

He handed the gift to me. I gently pulled off the ribbon and opened the paper. I raised one eyebrow as I lifted the lingerie up to admire it. He was full of surprises.

"Did you know my dress was red?" I asked, fingering the bra, panties, and garters.

"No," he said, a husky tone to his voice. "I just liked the way you looked when I imagined you wearing this. Besides, you will need these to attend one of Nikola's parties."

"Why?" I asked.

"You will see," he replied.

"That's hardly an answer," I said, worried about what he was hiding.

"You volunteered for this assignment, darlin'," he replied. "Some of the details will have to remain a mystery until we get there. For your own good."

"You sound like my father," I replied, a bit more sharply than I would have liked.

William frowned. "Hardly," he said. "You begged us to take you to this ball, despite the dangers. I agreed."

"And I appreciate it," I said. "I'll show you just how much sometime soon."

The stormy moment over, William helped me put on my lingerie, and then my dress. The air grew sultry, and for a moment I thought we would be delayed, but then I recalled my mission and briskly stepped away from him to grab my new heels from the shopping bag.

"You mustn't leave my side tonight, Olivia," he said, the two of us standing in front of a mirror at the dressing table. "The other vampires in the room will be ravenous when they see you." He continued, "I have a few other gifts—stay here for a moment." He left the room briefly, returning with three black velvet boxes in his hands. "May I?" he asked, indicating the first box.

I nodded, excitedly. William liked buying me jewelry. On our first date, he purchased a necklace for me at almost the same moment I was trying it on. He also gave me a set of bejeweled copper betrothal bands I now wore every day.

William opened the velvet case and pulled out a choker made of multiple strands of black glass beads. Old and exotic, it seemed like something a czarina would have worn to dinner inside her bejeweled Russian palace.

"It's beautiful," I said as he fastened the clasp. "Where did you find it?"

"You are not the only person who knows how to shop in Paris," he said.

"Can a girl dream that you also bought earrings and a bracelet?"

"Close," he said, opening the smaller of the two remaining boxes. There, inside, was a set of matching earrings.

"They're lovely," I said, fastening them to my ears. I glanced over at the last box, sitting on his lap. "What's that?"

William turned the long rectangular container, so the front of the box faced him and slowly opened it. He regarded the contents for a moment and then rotated it toward me. Inside was a small, beautiful, viciously sharp dagger. The blade was thin, the hilt made of gold. Small flowers and gems were inlaid into the handle. I looked up at William, unsure of the dagger's purpose. Quite able to hear my thoughts, he replied without further prompting.

"Olivia, you're a witch, traveling to a ball that's a front for a syndicate of vampires, the leader of which is set on killing you," William said. "If we were in America, I might have given you a gun, although it would be useless. This lovely dagger won't kill Nikola either. But it dates to seventeenth-century India, and it is thin, light, and very sharp. It is meant to be hidden on your body. You could surprise any foe with a stab from this blade. Even, perhaps, a vampire."

"You expect me to use this?"

"If necessary, yes," he said, placing the weapon in my hand.

I held the dagger in my palm, feeling its weight. Then I grasped the hilt in my fingers, tilting the weapon back and forth, all the while gazing at my 192-year-old lover, whose face bore not a trace of humor. For a moment, I tried to imagine the dagger's last owner. Had it been used as a weapon or merely an ornament? If I used it, I had no idea what to expect. As an A-list political consultant in San Francisco, I ran campaigns and solved problems for people on tight deadlines and in times of crisis. With razor-sharp precision, I might say, but my greatest weapon had always been my wit or perhaps my intelligence. Causing physical harm? Not so much. In my professional endeavors, the biggest risk was merely failure, and although it might feel fatal, it rarely was. Suddenly that world felt miles away. It occurred to me, as I turned the golden dagger in my hands, that the moment I met my William, I had begun to leave that world behind. I hadn't noticed at the time.

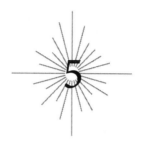

JOSEF, MY EVER-PRESENT ANTAGONIST, REGARDED ME SILENTLY as William and I emerged from the bedroom. His emotions were clear, but my empathic skills were almost wasted on it—the look on his face was so obvious. I was playing with fire, my attire too provocative. For a moment, I was tempted to lift my dress and show him the dagger—but there was no point in initiating a clash on our way out the door.

"It will be fine," I said, returning his gaze.

"So you seem to think," he said, nearly spitting the words.

Rather than rise to the bait, I decided to defuse the tension. An angry Josef could only hinder me, after all. I smiled at him with all the charm I could muster. "The vampire look becomes you," I said.

Both he and William did look incredibly sexy. They'd traded their normal sleek Armani suits for more old-fashioned bespoke suits paired with dark cravats at their throats. I half expected to see a top hat, but neither seemed prepared to go that far with his costume for the ball.

I thought I saw Josef relax slightly. "Maybe we'll get through this evening after all," he said.

As winter was in full swing, I put on a coat and scarf before exiting the building. William and Josef bundled up as well, although that was for show. Vampires don't get cold. A hat should have been a part of my outerwear, but I was too vain to ruin my hair and decided instead that my ears could brave the cold. I wanted to look nothing less than stunning for my first encounter with Nikola since he'd killed my mother.

Josef hailed a taxi, and soon we were standing on the sidewalk scrutinizing the long line of partygoers eager to get inside Club Rasputin. William walked directly into the line of sight of the club's twenty-something bouncer. To my eyes, his closely shaven head and Slavic features marked him unmistakably as a member of Nikola's entourage. As soon as he saw William, the man yelled out in French to his colleagues, "*Ouvrez! VIPs—ouvrez la porte*," and we were ushered inside the building and left in the care of a scantily clad coat check attendant who stowed our winter gear.

A well-dressed man in a dark suit appeared from behind a hidden door in the wall. He picked up the earpiece dangling at the collar of his dress shirt and positioned the small plastic device inside his ear, holding it firm against his head with his hand. "*Da . . . da*," he said aloud, speaking into his sleeve as he walked briskly toward a heavy red velvet curtain that I assumed covered the entrance to the club. It was almost midnight.

As we stood there, more revelers entered the hallway, and I tried to get a read on Nikola's guests. Of the half-dozen people standing behind me, at least two were vampires. I could feel them trying to read me, but I trusted my now well-honed defenses to keep them out. William and Josef turned and acknowledged them with the slightest of gestures, remaining silent. Clearly, the vampires of Paris wanted to keep their true nature a secret tonight.

Finally, responding to some unseen signal, the guard pulled open the curtain and ushered us into the party. As I walked through the doorway, the guard spoke directly to me and no one else.

"Welcome, Ms. Shepherd," he said in a thick Serbian accent. "Enjoy the party."

Josef looked at me, clearly trying to remind me of his warning.

"It will be fine," I said, repeating what seemed to be my mantra for the evening.

But soon after I spoke, I noticed a strange energy in the building. It was like a faint vibration lurking under the surface of my skin. Whatever the sensation, it felt . . . *wrong*. There was no other word to describe the pulse of energy, and I couldn't pinpoint its source. However vexing, I ignored it for the time being, intent on people-watching. William, though, picked up on my discomfort and asked me about it as he distributed the three glasses of champagne he'd grabbed off a passing tray.

"Do you feel it?" I asked, mentioning the odd energy in the room.

"I'm afraid that's your domain," he replied. "I'm not much good at sensing things like that. It sounds very San Francisco."

"This is more than just bad vibes," I said. "Let's go take a look around."

The club was dripping with red: the carpets, the drapes, even the shades on the lamps. Everything was adorned in crimson velvet, right down to the servers squeezed into uniforms of petite scarlet leotards. It was a cavernous place, with one expansive main chamber and a series of long hallways leading to side rooms. Aside from the dim light of the small table lamps, the club was illuminated by hundreds of candles placed on the tables and ledges. Adding to the ambiance was an eclectic ensemble of performers: jugglers, knife throwers, and magicians wandered through the crowd. Nikola's guests, all dressed in the most provocative Gothic couture money could buy, were clearly enjoying the nocturnal carnival.

We paused to observe as a young woman wearing a white dress cut down to her navel was led away by the knife thrower. She was blindfolded by her companion and then fastened to a nearby wall. I could feel her adrenaline rising as she anticipated the throw.

"Do you think he'll draw blood?" I asked my companions.

"Yes," William said, leaning in close to my ear. "He won't strike her directly, but as he cuts her loose, somehow he will contrive to prick her skin so he can take a small sip."

"He's a vampire?" I asked. "Are all of the performers?"

"No," Josef replied. "But that one is fairly notorious for tasting humans. Not that they ever realize what has happened. Let's try to avoid him. If anyone is going to drink your blood tonight, it should be one of us."

Ever the provocateur, Josef delighted in putting me on the spot by playing with my unspoken desire for him. I ignored his remarks, much like I ignored our attraction for one another. But for some reason, I felt the twinge of interest more keenly tonight. It needled me, much like the irritating pulse I'd been observing. I put that thought aside, too, and focused on my reason for being at the club: finding Nikola. The crowd was increasing, and the rooms began to fill with guests. A DJ started up, the dance floor suddenly pulsing to the beat of vintage David Bowie.

Watching the horde, I opened my mind to scan the guests in the room, allowing their emotions to wash over me. Nothing remarkable emerged, but once again, I detected the odd energy I'd experienced earlier. Its power was increasing slightly, making it harder to ignore.

My companions seemed distracted by it too. William left my side, despite all his warnings about the dangers of this party, saying he wanted to speak with someone he'd seen on the other side of the room. Josef also wandered off, determined, he said, to find a bar where he could commandeer a glass of whiskey. Left alone, I let the momentum of the mob carry me away. I moved along, content to wander until, to my great surprise, someone familiar popped into view. There, in the back corner of one of the smaller parlors, was Nadia, setting up the same fortune-teller wares she'd had in Montenegro. I blinked and looked down at my champagne flute, wondering if I'd unknowingly ingested some kind of hallucinogen. But she was no mirage. She beckoned me over to her table with a wave of her gnarled hand.

"*Chuvihani*," she said telepathically as I approached. "Don't be alarmed. It's me, Nadia. Elsa sent me to watch over you."

I pretended to examine her tarot cards, surprised at her presence but pleased to know I had an ally in the midst of this strange evening.

I was also trying to master the ability to communicate with Nadia without speaking. A few months ago, in her quest to restore my gifts as an empath, Elsa had given me a tea brewed from peyote. That night I'd run through Golden Gate Park like a wild animal until dawn, feeling my sixth sense emerge. The day after, my ability to read people's emotions and sense their intentions was revealed to me. I still had work to do to make the most of my gifts, but everyone seemed to agree they would be powerful when I finally mastered them. So far, in addition to having witchlike abilities from my father's side—like telepathy, the ability to communicate wordlessly—I'd also inherited gifts from mother and my grandmother: powerful, if human, empaths who'd been capable of reading the emotions of others.

"Where is Elsa?" I transmitted the question silently, testing out my skills.

"You'll see her soon," Nadia replied. "For now, I have something important to tell you."

I glanced up, indicating she should proceed.

"Your enemy is approaching," she said. "Although immortal, Nikola is obsessed with seeing his future. You must ask him to sit and have his tarot cards read."

I was about to ask how she came to know this information when a cold hand clasped my bare shoulder.

"*Bonsoir*, Olivia," Nikola purred.

I turned to regard my nemesis directly. In my brief time working for the Council, I'd never given the ancient vampire's appearance much thought. This time I saw him differently. Nikola wore his raven-colored hair pulled back in a ponytail, a dark velvet ribbon tied in a bow at the nape of his neck. His costume for the event was a midnight-colored velvet waistcoat and a pair of narrowly cut trousers that accentuated his lean frame. His hawklike nose and delicate mouth gave him an aristocratic air, and I wondered if he'd hailed from some powerful Serbian family before becoming a vampire. He looked magnificent and menacing. It was easy enough for me to overlook his beauty, however. When I stared into his cobalt-blue eyes, I saw nothing but my mother's broken body.

"You look ravishing," Nikola continued, surveying the people around us. "What are you doing without an escort? I'm surprised William let you out of his sight."

"*Bonsoir,* Monsieur," I replied.

"Monsieur?" he remarked. "Come now, don't we know each other well enough for you to address me less formally? We are colleagues, *n'est-ce pas?*"

"I like formality," I remarked. "And my friends will be back. William stepped away to speak with someone, and his brother, Josef, is also with us this evening."

"A human living with two vampires," he said. "How lucky they are. The way you look tonight, I should try to steal you away for my own. Perhaps you'll let me entertain you for a while."

"I'm afraid that is out of the question," Josef said, gliding to my side, a glass of champagne in one hand, a Jack Daniel's in the other. He leaned in and kissed my cheek possessively. "*Mon amie,*" he said, handing me the flute. "I thought you needed a fresh drink." He glanced sidelong at Nikola. "It's far too hot in here for the champagne to sit."

Nikola let out an almost imperceptible hiss as Josef inserted himself in the space between us. "The loyal brother arrives," Nikola said, sneering. "Like Sir Lancelot to save the day."

Josef tossed his head back and laughed. "Hardly, but I'm here nonetheless."

"I'm surprised to see you three out at all, with the recent death of Olivia's mother," Nikola continued.

I steeled myself so as not to give him the pleasure of seeing me react. This was his way of trying to wound me, make me feel weak. "Curious, isn't it?" I replied. "So much death upon us. I do wonder what fate has in store."

Nikola raised his eyebrows, incredulity upon his face. "You forever surprise me, Olivia," he said. "Mortals are often paralyzed by their grief."

"I wonder, Nikola," I said. "You have been dead for so long, do you really know what grief feels like?"

"Touché, my dear, touché," Nikola said, a chuckle escaping under his breath.

As he prepared to walk away, I remembered Nadia's instructions. "Nikola," I said. "I know you must see to your guests, but I wonder, would you have your cards read with me? It's one of my obsessions, *le tarot*."

Nikola's intense curiosity hit me like a wave. He was trying to determine if my interest was authentic. "You consult the tarot?" he asked.

"Yes," I replied, "but I am afraid I left my cards behind in my haste to leave town. I've been making do with a woman nearby."

"Here in Paris?" Nikola asked, clearly hoping for a clue to my whereabouts.

Josef placed his hand on my shoulder, telling me he did not want me to answer the question. He said, "At this point we're citizens of the world."

"I don't want to impose," I said, trying to get the conversation back on track. "But will you stay for a reading?"

Nikola's gaze locked onto mine, as if his eyes could probe into my soul. Unable to detect any guile on my part, he relented. "*Si tu veux*," he said. "If you want."

I nodded in satisfaction. It was a small victory—but still a victory. I could read his emotions, and he could sense nothing of mine.

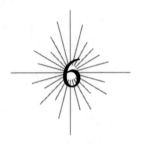

NIKOLA TURNED TO FACE NADIA. JOSEF REMAINED ONE STEP behind, his displeasure like a knife in my back. In preparation for telling fortunes, Nadia had draped a rich red velvet cloth over the table and had lit several candles housed in small, slightly tarnished silver cups.

"Good evening," she said. "Are you here to have your cards read?"

"Yes," I said, brazenly answering for us both. "But I wonder, can you do our readings at the same time . . . side-by-side? A simple five-card spread."

"Yours is a highly unusual request," she replied. "Your fates, now separate, could be linked together."

"I'm willing to risk it," I replied, glancing up at my host.

Nikola regarded me curiously but simply nodded.

As directed, we sat, and I split the deck of seventy-eight cards into two halves, leaving Nikola to split the deck further. We placed the smaller stacks on top of each other until we'd restored the cards back to one whole deck.

Looking at Nikola, she said, "I will place your cards on the left side of the table. The lady's cards will be placed on the right."

I shot a sideways glance at my companion. I could sense his anticipation.

"The first card represents your past," Nadia said.

She drew from the deck and laid a card in front of Nikola. It revealed a man standing before a table, facing a cup, a sword, and a wand.

"The Magician," she said. "This card represents manipulation of the physical world. It indicates a mastery of special knowledge."

Nikola smiled a self-satisfied smile but said nothing. Now it was my turn.

"Five of Cups," she said, dealing my first card. "For your past we see the numeral five, which suggests great disruption and instability. This is the card of loss and disappointment, regret, and self-blame."

Her remarks set me back on my heels a bit. I hadn't thought about whether she would give me an honest reading in front of Nikola, but I forced my chin up as I acknowledged her remarks.

"The next card is for you, monsieur. It tells of your present circumstances. Let's see . . . King of Cups reversed." She set the upside-down card upon the table. "Hmm. This is a sign of untrustworthiness . . . of insincerity and manipulation. It tells of a con artist without scruples . . . of someone who preys on the emotional pain of others. You must watch out for this man, monsieur."

"You can be sure I will," he replied, a thin smile across his lips.

I watched as she turned over the next card and placed it in front of me. "Three of Swords," she said. "It shows that heartache is upon you. This card represents a grief-stricken person, someone who has experienced loss through death. Tell me dear, has someone you loved died recently?"

"My mother," I replied, quietly. "A few days ago, here in Paris."

"How unfortunate," the old woman replied. "Death comes to all of us eventually, but you must be terribly distraught."

"I'd rather not discuss it," I said, feeling uncomfortable.

"But here, tonight, this reading reveals someone who has been pierced to the quick," she continued. "A wounded soul. I urge you to use caution with your emotions. Grief can be dangerous.

"And monsieur, now we return to you and the hidden influences in your life," she said. "Ahh. The Devil."

Nadia paused and leaned back, taking her time.

"It seems," she said, "that you must watch out for uncontrolled passions. Beware allowing one's inner demons to rule the roost."

Nikola leveled a cold stare at her, no doubt insulted at the idea that he'd ever lose control. His anger was rising. I could feel it.

"Shouldn't we all," I said, trying to defuse the moment.

My comment didn't lighten his mood, however. I sensed another wave of displeasure and thought for a moment he might get up and walk away.

As if trying to prevent such a move, Nadia drew another card with a flourish and presented me with an image of a beautiful woman with long, dark, flowing hair. In one hand the woman held a crystal ball, and in the other, an open book.

"The High Priestess," she remarked. "This is a card of knowledge long-hidden that will soon be yours. You must concentrate and focus on your inner self. A woman with great skills may come to your aid."

"I believe it's my turn," Nikola said abruptly, his restlessness coming in loud and clear. Sharing the spotlight was obviously not his thing. I lifted my gaze to see a small group had gathered around us, a gaggle of the half-undressed women whose presence inside the club seemed designed for Nikola's benefit. Next to me, Josef's gaze was as fierce as I'd ever seen. He was very angry with me. I could hear his voice inside my head when I relaxed for a moment and let him in.

"Reckless," he scolded silently, while standing at my elbow.

I ignored him. I would never achieve my goals if I asked first for his permission—or anyone else's, for that matter. "Yes, it's your card, Nikola," I said.

Nadia pulled another card from her deck and set it in front of him, this time revealing the upside-down image of a man with nine goblets surrounding his head.

"Nine of Cups, reversed," she said. "This indicates too much of a good thing. Overindulgence and greed."

"An appropriate card for a party like this," Nikola replied. "You have managed to say nothing unexpected."

"Monsieur is of course the host tonight," I said, also sending Nadia a silent message to complete the reading quickly. I wanted to keep him until the end but felt his urge to walk away growing stronger. "He surely must return to his duties."

Nikola scrutinized my face, his anger increasing. "Indeed," he said.

Eyes on Nikola, Nadia set a card down on my side of the table with a snap and no comment. Then she selected a fifth and final card for Nikola, the card representing final outcomes.

"Death," she said.

I wasn't sure if she was orchestrating our cards or if fate was in charge; whichever, Nikola was receiving a grim reading.

"Monsieur, change is coming," Nadia said. "This card means the end of a cycle and the beginning of new circumstances. You may need to say goodbye to an old way of life."

For all my talk of revenge, I squirmed inwardly at the overt challenge. "Madame," I said, embarrassed to notice my voice wavering, "what is my final card to be?"

Nadia took one final card from the deck. She reached over slowly and placed it in front of me. A disrobed woman, kneeling in a cauldron of flames, with a phoenix rising in the background.

"Judgment," she said, looking up at me with mischief in her eyes. "Rebirth. This is the card of metamorphosis, of final reckoning. A major event is coming, one that will elevate you to a new position in life."

I opened my mind to Josef's thoughts for just a moment and caught acute feelings of distress. He'd asked me not to provoke Nikola. Instead, with this reading, I'd done exactly that.

"Well, Nikola," I said. "It seems we're both in store for interesting times. But perhaps we can still change our fates."

Nikola regarded me silently. "What are you?" he said, his voice soft and yet somehow vicious. "You manipulated this somehow. I'm not certain yet, but I know that you're not what you seem."

"That can be said about so many of us," William replied, materializing at my side and extending his hand to help me up from my chair.

Nikola was on his feet in a flash, startled by William's abrupt arrival, his face darkening with fury as he scrutinized us. "What an odd little threesome you are," he hissed. "Now if you'll excuse me, I've wasted far more time than I should have on this little *divertissement.*"

"By all means," Josef said. "We will of course bid you *adieu.*"

Nikola laughed, his jet-black hair gleaming in the candlelight, a sneer upon his lips. "Hardly *adieu, mon ami,*" he said. "More like *à bientôt,* see you soon. I'm certain it won't be long.

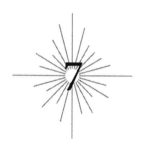

7

THE MINUTE NIKOLA DEPARTED, JOSEF POUNCED, PULLING US away from the table.

"Jesus, what were you thinking?" he hissed. "The tarot is a serious form of the occult, not a parlor trick for amateurs."

"I asked to have the reading on the advice of the fortune-teller," I said. "I know her."

"How do you know her, Olivia?" William asked. "This is the first we've heard of it."

"I meant to tell you, but my father arrived. You know Nadia. She's the witch who helped heal my leg after the bombing. I saw her again in Budva. She gave me a reading the same day Gabriel appeared on our doorstep. I think she may have disguised herself a bit. At first I didn't recognize her. It was only after I'd sat with her for a moment that it all clicked into place," I said.

Two sets of eyes blinked at me.

"I didn't have a chance to mention it in Montenegro. Gabriel showed up, and all hell broke loose," I explained. "After that, I sort of put the whole thing out of my mind. I was surprised to see her here, in the club. It was after you two wandered off and I started exploring by myself. She told me Nikola was obsessed with the tarot and encouraged me to have my cards read with him."

Again, a wall of silence met my remarks.

"There was no way to find you," I continued, dismayed at the pleading tone creeping into my voice. "By the time Josef arrived with my drink, Nikola was already at my side."

"Olivia, what did you hope to gain by letting him get so close to you?" William asked, in a tone that should be reserved for small children.

I gritted my teeth. "I didn't get that far, to be honest . . . but I think he came out worse than I did. Besides, no tarot reading is absolute. It's only one possible version of the future."

"Yes, but now he has a possibly accurate glimpse of both his fate and your own," Josef said angrily. "Fates he'd no doubt like to manipulate." He looked past me. "Where's this fortune-teller? I'd like to have a word with her."

I turned back to find her, but she was gone. Vanished into thin air, along with her table.

"Clearly she had to leave," I replied defiantly. "I'm sure she'll turn up again."

"You must see how this looks," William said gently. "How do we know she's really on your side?"

Their skepticism was insulting. To think they believed I could be so easily duped!

"Enough," I said. "You weren't in Budva. I was. She warned me about Nikola and told me that my father was coming. And we *know* her. She's connected to Elsa, which means we can trust her." Of course, privately I wished Elsa was with me to make my case, but she wasn't, and I didn't know when I would see her again.

"It could all be for show," Josef said. "I think we should look for her. I want to speak with her myself."

"Fine," I replied.

We made our way through the various rooms and chambers, past fire-breathers and snake charmers entertaining an enthralled crowd. As I watched the guests, drinking their cocktails as fast as they could be replenished, I detected an air of desperation. It struck me that this party seemed better suited to the end of the world than to a random evening in Paris . . . and yet again, the descent into drunken revelry began to feel oddly right. Around me, I saw men loosening their shirts and women moving more fluidly, moving in a way that drew me to join them.

Only one thing kept me from giving into the desire to relax: the constant, troubling pulse of energy I'd felt since we first arrived. It was growing—and rubbing my nerves raw. It clearly derived from something supernatural. It was nothing like the emotions humans give off. And beyond emotional discomfort, I felt a slow physical weakening, like Superman locked in a room full of Kryptonite. As we moved from room to room, I racked my brain for a clue to the source of my discomfort.

We finally arrived at the doorway of the main room of Club Rasputin. There, in the middle of a great field of energy, was Nikola. As I stood observing him, I began to realize that Nikola wasn't putting out the energy, he was *collecting* it. It swirled around him like a giant force field.

"Can vampires feed off of emotions?" I asked, as we paused just outside the room.

"There is such a thing as a psychic vampire," William answered. "They're rare, but they do exist. They drain the energy out of people— either on purpose or unwittingly."

"Instead of blood or in addition?" I asked.

"Both." William replied. "Why?"

"Behold Nikola, the psychic vampire," I replied, gesturing toward our nemesis. "These parties aren't meant for fun. They're his feeding ground. He's eating their experiences—their joy, exhilaration, desire . . . even fear."

"They don't seem to notice," Josef remarked. "The guests, I mean."

"They're absolutely frantic to have a good time," I said. "I think they're trying to replace all of the sensations he's stealing from them. Look closely. Do you see how much they're all drinking? I think it's a sort of sedative to calm their nerves. What I want to know is, how does the evening end?" I added. "There must be some kind of finale."

William came close and kissed me on the lips. "Olivia, you may be on to something," he said. "That would explain why all of his parties usually end the same way."

"What way is that?"

William gestured toward a corner of the room where two women had begun to dance intimately together. A Roxy Music song played over the sound system as they swayed arm in arm, caressing one another. Quiet giggles escaped their lips. They nuzzled, then began to kiss each other gently, exploring the contours of the other's face. After a few moments, a man, their companion I presumed, walked over and gently unfastened the halter top on one woman's gown, allowing it to fall to her waist, exposing her small, pale breasts to the crowd. The room shifted at the first sign of flesh: the humans aroused, the vampires hungry.

Even I wasn't immune. I felt my own core grow warm as I observed their display. The power of suggestion was strong, or perhaps the will of the audience weak. In either case, more dresses came undone. People dropped to their knees, buttons and zippers were unfastened in haste. In a few short moments the club began to undulate.

Nikola stood in the center of it all, a handful of half-dressed women encircling him. He kissed them all lavishly, finally choosing a tall brunette to drape across his arm as he spoke.

"*Bienvenue, zdravo,* hello, and welcome, *mes amis,*" he said, instantly capturing the attention of his guests. "As you know, from time to time I like to throw these little parties."

The room exploded in a burst of knowing giggles. Nikola laughed, too, enjoying his moment as the libertine of the ball.

"I'm so glad you could join me tonight and share in the evening's diversions. Life is short, my friends. The world is filled with so many restrictions and rules. If only for a moment, be immortal . . . live as if you had no clock to check, no calendar to consult. You must take fate into your hands and forge your own destiny."

The crowd cheered him on, clearly enjoying the carefree atmosphere.

"And now," Nikola continued, "let us drink to seeking life's greatest pleasures."

I watched, disgusted, as Nikola abruptly pulled the woman he'd been holding close, lifted her dress, and unzipped his pants. She never opened her eyes as Nikola penetrated her, her body a barbaric appendage on display for the room. Finally, after what seemed like an eternity, he carried his plaything off into the shadows, where I imagined he'd drink directly from her neck, with none of the other humans in the club the wiser. I caught another glimpse of him, minutes later, descending into a pile of bodies awaiting his arrival. In fact, as I scanned the room, I realized with consternation that everyone was getting into the spirit of the evening in one way or another.

"Welcome to the bacchanalia," Josef whispered in my ear. "Have you noticed we're the only ones not participating? It's considered rude to only watch."

It seemed fitting that Josef would be the one to point out our faux pas. We could, of course, walk out, and leave the rest to our imagination. But what if Nikola had more up his sleeve?

"Is it?" I asked, looking directly at William. He half smiled, but said nothing. "I guess we better do something to fit in," I said, feeling slightly confused as I leaned over to kiss him. Up to now, William hadn't been keen to share our bed, but the landscape, it seemed, was shifting.

I turned to face Josef, who regarded me with an amused look upon his face.

"This time I intend to make you finish what you start," he said, referring to a night weeks ago when I'd declined to go forward with a steamy threesome. Even then I'd known my desire for him would only complicate things down the road. Our attraction had been unmistakable since the day we'd met, but, unlike in other areas of my life, I'd never let my impulsiveness hold sway.

"Perhaps," I replied. Giving in to my desires, I grabbed his bottom lip between my teeth, ever so gently. "But I'm not going to sleep with you both here in the middle of this circus," I said between kisses. "We can stay a little longer for appearances, and then I want you to take me home."

I felt a vague acknowledgment from my companions as they led me to a wall nearby and unzipped my dress. I thought William would pull the dress down to my waist and leave it at that, but he continued on toward the floor, helping me step out of the gown.

"It's couture," he said as he draped it on a chair. "We shouldn't crease the silk."

Goose bumps appeared as I stood in nothing but lingerie and heels. Well, not exactly nothing. The dagger was strapped to my thigh—a detail Josef noticed immediately. Kneeling, his hand upon my leg, he removed the blade from its sheath.

"What a lovely gift," he said. "We'll have to teach you to use it wisely."

Josef met my eyes, then focused on the dagger, running the blade along my right leg. He smoothed the cold flat side of the metal along my skin until he came to my knee. Very quickly, he made a small cut. I gasped as he placed his mouth over the nick, licking away the blood trickling from the wound.

"Just a taste," he said, rising to kiss me, my own blood upon his lips.

His gesture incited a great moan from William, who grabbed me and began to kiss me with a heat that would have melted a glacier.

Josef meanwhile, busied himself with other matters, and I soon found myself near collapse, my knees buckling from the pleasure of it all. They were thorough seducers, working hard to bring me enjoyment.

Then, as I lifted my head in ecstasy, my pleasure-dulled gaze sweeping over the crowd, Nikola's piercing gaze met mine, and I felt a cold shock. Willing myself not to recoil, I held his stare. In that moment, I knew he had been watching us, and it instantly killed my desire. Breaking our visual connection, I whispered to my companions that I was ready to leave.

A short taxi ride later, we arrived at the apartment. William threw more euros than necessary into the front seat next to the driver as we exited. The trip up in the elevator was a blur, and then we were inside, the front door closed and locked. Once again, my dress came off. William picked me up and carried me into our bedroom. I was aware of Josef trailing us, discarding his clothing as he approached the room, and for a moment I thought of slamming the door shut on the whole threesome idea, for a second time. But my body betrayed me, insisting that we finish what we'd started.

As William removed his suit coat and came to lie next to me on the bed, I knew I was entering dangerous territory making love to both men. Perhaps sensing my trepidation, William took my head in his hands for a long, slow kiss that seemed to be a gesture of reassurance.

Josef's lips, meanwhile, hovered a hair's breadth above my skin and feathered me with kisses. For a moment his gaze caught mine, and I could sense his feelings of uncertainty. I nodded, offering my silent consent. Assured, he continued, caressing me with his lips until he reached his intended destination and pulled off my panties. Soon I was being kissed in every way possible. Josef was a determined lover, and his efforts caused me to squirm in delight. Meanwhile, William shifted his attention to my breasts. I arched my back in pleasure as he latched on to one of my nipples and began to suck, with the force of a vampire, not a man. Josef, seeing my frenzy, came up and latched on to the other, eliciting a shriek of pleasure.

"*C'est rien, ma chérie*," he said, pausing for a moment. "This is nothing. We've only just begun."

True to his word, we continued for several more hours. I was unsure how much time passed, but I know we stayed in bed together, exploring one another, until it seemed there was no possible mystery left to uncover.

As I was drifting off to sleep, it occurred to me that I might wake up feeling remorse for our evening's activities. William, sensing my distress, spoke to me. "You mustn't regret this night, Olivia. There is no shame in knowing great pleasure, especially with those who love you."

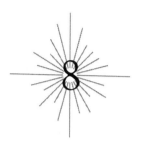

RISING FROM BED THE NEXT AFTERNOON WAS DIFFICULT. I'D been sleeping too heavily at the wrong hours. As I was waking up, lying there, I braced for a wave of shame, but none came. Instead, resignation. *In for a penny, in for a pound*, I reminded myself. I'd been the one to insist on attending the party. I'd been given what I asked for, which is always a tricky thing.

Once up, I found William alone in the living room, a book by his side and a guitar on his lap. As I stood silently in the doorway regarding him, my heart thumped hard in my chest. This was the man I'd fallen in love with—the musician, the thinker. I wanted to go back to the beginning, before the Council, back to our first starry-eyed encounters, like the one at the bluegrass festival in Golden Gate Park, before all of the violence and obligations arrived at our doorstep.

Not to mention threesomes. I didn't regret it, and William had seemed more than happy to participate, but it wasn't for me. For us. Not long term. Still, it was done—and good to have the craving for Josef out of my system. Now we could go back to the ways things were meant to be.

"Don't fret," he said, sensing my brooding.

"I was remembering how things were before Aidan died," I said. "When we were alone and no one bothered us."

William set down his guitar and opened his arms, inviting me to join him. "I don't think it was ever that easy, darlin', but I do agree it would be nice if things quieted down a bit."

"That's not going to happen though, is it?" I asked, already knowing the answer.

William shook his head as I climbed into his lap. "No, not for a while at least."

For a little while though, we pretended we were untethered to this world. Wrapped in each other's embrace, we silently transmitted our love in small movements: a press of the lips to the forehead, a squeeze of the hand. It was pure bliss, but eventually my curiosity got the better of me and I felt compelled to interrupt our peace.

"Why did you say Josef loved me?" I asked, recalling William's last words the night before.

"He does, in his own way," William replied, adjusting our bodies so he could look directly at me as he spoke. "When you love someone who lives centuries," he asked, "what matters most, monogamy or fidelity?"

"Fidelity."

"Good answer," he said. "Did you enjoy your time with Josef?"

There was no point in lying. "Of course. You were there. But . . ."

"I understand. It is uncomfortable to acknowledge that you can be attracted to him also. But consider this: watching you with him gave me great pleasure. I know he enjoyed it immensely, but Josef knows you're mine, meant to be my wife. Joseph understands fidelity. He loves me, we love you, and for one night, we shared our passion with one another."

"What changed? Before, on our first night in Paris, you were glad I didn't invite him into our bed."

"The only constant is change, Olivia," William said gently. "You must promise to keep your options open."

"I don't like the sound of that," I said, suddenly feeling alarmed.

"I have an idea. Let's elope. Today. You said yourself that I'm meant to be your wife. Let's go now and ensure nothing can separate us."

"You will *never* be rid of me, Olivia," William said. "But you are Gabriel's daughter and a witch, perhaps a powerful one, and we must learn to be flexible. Who knows how your life may change? Last night is a good example. Those with even the wildest imaginations would have had trouble conjuring up such a scene."

"It would have been nice if you'd been more honest with me," I replied. "I don't like surprises."

"You wanted to find Nikola, regardless of the circumstances," William said. "Nothing we said would have deterred you, and it's unlikely you would have believed us. As you can see now, anything is possible in his world. Things escalate."

I probed William's mind as best I could to try to fully understand the hidden meaning in his words. "You're keeping something from me," I said. Impulsively, I untied my robe and tilted my neck toward him. "Drink," I demanded. "Complete the cycle so our bond is sealed. Back in San Francisco you refused, but now my leg is healed and I'm fine. So drink."

William shook his head. "No," he said. "I will not bind us together until the time is right."

"When, then?" I asked, suddenly feeling desperate to see us bound to one another.

"Let's get your mother buried and see her safely to the next world, and then we can decide," he replied. "For now, we should enjoy what we have, which includes Josef. You can trust him, Olivia. One day he may save your life."

My potential savior did not return home that evening, which was fine by me. William and I passed a quiet night together, eventually retreating to our bed, where William demonstrated that he was perfectly capable of bringing me great pleasure with no assistance from others.

Early the next morning my father called to tell me the police were ready to release my mother's ashes.

"I'll pick them up and be home on the next flight," I said, realizing as I spoke that home was an ambiguous place at the moment.

"*Bon,*" Gabriel said. "I've been staying at your mother's house, in the guest quarters. I hired some workers to look after the place." He paused. "I had forgotten how easy it is to feel at home here in Bolinas."

"I'm glad you're comfortable," I replied. "And thanks for all you're doing."

"Oh, and Monsieur Rawley, your mother's agent, has been calling. He wants to meet to review her work."

The idea of seeing my mother's paintings without her there revived my grief. At the same time, if I had to do it with anyone, Jason seemed like a good choice. His comforting manner was appealing. I exhaled slowly, hoping to push the sadness off my chest.

"*Oui, Papa.* I'll call him. I assume we're going ahead with the service."

"*Bien sûr . . .* yes, of course," he said. "I've arranged for a tent and chairs to be delivered. It's California, so it's not supposed to rain, but you never know this time of year."

I paused for a moment, trying to put words to the feelings bubbling up inside me.

"I hope when I get back, we'll have a chance to talk," I said tentatively.

"Yes, of course," he said after a pause. "For as long as you like."

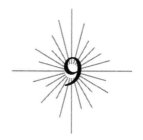

9

"WE HAVE LANDED," WILLIAM SAID, GENTLY SHAKING MY ARM
to wake me.

I rubbed my eyes and quietly asked Josef to lift the plane's window
shade so I could take in the first glimpse I'd had of San Francisco in
what felt like ages. Outside, rain fell in furious horizontal sheets. The
storm continued even after we picked up our luggage and Gabriel
collected us from the arrivals curb.

"See," he said, his hands popping off the steering wheel for a
moment to help illustrate his point. "I said it would probably rain."

As we drove out of the city toward Bolinas in his black Suburban, I
fell asleep, jet lag pulling me into slumber as our car merged onto the
freeway.

When I woke, we were parked in my mother's driveway. While
the men gathered the luggage, I walked ahead through the cool
night air—it had finally stopped raining—and felt a wave of relief
that I'd succeeded in bringing India home. Her ashes, housed in a
small ceramic jar packed carefully inside my carry-on, had completed
the journey.

Inside, I contemplated the familiar scenery. Brightly colored up-
holstered furniture, Persian rugs, eclectic bits of pottery, a 1970s
edition of *The Hobbit*, matchbooks from Parisian cafés, and endless
issues of the *New Yorker* dotted her domestic landscape. All of her

belongings were where she'd left them, waiting for the return of their mistress. Carefully, I lifted the jar from my bag and placed it on the mantel of the fireplace. My father appeared behind me, placing a hand on my shoulder.

"*Un malheur ne vient jamais seul,*" he murmured, uttering a French version of "when it rains, it pours."

"Yes." I nodded. "Misfortune never arrives alone."

Our group split up after arriving. The vampires left to hunt in the hills surrounding my mother's home. William's reluctance to leave me was obvious, but Josef prodded him—in part, I think, to give me some time alone with my father. I promised them it would be a worthwhile diversion; the forests around Bolinas are rich with deer and other wildlife. Then, after they left, my father added a surprising comment.

"I'd forgotten that your mother's property is sacred ground," he said. "I can't recall if India made it so by allowing magical beings to roam or if her family knew when they bought it decades ago. I'm afraid my own conjuring has stirred up even more attention, so be careful when you walk the grounds."

"Be careful?"

"You'll see," Gabriel replied sheepishly. "Just pay attention when you go out."

"Should we have warned the brothers?" I asked.

"They'll be fine," he said. "I just didn't want you to be surprised."

I chewed on my father's bit of news while I unpacked. I'd spent so much of my early years blocking out my gifts and those of my family that I wasn't sure I could trust my memories of living in Bolinas. Maybe it had always been magical, and I'd ignored it—or *avoided* it. I had a niggling sensation that maybe I'd seen things in the morning or evening light, but it was a hazy memory at best. Once I'd decided to subvert my gifts, well, that had been the end of things.

My mother would never have forced me to acknowledge any of it, but now I was living with my father—a witch. It was a whole new ball game. There would be no more avoiding the supernatural.

I had managed to avoid one awkward issue by deciding to stay with William in the guest cottage next door to my mother's studio. Assuming the status of visitor was about all I could manage at the moment. The idea that I would inherit my childhood home was too much to fathom, and I was not yet ready to visit her art studio. Once my things were put away, I returned to the house.

I found my father sitting in an old leather chair in the living room reading *Mahomet*, a play about religious fanaticism written by Voltaire in the 1700s.

"Just a little light reading?" I joked as I entered the room.

Gabriel looked up, clearly lost in the story, and smiled. "'Anyone who has the power to make you believe absurdities has the power to make you commit injustices,'" he said. "At least that is what I take away from this particular work of his."

"Was Voltaire a member of the Council?" I asked.

"I wasn't around then, of course, but I believe he was a major force. He felt strongly that religious fanaticism was poisonous to humanity, so he encouraged those around him to do something. As you know, he was also something of pragmatist. He had no patience for hysteria in politics and science."

I smiled but didn't comment, too weary to participate in such a deep discussion. Gabriel laughed and put down the book.

"Forgive me," he said, shaking his head. "I'm too much in my head, too much about my politics and causes, never making time to enjoy the moment."

"Here's your chance," I replied, settling into the couch to stare at my father. This was the first opportunity I'd had to examine the man who had caused my arrival into this world, then been conspicuously absent since.

"I know you have a million questions for me," he said. "I will answer as best I can. I do want to tell you how I met your mother. It was the seventies, you see. We all felt free and happy then. The war was winding down, but here in Northern California, we were more concerned with music and, well, sex."

I cringed inwardly, not wanting that image in my head.

Gabriel nodded, easily hearing my thoughts. "Yes, well . . . I'd been living in Marin trying to decide what to do with my life. This was years before I started my current company. George Lucas was building his career as a filmmaker there, and I spent some time with his entourage learning about film and special effects. I can make fireworks with my own skills, of course, but I liked learning to manipulate human tools to make magic—or at least what they thought was magic.

"One evening, I went to a party in Stinson Beach. Your mother had come alone, which surprised me, that such a beautiful woman would be unescorted. I asked my host who she was and was told that she was an artist of some early notoriety."

Gabriel closed his eyes for a moment, clearly transported back in time. It was a few seconds before he spoke again. "That night, I managed to introduce myself, and I could tell right away that she was different. She had so much energy radiating from her." He looked at me. "I sensed the same qualities in you the first time we met," he said. "Needless to say, we were inseparable after that. At least for a while."

The room was growing chilled, so I got up and turned on the gas fireplace.

"Would you like some wine?" I asked.

Gabriel nodded. I grabbed a bottle of Côtes du Rhône from my mother's wine rack and walked into the kitchen, returning with two glasses of red wine. After he'd taken a sip, Gabriel continued his story.

"Not surprisingly, we had a fiery relationship. Your mother, as you know, could be mercurial. I was a young man trying to build a career and navigate my work with the Council. My parents were alive then, you see. And then there was the fact that I was a witch. My family had made it clear that I was to marry someone who could help carry on the bloodlines. Meanwhile, your mother was pressing me to get engaged."

"So soon?"

"It was a different time," he replied, smiling. "People didn't wait years to get married, after they had gone to graduate school or climbed a mountain."

"Did you have an argument?" I asked.

"I'm afraid so," he replied. "I tried to convince her that marriage was an outdated practice and that we should just live together. She refused my offer and asked me to leave."

"So you just left?" I asked. "You never saw her again?"

"Not until that night in Paris," he replied. "I know how unbelievable it must sound, but not long after our argument, my parents were killed in a car crash. I moved back to France to manage my family's affairs and eventually started my own business in Marseille. I often thought about your mother, but by then, too much time had passed."

"Did you ever marry?"

"No," he said quietly. "I realize now it's probably because I still loved your mother."

"Really?"

"*Bien sûr!* When you left the two of us alone in Paris, we spent hours talking. All these years later, it seems foolish that we didn't try to stay together."

"You didn't know she was pregnant?"

"*Mon Dieu*, no," Gabriel said emphatically. "It's not exactly forbidden for humans and witches to mate, but it is not encouraged. Human women often cannot carry the babies to term. It's risky. And of course, the bloodlines are not pure, which to some families is all that matters."

"What would you have done if you'd known?"

My father drained the wine from his glass before he spoke. "I don't know. The young man I was back then might have done what India suggested. I might have felt compelled to bring you back to France to be raised by Maman."

"I can't imagine life without her," I said, and rose to retrieve the bottle of wine from the other room. When I returned, I refilled our glasses. "I'm ashamed to admit that when she was alive, she drove me crazy," I said. "All my life, I tried to be different, and yet many of the traits that I like most about myself come from her or her influence."

"Well then, I guess we should propose a toast," Gabriel said, raising his glass. "To India, may she rest in peace," he said, adding, "And may we be *loyal au mort* . . . loyal to the dead."

"Why didn't you tell me who you were when we first met?" I blurted, emboldened by two glasses of wine.

"It's a question I've asked myself," he said. "My only answer is that I was a coward. I knew if I told you too early, you'd probably refuse to join the Council and I might never see you again. Then, once you started working for us and were put in danger, I was afraid if I revealed the truth you'd leave and I wouldn't be able to protect you. As is the case when you spin lies, you get farther and farther away from the truth and your opportunity to put things right diminishes.

"That night after Aidan's death, I promised William I would tell you everything. But of course, India got to you first."

"How did you know I was your daughter?"

Gabriel leaned back in his chair and smiled. "Yes, that was a great surprise. When Elsa came to us and said she was visiting a young woman who was troubled, I didn't pay much attention. That changed after she described your skills and mentioned your grandmother. Once we were introduced, I knew without a doubt that you were my daughter. Elsa was furious that I made her a part of the lie, but as I said, I couldn't seem to find the right moment."

I closed my eyes, preparing to pose the last question I was harboring—in some ways the one I feared the most. Hearing the answer meant I would have to acknowledge I was a witch, at least partially.

Gabriel laughed out loud. "My God, daughter, your thoughts can be loud. Did Elsa ever mention it to you?"

"Yes. It's something I could use some help with," I said. "If you know my question already, will you answer?"

"You want to know what kind of witch you are," he replied. "What kind of powers you have? The short answer is, I'm not sure. You are a rare thing, Olivia. Not only because you survived, but because the women in your family all possess great intuitive powers.

"My family is known for its mastery of telepathy and control of the weather. We pull *la brume*, the fog, from the sea across the land when it suits us. I'm told my great-great-grandmother used to delight in conjuring a fog bank that would send the monarchy's ships crashing into the rocky cliffs when a king or queen had displeased her. But you don't seem to possess that skill, and instead, you can disappear. How does one become invisible, exactly? What can *you* tell me about that?"

"Not much," I admitted. "It seems to happen when I'm in danger or scared. I didn't show up on the security camera footage from the robbery, and I'm guessing that was because I felt frightened. According to Josef, I also disappeared into thin air after the car bomb that killed Aidan. He was unable to find me until I literally bumped into him. I'm really not certain how it works."

Gabriel looked at me thoughtfully. "What else? You're telepathic; I hear your thoughts when you try to communicate. So you can read the thoughts and emotions—only of humans?"

I looked at my father, wondering if I should tell him everything, and then I recalled our pact: no more secrets between us.

"It's not just humans," I said, looking him straight in the eye. "I can read the thoughts of the undead, too."

"*Vraiment? Tu es certain?*"

"Yes," I replied. "I'm certain. William and Josef know, but no one else."

Gabriel let out a slow breath. "Olivia, there are prophecies through the ages concerning witches who can control the thoughts of the living and the undead. Whether you might be *that child*? Deciphering the prophecies is something I never imagined would be my responsibility. We're entering unknown territory. But of one thing I am certain: if Nikola knew there was even a possibility that you were that powerful, he'd kill you in an instant. The last thing he wants is my daughter lurking around listening to his every thought."

"I don't want to waste time on ancient stories. I can barely make sense of my powers myself. But the good news is, I don't think he knows I'm your daughter. Not yet. And in any case, reading the mind of an ancient vampire like Nikola isn't easy," I said. "I suppose what I can do is sense his intentions rather than actually hear his thoughts."

My father shook his head. "We don't know the extent of your powers. We'll need to test them. Mark my words," he said. "If you can perceive their intentions, chances are that you can do more. It's a powerful tool, and one that might come in handy."

"'Come in handy,'" I repeated, incredulous. "How so?"

"Olivia, think of our work with the Council. Being able to convince someone to do something in politics is a great weapon."

"I don't want to be a weapon."

"Olivia," my father said, a touch of frustration in his voice. "I thought we were past this. You are a *Laurent*—a witch and an heir to the family's seat on the Council. You must use every skill at your disposal. It's your obligation and, frankly, a matter of survival. Nikola wouldn't hesitate for a moment if he had such a gift."

"He has his own weapons," I replied. "When we were in Paris we learned something about him. We attended one of his parties—you know, his Bal des Vampires."

My father raised his eyebrows. "I'm sure as your father I don't want to know any more about your activities there," he said. "*Ces soirées sont infâmes.*"

"*Oui, Papa,*" I agreed, blushing. "The point is that Nikola is a psychic vampire. He feeds off of other people's emotions. That's one reason he enjoys such—how should I put this—robust parties."

"What do you know!" Gabriel replied. "I just assumed he was a little kinky. Most vampires are."

"Kinky doesn't begin to describe it," I said, no humor in my voice. "I'm not sure how all of this fits together. As we discovered when we first began looking into his background, he's deeply connected to the Serbian mafia. His behavior at the party in Paris suggests someone with very dangerous tastes and habits—even for a vampire. The robberies last year, killing Aidan—all of it is *linked*. I just don't know how yet. I suspect he hopes to become the leader of the Council and use his authority to further enrich himself and his criminal gang. Because he can. Because it's fun to play a game that he knows how to win." I unclenched my fists and cleared my throat. "It was plain old bad luck that I happened to be in Union Square the day his associates robbed that jewelry store. William warned me my curiosity could be dangerous, and he was right. If I hadn't asked you to pry into Nikola's affairs to see if there was a link between his misdeeds and the Council, none of this would have happened. Two people would still be alive."

"We don't know that," Gabriel said. "Nikola was a bad seed before you arrived. I just preferred not to pay attention. You reminded all of us that we have an obligation to protect the Council and its mission."

"I don't know," I said. "My impulsiveness attracted a powerful enemy, one whose skills dwarf my own."

"For the moment. This just reinforces our need to learn more about your powers and how to use them," Gabriel said. "You can't expect to best a thousand-year-old vampire without a few special tricks up your sleeve. Now come, I'm famished. Let's make some marrow bones and a nice salad while the boys are out having their meal."

"Hopefully safely," I said.

"They can protect each other," Gabriel said. "They are strong, Olivia. Perhaps stronger than you realize."

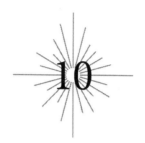

10

DAWN CAME TOO EARLY, AFTER SLEEP TROUBLED BY A THOUGHT I chased but could not grasp. I got out of bed and found some athletic clothes, hoping an early morning walk would soothe my mind. On the way out of the room, I grabbed an orange ski hat in honor of the San Francisco Giants, my favorite baseball team. Properly outfitted, I strolled into the living room and found William seated in a chair by a fire, curtains drawn, a new biography of Charles de Gaulle in his hands. Several guitars were propped up against the wall, telling me that he and Josef had driven back to San Francisco during the night to fetch some things from home.

"I don't suppose you stopped by my house and raided my closet?" I asked. "Otherwise, I'll go back today and pick up a dress for the service."

William rose and stretched his long, pale limbs as he walked toward me. I held on tightly as we embraced, feeling a connection at the place where our two hearts touched, even though I knew his had no beat. It mattered little, because I felt William's love like an electric pulse, one that could warm me if I were in the coldest and darkest of places. His red hair fell across my face as he kissed me deeply. I kissed him back, feeling as if we'd been separated for weeks instead of one day.

"Did you eat well?" I asked.

"Yes," he said. "Josef was right to take me out. I feel much better. But why did you not tell me your mother's property is crowded with supernatural types? I haven't seen so many ghosts since the Civil War."

"I didn't remember—or, maybe, I intentionally forgot." I stared at him. "Did you say ghosts?"

"Yes, and other creatures as well, some of them a little mischievous. We used to call them bogeymen in the South."

"But bogeymen aren't real," I said.

"Neither are ghosts," said William, smiling. "Some people call bogeymen by other names—like pookas or gremlins."

"Doesn't ring a bell," I said. "Are they dangerous? My father warned me to be mindful of my surroundings when going out."

"Not dangerous, but they do like to play tricks," he said. "They're nocturnal, though, so you shouldn't see them this morning."

"Well, that's good news," I said, leaning in for one more kiss, "since I'm headed out for a walk. Care to join me?"

"No," he replied. "I am enjoying this biography of de Gaulle. History is funny. Even the most difficult of men become geniuses after they're dead."

"Yes," I agreed. "Death makes everyone heroic. It's in our nature to remember people more generously."

"I hope you'll keep that in mind tomorrow when you speak of your mother at her service," William said.

At William's words, my throat tightened. Honoring the dead is a tricky business, especially when your business with that person is unfinished. My mother and I loved each other in spite of our differences. But did I truly *know* her? Not really. You can't look too closely at a parent for fear of seeing yourself in the reflection. But I had wanted to know her. I'd never intended to ignore her—or walk away, like I did in Paris. I was reminded once again that I'd acted like an angry, petulant child, never imagining for a moment, when I turned my back on her, that it would be the last time I'd see her alive. I hoped one day to be able to forgive myself.

Darkness still held sway outside, the violet light of dawn not yet giving way to sunrise as I left the guest quarters. My running shoes grew damp from the dew as I pressed through the tall grass heading west, toward the coast. I scanned my surroundings as I went, looking for anyone, or anything, out of the ordinary, but thankfully there was nothing. Perhaps there'd be no sightings of magical creatures this morning. Perhaps they'd bide their time until the witching hours—which, I'd been told, took place between midnight and three in the morning—hours when the window between the living and the dead is at its thinnest. During that special hour, certain kinds of creatures are at the peak of their powers. With the sun about to rise in earnest, that time was well past, and I was relieved.

As I neared the western edge of our property, which overlooked the ocean, the sound of the waves crashing on the rocks below became louder, sounding like an eerie, mournful melody. At the cliff edge, I paused to stare out at the Pacific. Although the sun had not yet fully risen, there was enough light to see the churning water and white spray below. I stood still, watching the powerful waters surge, my ears filled with their song. I looked down into the froth and thought for a moment that I'd glimpsed a set of tails or flippers. Then, as I stood at the precipice, I heard a set of shrill female voices calling to me.

"Come," they said. "Come join us in the sea."

All it once, it was as if I were in a terrible dream, my skills useless against whatever dark magic lurked below. I half realized I was not myself—but the bigger part of me was lulled into a trance by the pernicious melody I could not block out. My senses fogged, and all I could think was, *What is the point of staying?* I wobbled at the precipice's edge, and a cold fear spread across my body as I felt bottomless despair and realized I was about to jump. Then, just before I took the final step, a powerful arm grabbed me and kept me from tumbling into the churning waters below.

"Olivia!" a familiar voice chided, and a hand slapped me across the cheek. "Wake up. It's a spell."

I knew the voice instantly; I'd grown used to its owner's barking tones when she lived with me. I turned, blinked, and found myself facing Elsa, my mentor, the woman who'd saved my life when she'd first appeared in my dreams a few months ago—the woman who'd then stood by me and helped me reclaim my skills as an empath.

"Your timing is impeccable," I said, rubbing my cheek and hoping a little humor would calm my nerves. I wasn't sure what was a greater shock, that I'd almost been cajoled to jump to my death, or that Elsa had reappeared after her long absence. She looked exactly the same— long and lean in black leather pants, a small gold ring in her pierced eyebrow.

"Was it you who kept me up last night?" I asked. "I felt as if I were chasing something in my sleep."

Elsa grimaced. "It was me," she replied. "I knew you were headed for trouble again. It's a good thing I arrived when I did. *Rusaki* are dangerous. Their wailing has driven plenty of ship captains to their death upon the rocks."

"What did you just call them?" I asked.

"*Roo-sa-kee*," Elsa replied. "I'm using a Russian word, but they go by many names, including sea siren or nymph."

I took a deep breath. Ghosts, bogeymen—and now sea sirens. Yes, Bolinas definitely qualified as a magical place. It was hard to be-lieve I'd never been aware of these malevolent sea creatures when I was a child. Then again, my father had warned me about the effects of his conjuring, so perhaps their presence was new. The Laurent family did like to play havoc with the elements. Maybe my father's presence alone was enough to call these sea-bound creatures into being.

"Thank you," I said. "This is the second time you've pulled me back from the ledge."

Elsa shrugged. "I promised to look after you."

And I was grateful, even if I wished I didn't need such looking after. "So where have you been? I haven't seen you since the night Aidan died. You left without saying good-bye."

"Aidan was my mate," she said, turning away from me as she spoke. "I needed . . . to get away. To be alone."

"I understand. It was a terrible night. I wish I could have been there for you. I knew you and Aidan had grown close," I said. "In many ways I feel like his death is my fault. I hope you can forgive me."

Elsa faced me again, her chin lifted slightly. "This is why I came back. You need me," she said. "You're still thinking like a human. You didn't cause this, Nikola did."

"I do need you," I said. "Maybe more than before. Nikola murdered Aidan and he killed my mother. But William and Josef won't kill him."

"They cannot," Elsa said. "We'll have to do it."

"Yes, but we have other problems to tackle too," I replied, happy to unburden myself. "You taught me how to use some of my gifts, but I still feel . . . I feel powerless. I'm a witch who doesn't understand her skills. My mother's dead and it's my fault. My father hasn't a clue what to do. I need someone to help me figure this all out."

"Calm your mind, Olivia, or it will be your undoing," Elsa chided, sounding just like the day she'd first installed herself in my guest room, months ago. "We cannot change the past. We can only learn from it. Honor your mother's memory by embracing your heritage and completing your training."

I sniffed and shook my head in agreement, moving a step closer as I spoke. "I missed you. And Lily," I said, referring to my best friend and the third woman in our triumvirate.

I'd only recently discovered Lily was supernatural—a descendent of a long line of powerful fairies. Inseparable since we'd first met as new arrivals to San Francisco, the last few months had tested our friendship, first when I lashed out, depressed and mostly drunk, over Stoner Halbert's sabotage of my career, and then when Lily left to recover with her family after the explosion at the museum. I'd gone to Paris, been informed of my true parentage, and fled, leaving word with no one, not even Lily—not that I would have known how to find her. Reuniting with Elsa made me realize how important they both were to me.

"I want to find her. I want her at my mother's service tomorrow," I said. "I need my friends by my side."

"Is that what we are?" Elsa asked, with seemingly genuine curiosity.

I smiled. "*Friends* doesn't quite fit, does it?" I said. "Maybe *sisters* is a better description. I do know we're bound to one another, you and me. Our fates are crossed."

Elsa's stance softened. "You're not angry that I didn't tell you?"

"I was," I replied. "But what's done is done. And Gabriel told me you didn't like being caught in the middle. Anyway, it's cold outside. Come back to the house with me. We'll have some tea and call Lily."

"There's no need," Elsa said. "She's here."

True to her word, when we were just a few steps from home, the door opened to reveal Lily standing in the entryway. I smiled at the sight of her, tears of joy and regret brimming in my eyes. Our last moments together had been spent in the chaos of an explosion. Separated by smoke and fire, we'd both been seriously injured. By the time I regained consciousness, she'd already gone. William, Josef, and I had left for Paris soon after, and then weeks later, when we left for Montenegro, a combination of embarrassment and remorse kept me from trying to contact her. Even now, I felt as if my feet were rooted in the ground. I wasn't sure what to do next.

Lily made it easy by walking toward me, arms outstretched. I could hear her thoughts, which were full of love and understanding, and I ran to her and threw myself into her embrace.

"I love you," I babbled as we held each other. "I'm so sorry for everything."

Lily did not release me as she spoke. "I love you too. I've missed you," she said. "I'm sorry about your mother. Let's not be separated again, my dear, dear friend."

Elsa stood by, her eyes wet as well. I smiled a secret smile to myself. Her tears confirmed that years of time-walking hadn't robbed her of her humanity. Surrounded again by my friends, a sense of peace that had been missing for some time settled into my heart.

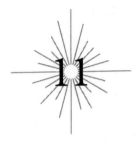

TOGETHER WE WALKED BACK INSIDE. I FELT LILY'S JOY AT seeing Josef, reminding me that before the explosion, the two of them had begun a fledgling romance. A brief pang of jealousy flared, which I quickly doused. Josef's love life was no concern of mine, I reminded myself. His appearance in my bed had been a fluke, a rare occurrence like an eclipse that was not destined to happen again in my lifetime.

"OK, who's hungry?" my father asked, clearly delighted by the full house. "I'm in the mood to make crêpes."

"Not so fast," I said, despite the growling from my stomach. "I almost fell off the cliff, nearly lulled to my demise by a bunch of *sea sirens*. I know I ignored my skills when my mother was alive, but I would have *noticed* those creatures lurking in the sea."

Gabriel grimaced. "Magic has three functions: to produce, protect, and destroy," he said, eyeing us uneasily. "I told you that I come from a long line of witches who control the sea and *la brume* . . . the fog. Occasionally our efforts attract other creatures. It's a symbiotic relationship. I did warn you to be careful."

"I guess I misunderstood the level of severity attached to your warning," I replied. "I'll be more careful next time."

"*Bon!* Now can I start cooking?" he said, walking toward the kitchen.

The two vampires kindly demurred and left the room as my father began pulling ingredients from the pantry. You'd think he'd lived here all his life. Lily paired her phone with a wireless speaker in the kitchen, filling the room with French café music. Elsa put on the kettle and pulled a box of chai from the cabinet. Suddenly the house was alive, a family of sorts occupying its center. I felt an ache in my chest. If there was an afterlife, I hoped my mother was looking down with satisfaction knowing her home was filled to the brim with people and activity.

After brunch I worked on my remarks for my mother's service, choosing to close with an excerpt from Tennyson.

> Gone.
> Gone! . . .
> Gone, and the light gone with her, and left me in shadow here!
> Gone—flitted away,
> Taken the stars from the night and the sun from the day!
> Gone, and a cloud in my heart, and a storm in the air!
> Flown to the east or the west, flitted I know not where!
> Gone.

Lily's delivery of clothing from my closet to wear to the memorial service robbed me of my last good excuse to avoid my mother's studio. The one saving grace was that when I explained my obligation to catalog the paintings, Lily and Elsa agreed to assist. I tried to prepare myself as I slid the barn door open. This, if anywhere, is where the ghost of my mother would lurk: among the rough sketches, haphazardly drawn and taped to various walls, the jars of brushes and pencils lining the waiting worktables.

"OK," I said, breathing in the mix of stale air and turpentine. "We need to create an inventory of India's work to give her dealer. He'll use our list against his records to see if anything in here is unaccounted for. Then, when everything has been reconciled, we can create a final catalog."

"Leave it to the librarian," Lily said. "I'll give every painting, every drawing a name, number, or identifier with a corresponding photograph."

"Perfect," I responded gratefully. "Elsa, what would you say to opening my mother's laptop and checking her email and files for any requests for commissions or exhibitions? The police in Paris gave me her computer when I claimed her body, but I haven't been able to bring myself to do it."

Elsa smiled, and I sensed her relief at having a purpose. "I can do that," she said. "Do you know her password?"

I didn't, off the top of my head, but I knew my mother. My throat hurt.

"Try Olivia," I said, my voice catching. "Try typing in my name."

A FEW HOURS LATER, STIFF FROM SITTING, WE DECIDED TO GET some fresh air and walk through the meadow and forest that surrounds my mother's home. The fog had rolled in wet and thick. I thought again of my father and his tricks, but we were antsy to stretch our legs. As we headed for the door, the persistent music of the lighthouse reminded me of my ancestors' ability to call the fog, like a fisherman pulling a net into a boat. Why didn't I have the same gift?

Elsa, as always, was listening closely, and she replied aloud to my silent query.

"It's like eye color," she said. "A couple with blue eyes might have a child with brown eyes. There is no predicting what will show up in powerful families like yours. And your half-human side is going to make it difficult for us to know how your gifts will play out. Things won't work the way we expect. Still, it's a miracle that you were even born."

"You don't know how sick I am of hearing that," I said, huffing and puffing as we climbed briskly into the forested hills. "The question is, how do we figure out what I *can* do?"

Lily paused to wipe moisture from her forehead that had fallen from the tree canopy above. "It's almost raining out here," she complained. "Can we turn around?"

It didn't take much convincing, with all of us drenched, for us to head back to the house.

As we turned, a flicker of something dark and shiny caught my eye. Already on alert for new and potentially *more* dangerous creatures to appear, I held out my arm to stop my friends from moving forward. Elsa opened her mouth, but Lily's hand shot out to grasp her in warning. There, in front of us, was a single black wolf, his teeth bared in a growing snarl. A quick mental calculation told me this creature was not native to my mother's property. Coyotes yes, occasionally even a fox, but without supernatural assistance, a large *Canis lupus* in Bolinas was unlikely.

"Be gone!" Elsa yelled, pulling a small dagger from her boot and lunging at the animal. "Tell your master to stay off our property."

The wolf, confirming the fact that this was no ordinary creature, raised its head and gazed directly at Elsa. For a moment, the two were in a standoff, but the beast finally relented and trotted away, quickly disappearing.

"Werewolf?" I asked, thinking that it hadn't *felt* like a normal animal when I'd tried to reach out with my mind.

Lily nodded. "It smelled like one, and I have an exceptional sense of smell."

"We have the most fascinating conversations when we're together," I said, letting my sarcasm loose. "But what the hell was *that thing* doing here?"

Lily and Elsa exchanged glances. "Nikola," they said in unison.

"I think he's looking for you," Elsa said. "Nikola likes to use werewolves to deliver messages and run errands."

"Great. In addition to learning about my skills, now I have to worry about Nikola showing up. Nadia was right: I am out of time."

"I don't know about out of time, but the other part of this is just like your mother's artwork," Lily said as we hiked back down the hill, our senses on guard for another encounter with a dangerous creature.

"We need to catalog our observations about your current skills, and those of the women in your family and Gabriel's."

"And then what?"

"Then we see if you can do any of the things on the list we create," Elsa replied. "We know you are telepathic and empathic, and you have the ability to disappear. Have any new tricks popped up since we were all separated?"

"I don't do tricks," I said, feeling snippy.

Lily, hair plastered against her head from the damp, began to howl with laughter.

"What's so funny?" I said.

"Oh, I'm just reminded of the night not long ago when you were the one asking us these questions," she said.

Lily's remarks snapped me out of my funk.

"You're right," I agreed. "I didn't know then how different things could be."

"But they're also very much the same," she replied reassuringly. "After all, we're all here together again."

As soon as we entered the house, the smell of a rich meal filled our nostrils. Gabriel, once again, had prepared a sumptuous dinner of beef stew with plenty of red wine and a cheese course for dessert. Even the vampires stayed at the table, drinking wine and enjoying the languorous tempo of the evening. Perhaps it was the knowledge that the memorial service was the next day, but no one—myself included—seemed to have the stomach to bring up the wolf sighting, Nikola, or the work that remained. Instead, we traded stories about exotic cities, amazing meals, and worthwhile books to read in free time that no one expected to have in the near future.

Despite the lovely evening, I went to bed that night restless and worried about the encounter with the wolf and about the small window of time I had to learn about the skills I possessed as a witch. Since we'd first met, William, although a vampire, had been able to hear my thoughts clearly. We didn't question it—we saw it as a sign that our relationship was meant to be. But tonight it proved exasperating, and finally, having had enough of my thoughts in his head, William admonished me to take a deep breath and go to sleep. I took his advice, and awoke with a start the next morning, groggy from too much red wine and too little sleep. William was kneeling next to me, gently shaking my arm.

"We need to get ready, Olivia," he said, a sad smile on his face. "The caterers are here; the guests will arrive soon."

I nodded and forced myself up and out of bed. William escorted me straight to a warm shower. I appeared in the kitchen sometime later, wearing a simple midnight-colored wool dress topped with a matching velvet jacket and black suede boots.

I gulped down one cup of coffee, and then the guests began to arrive. I watched as my mother's friends stepped into the living room, grim masks of grief affixed to their faces. These were the artists and thinkers of her generation, her fellow rebels, determined to show the world as they saw it.

I felt their emotions roil. India's alleged suicide didn't sit well with them, and although I pitied their pain and suffering, it was a great relief to feel such loyalty. They were all watching me, the distant, difficult daughter whose entourage had taken over India's home. Oddly, I wasn't the least bit offended. Their indignation was a fitting rebuttal to the indifference my mother's broken body experienced at the morgue in France. It warmed my heart.

The day became a blur punctuated by Tennyson and grief. Hours later, when the last guests had departed, I sank into a chair and wept, exhausted by my hostess duties and the realization that my mother was now well and truly gone, sent away from this world with the blessings of those who loved and respected her. Feeling melancholy, I pulled a collection of poems by T. S. Eliot off the shelf and began to read.

Lady of silences
Calm and distressed
Torn and most whole
Rose of memory
Rose of forgetfulness
Exhausted and life-giving
Worried reposeful
The single Rose
Is now the Garden.

13

THE DAY AFTER THE SERVICE, OUR GROUP SPLIT UP, everyone—except Lily, who had a previous appointment—promising to reassemble in Bolinas later for dinner. It was January, a new year, and paying a visit to my house near Golden Gate Park and having lunch with my mother's art dealer seemed like a good way to occupy my time.

In fact, everyone seemed eager for a trip across the bridge, and perhaps a break from Bolinas, which was proving to be almost *too* magical. Gabriel wanted to visit his apartment on Nob Hill. Lily needed to go home to change for work and get to her job at the library. William and Josef had set off in William's black Subaru wagon before sunrise, heading for William's lovely Victorian house near Dolores Park.

A short drive across the bridge and I was perched on my doorstep, unsure for a moment how to navigate the lock on my front door. Elsa stood behind me watching, perhaps understanding the odd sensation of returning to a familiar place after a long absence. Finally, I turned the key and entered. A quick glance confirmed that my belongings were just where I'd left them, which helped me relax. It was just like coming home from a vacation, I told myself—the one where you fled from country to county to avoid personal responsibility and great bodily harm.

"How come all of your plants are still alive?" Elsa asked as we walked inside.

I looked around and noticed that not only were they alive, but there were also new orchids sitting on some of the tables.

"I'm not sure," I replied. "Either Lily or my father must have arranged for someone to look after the house."

"It's nice to have a family to look out for you," she said wistfully.

"Why do you say that like you don't have the same thing? I know Aidan is gone, but you're a part of this family now," I said earnestly. "It's unconventional and certainly I have no idea what will happen next, but you *are* a part of it."

Elsa, never overly effusive, nodded, a hint of a smile upon her lips.

"OK then," I said. "Let's get organized and head downtown."

"What's downtown?" Elsa asked.

"The gallery that represents my mother," I replied. "I'm going to meet Jason Rawley, India's dealer, for lunch. I don't think my mother had a will, or left any directions about what should be done with her art. I need to speak to him and form a plan."

"If you don't mind, I think I'll pass on lunch," she said. "I was going to go for a walk in the park and then maybe do some yoga. When you get back, we should go for a run. You could use some exercise."

"You sound like Josef," I chided playfully.

"Actually, he sounds like *me*," Elsa sniffed, disappearing up the stairs to my bedroom to borrow some workout gear.

Jason and I were to meet at Café de la Presse, a French bistro and international newsstand on the corner of Bush and Grant Streets. While I waited for my companion to arrive, I perused the bistro's newsstand, which still featured a collection of European versions of magazines like *Vogue* and *Elle*, and made a mental note to bring a few home for our group.

My back was to the door when I felt the wave of curiosity hit the room. I looked around just in time to meet the eyes of a man in his mid-thirties, wearing a collarless black leather jacket over a dark gray T-shirt and jeans. He had curly black hair, cut short enough to be tousled but not messy, and a neatly trimmed beard with a few wisps of gray. A pair of round tortoiseshell glasses completed the picture. I hardly ever thought about my skill at reading auras anymore, it had become so much a part of my senses. But looking at the brilliant blue and green band hovering around Jason Rawley, my stomach did a little flip. It was rare to encounter a human who seemed so . . . *alive*. Having this gorgeous man meet me for lunch was not what I'd expected.

"Olivia," he said, coming to take my hand. "I recognize you from your mother's photos. Although you look better in person."

I smiled, shocked to feel myself blushing at such a clichéd complement, although I knew I looked good in my jeans, knee-high boots, and fitted sweater.

Listening to him speak, I quickly realized that Jason was nothing like his father, who'd founded the gallery in the late 1960s. Peter Rawley had been a sculptor and had wanted to create an institution that would attract serious collectors interested in San Francisco artists. But art wasn't an avocation that ran in the family; instead, Jason was the well-educated native son, intent on seeing his father's legacy survive.

"I love my father," Jason said, dunking a *frite* into a little silver dish of aioli. "But growing up, he always seemed to be angry about something. The war in Iraq. Censorship. Yuppies in San Francisco. I found it exhausting to be so upset all the time. And, of course, I secretly suspected he saw me as one of those capitalist types, more interested in money than art. The types he professed to hate so much."

"When did he die?" I asked, pouring some more Rosé into our glasses.

"He's not dead," he said, directing his gaze away from mine. "I didn't realize I gave you that impression. He's in a home in Marin. Alzheimer's, I'm afraid. At this point, he doesn't really remember me."

"I'm sorry," I said. "What about your mom?"

"There isn't one," Jason said, pushing the haricots verts around on his plate. "She left us when I was little. My father raised me on his own."

"Wow," I replied. "You and I have been living somewhat parallel lives."

Jason smiled, small crinkles forming at the corners of his smoky green eyes. "I know," he said. "I find it odd we never met before now."

"Not really," I replied awkwardly. "I gave my mother a wide berth these last few years. I didn't expect . . ."

Regret caught my tongue. Books could be filled with all the things I hadn't realized, but dwelling on it made no sense.

"Enough said," Jason agreed. He emptied the last of the wine into our glasses. "OK. Let's discuss your mother's work and what to do with it."

I nodded, grateful for a concrete task.

"Are you the executor of her estate?" he asked.

"I haven't found her will yet," I replied. "I wondered if you should be the executor though, since you know her work so well."

"It shouldn't be me," he said emphatically. "There's too much temptation as a dealer, too much conflict of interest. I'm happy to act as an advisor, but you should decide what pieces should be sold and what pieces should be donated to schools or smaller museums. If making money is a priority, let me know. If you'd prefer to move slowly, even better."

"I'm in no hurry to sell anything," I replied. "I'd like to finish cataloging her studio with my friends and turn my findings over to you. Then perhaps we could arrange an exhibition to honor her work? I've found a number of her journals and sketches in the studio. It could be a tribute to her."

Jason sat back in his chair and stared past me for a moment, thinking. While he ruminated, I found myself studying the curve of his neck and his earlobe, where the faint trace of a piercing was still visible.

Finally, he broke his silence. "We're a lot alike, you know," he said. He leaned forward again and briefly touched the back of my hand. "We both admire and dislike our parents."

"Maybe once," I said, trying to ignore the tingling sensation his fingers left behind on my skin. "But loathing your parents is something you do when you know you can see them again." I grabbed my glass of water, my throat suddenly dry. "My mother is *gone*," I said. "Now is the time to honor her life and make sure she's not forgotten."

"She won't be forgotten," Jason said. "But the show you're describing—that kind of retrospective will take some planning. Give me some time to organize. In six or eight weeks we could pull something together."

Would I be around in two months? Hard to tell, with Nikola nipping at my heels. But something about Jason put my mind at ease, causing me to forget my woes, lean back in my bistro chair, and gaze out the dining room windows at the people walking past on Bush Street. In fact, I was so absorbed in the view, I barely heard his next question.

"Are you free this weekend?" The unmistakable feelings of attraction attached to his query made me squirm a little in my chair. For the first time in my adult memory, I was actually attracted to a human man. *Really* attracted. Of course it coincided with another first: having a vampire boyfriend—a fiancé, really—who wouldn't enjoy any competition.

And yet, I didn't exactly shut things down. "I can't this weekend," I said. "There's a lot going on at the moment. My father is staying with me in Bolinas, and I want to check in with him before I make plans."

It was a version of the truth. Why the white lie? I suspected it went back to the fact that Jason was the first human male I'd ever felt this at ease with. Whatever my motivations, I didn't mention William or Josef.

"I should have told you earlier that my father and I only just met recently," I continued. "My mother kept his existence from me until just before she died."

Jason's eyes widened in shock. "Oh my God," he said, reflexively reaching for his wine glass, which was now empty. "Is that why she was so . . . despondent?"

His assumption of the motive for my mother's so-called suicide chilled my attraction and reminded me once again of Nikola and the ugly charade he'd forced upon me. Or was it a bed I'd made for myself? Either way, the mood was ruined.

Suddenly feeling done with the situation, I stood up, looking directly at Jason. "Maybe, but I don't think we'll ever know," I said. He stood up, too, looking confused at the abrupt end of our lunch. "I really wish I knew what happened," I added, knowing that at least in that moment, I was telling him the truth.

"Of course, you've had a terrible shock with all of this," he said, empathy coming off him in waves.

"Yes," I said. "I'm sorry to wrap up so quickly, but it's for the best at the moment."

"Olivia, I understand," he said.

I nodded as politely as I could and walked away from the table. I was relieved at least that I'd been able to leave before he could ask a second time to see me again.

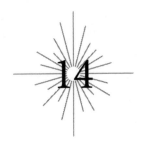

14

DESPITE A FOUL MOOD AND A BELLY FULL OF WINE, I KEPT my promise to take a run on Ocean Beach with Elsa. Dusk was approaching when I turned into my mother's driveway. Gingerly, I peeled myself out of the driver's seat, my legs aching from the first real exertion I'd had in weeks—unless of course you counted a Parisian sex party as legitimate exercise. I made my way slowly toward the front door, rubbing my aching lower back along the way. Josef stood in the doorway, his dark hair shorn to his scalp, old, knowing eyes following me.

"I told you," he said. "We need to restart our training. You're getting soft."

"As much as it pains me to agree with you, I think you may have a point," I confessed. "But you're late. Elsa already chided me."

"Agreeing with me is the *least* painful thing you can do," he muttered under his breath as I passed.

I choked back a snort as I moved beyond his grasp. Ever the bad boy, Josef loved to taunt me with suggestive comments. Since Paris, they tended to amuse more than annoy me, but I knew better than to take his bait. I dropped my purse and keys in the kitchen, and not long after, Gabriel arrived, carrying several bags from Whole Foods.

"I met with Jason Rawley today," I said, watching him place several bottles of Côtes du Rhône, a rotisserie chicken, a baguette, and a head of butter lettuce on the counter. "He'll arrange for a retrospective of Mom's paintings for the spring or early summer."

Gabriel's back was to me and he made no response.

"Gabriel?" I asked again.

"What? Yes, that is excellent," he said. "Forgive me. I've had a terrible day. Nikola arrived unannounced at the Council's offices and demanded a meeting."

That caught everyone's attention. William, who'd been reading in the living room, stepped into the kitchen, and all of us inched closer to hear the conversation better.

"What did he want?" I asked as I opened one of the wine bottles on the counter. I poured myself a glass and handed the bottle around.

"First and foremost, he wants to know where you are," Gabriel replied. "You must have managed to irk him deeply in Paris." He poured himself a generous serving of wine. "His stated purpose was merely to inform me in person that he's ready to assume control of the Council early. He says if necessary, he will seek the votes to force an early transition."

"There is no such thing," William remarked grimly. "Not unless he's decided to rewrite the bylaws of the organization."

Gabriel responded with a thin smile. "*Exactement!* What's the expression? He's bluffing. I'm not sure why Nikola would need the Council to bend to his will in this. For decades we have maintained a transition every five years, rotating leaders from one geographic region to another. The Council is a well-oiled machine—a thoughtful instrument of good working to protect humans. I'm beginning to think that Nikola relishes rewiring the machine to subvert our mission or create conflict. He's always been this way, testing boundaries. He's trying to generate chaos, but I will—"

Gabriel stopped midsentence when his wine glass flew off the counter, then burst into shards as it hit the hard tile floor of my mother's kitchen. For some reason, all eyes turned to me.

"What?" I asked, feeling an odd tingling in my chest.

"Olivia, did you move that glass?" Elsa asked, breaking the silence.

"I don't know," I replied. "I was only half listening to all of you. I got distracted thinking about how angry I am at Nikola."

The group exchanged glances. "And then what?" William asked, coming to stand next to me.

"I'm not sure," I admitted. "I just felt this pressure in my chest and exhaled. A second later the glass flew off the counter."

"Well, I think we know what your other skill is," Gabriel remarked, beaming like a proud father.

"How can you be sure it's me?" I asked.

"Just a hunch," Elsa said calmly. "Do you remember moving objects like this before?"

I hesitated. "Not exactly like this, but to be honest, from time to time I've had things happen . . ."

"Such as?" Josef asked.

"Sometimes I've walked past a window that I thought should be open or a drawer that should be closed and made a note to come back to take care of the task. But when I returned, it was already done. I always assumed I'd actually done it myself but had been too busy to remember."

"How could you not notice you have telekinesis?" Josef grumbled.

"Because until recently I thought I was human," I spat back. "Generally, humans can't move objects with their mind, nor can they disappear in scary circumstances. I wasn't expecting to have any special powers beyond my empathy skills."

Elsa stepped in between the two of us. "Olivia hasn't known what she was looking for," she said sternly. "Now she knows. And so do we." To me she said, "Let's try now. Can you move the wine bottle? See if you can focus on it and forget everything else."

I exhaled, looking to William for guidance. His lively green eyes held mine. "Go ahead, darlin'," he said. "We'll make sure you don't break the place up."

I looked over at the counter and tried to recall the sensation I'd felt in my chest. It had felt like anger, pure, unbridled anger. I turned my thoughts to the morgue in Paris and my mother's broken body as I focused on the glass bottle on the counter. I exhaled as I had before and watched the bottle begin to vibrate on the counter. It moved ever so slightly toward the edge, but stopped.

"Again," Gabriel encouraged. "But don't use anger. This time, try to forget your emotions. Just think about moving the bottle."

I glanced at the wine and emptied my mind of everything but the intention to complete a physical task. This seemed closer to how I'd likely moved things in the past, before I'd found out I was part witch. As I simply made a mental note to put the bottle away, and pictured it happening, there was motion. Sure enough, the bottle slid off the counter toward the refrigerator. William grabbed it midair and set it back down on the marble countertop.

"What did you do that time?" William asked.

"I just imagined doing it," I said. "I made a note in my mind to put the bottle away and then . . . well, then you caught it midair."

Josef rubbed his hands together. "I wonder if you could summon an object to yourself on command. Like a knife or a dagger."

"Probably," I said, shrugging my shoulders, feeling self-conscious. Once again, I was a sideshow in which everyone else seemed to know the act better than me. "Maybe we can try tomorrow."

"OK, enough hocus-pocus for now," Gabriel teased, breaking the tension. "We need to eat dinner."

Once we took our seats for the meal it felt easier to get down to business. "What are you going to do about Nikola?" I asked, between mouthfuls of roast chicken and silky mashed potatoes. "He wants to run the Council for some reason, but it's not to help humans."

My father frowned. "There is a saying in Serbian," he remarked.

"'A greedy father has thieves for children.' The answer to his motives lies in Serbia, but I don't know if we have the time to find out."

"Stall," Josef said. "He has no legal way to assume leadership until the fall. That's months from now. Surely you and your team can create enough diversions to keep him busy until we can find out what he's up to."

My father leaned back in his chair and exhaled, a heavy breath of discontent. "I've been a fool," he admitted. "Aidan's death, the bombing, India Rose—on and on Nikola goes, destroying people, and I sit in my bureaucrat's chair pretending that rules and regulations will save me. But we all know that Nikola must be prevented from becoming head of the Council. The only way to do that is to present enough evidence of his misdeeds to require that he be replaced."

"You're making the Council sound like a law firm that can get Nikola disbarred. But it's hard to imagine he'd go for that," I said.

Josef snorted. "Olivia's right. You think a criminal file will convince your colleagues to remove him from his seat? He's ancient and powerful. Why would they risk his wrath?"

Elsa answered for Gabriel. "We're not so complacent as you make us, Josef. The other directors could vote to skip Eastern Europe's turn at the helm and move on to Russia or China, which are next in line. If we made a compelling case."

"What would be a compelling case?" I asked.

Gabriel glanced over at me and took my hand in his. "You'll know it when you see it," he said. "It must be something that proves without a doubt that his actions are a danger to the Council and its mission."

"What are you suggesting, Gabriel?" William asked, frowning. I could feel his unease growing.

"As it happens, there is an election coming up in Belgrade," Gabriel said, pouring more wine into everyone's glasses. "National elections will take place in April. Given Serbia's tepid advance into democracy, there will be plenty of work for election monitors in the country. What better cover for Olivia than to go and work as an election monitor for the Organization for Security and Co-operation in Europe? The OSCE will hire Olivia in a minute, with her vast elections experience. She's perfect, especially if she arrives with an associate who speaks Serbian and reads Cyrillic.

"It's common knowledge in Serbia that Nikola uses his money to influence elections and local politicians to ensure his hotels and casinos get built without having to go through all of the normal reviews and permits. He built an empire while his competitors were still filling out forms. I suspect he uses his political connections for much, much more nefarious deeds. You can investigate while you monitor the elections. Chances are good a few candidates he supports will be running in the smaller towns. You should be able to find some connections to his criminal efforts."

"Suddenly your clarity about Nikola is remarkable," William said. "Why didn't you do anything about this before?"

"There was no reason to poke a stick at a beehive," Gabriel replied. "But now—"

"You can speak Serbian?" I asked Elsa.

"He means me," Josef said.

The room was silent. For the moment, I let drop the absurdity of Josef traveling with me in Serbia. "Fair enough," I said to Gabriel, jumping back into the conversation, "but you would never leave this to chance. I assume you've already contacted someone there and secured me the job."

A sheepish look appeared on my father's face. "You know me too well," he said. "I did call the director, and you have a job waiting in Belgrade."

"Nikola's intentions toward Olivia are clear," William said. "Are you sure it's smart to send your daughter into his territory?"

"Olivia wants to do this," Gabriel said, lifting his noble chin to glance at me for support. "After Nikola's visit today, I realized we had to act fast. Besides, is she in any less danger here? We have no idea what Nikola's plans are. The sooner we understand his activities, the better."

Gabriel's comments reminded me that I'd neglected to mention the wolf sighting. "Nikola has been here," I said. "Or at least one of his minions. When we went out for a walk a few days ago, we encountered a wolf in the forest. Elsa thinks it was a werewolf sent to look for me."

"*Zut*," Gabriel said. "You see, we have no time to spare."

"I disagree. Now is the time to slow down and strategize," William said. "Let me state the obvious: Olivia is not a soldier. She has never functioned as a tracker for the Council, as Josef and I both have in the past. Nikola is a brutal vampire who engineered the car bomb that killed Aidan and then murdered Olivia's mother. Now we are saying the best solution is to send her directly into his path in Serbia?"

"I think I should go," I said. "Someone has to act before he takes down the whole Council. It's my mother who was killed. I want revenge, and I plan to take it."

"It's not worth putting yourself in danger," William said.

"Why not? You said yourself that you can't kill him," I said. "There is no one else but me. I'll train with Josef. I'll improve my skills with the dagger and work with Elsa to learn to control objects. With the election monitoring, I'll be able to travel easily. I will find out what Nikola is up to. Someone has to rid us of this problem once and for all."

"I cannot tell you how it pains me to hear that the woman I want to marry and have a life with is hellbent on confronting a lethal foe despite the great risk," William said. "I asked you to train to protect yourself, not to seek out a confrontation with a monster."

"Perhaps it is destiny," Gabriel said. "She was born to be a leader, this child of two worlds. She has skills no one else possesses."

"All the more reason to keep her close to us," William said, rising from the table. "Let someone else go and build a case against Nikola. It's too dangerous."

⁂

Later that evening, after the dishes had been cleaned and put away, I crawled into our bed in my mother's guest cottage to find a welcome that was not exactly warm. William, perched against a pillow, a copy of *World War Z* in his hands, refused to look at me.

"You, of all people, should understand," I said.

"Why go to him?" William asked, putting down his book. "He's waiting for *you*. He's baiting your father to ensure he sends you straight to him."

"There will be no peace until we stop him," I said. "Nikola will overtake the Council and remove Gabriel. And then what? What will he do when he's got real power at his fingertips? How will we stop him then?"

"This is my greatest fear coming true," William said. "That you become the target, a pawn in their games."

"What other choice do we have?" I asked, knowing William had no answer.

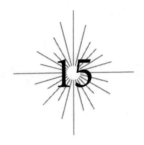

I FELT PENSIVE AND MOODY THE NEXT MORNING AS I greeted Elsa in the kitchen. Beautiful as always, her dark hair fixed in a tight braid, she was sitting at the counter sipping mint tea, a piece of half-eaten toast on a plate before her. The house seemed unnaturally quiet.

"Morning," I said, turning on the espresso machine. "Where is everyone?"

"Out," she said. "Everyone went back to the city. Josef left last night. Gabriel and William took off before the sun came up. But here's the good news: Lily texted. She's taking the day off and will be here shortly."

"You told her?"

"I did," Elsa said. "I heard your thoughts. I knew you wanted to talk to us. It's better if the men aren't here. They won't be any help, anyway. If we need to kill Nikola, it will come down to either you or me."

"Do you remember when we first met and I asked if I could just go back to my old life?"

Elsa pushed the plate farther away from her before she spoke. "I remember," she said. "I told you that there would be no turning back. And that was before you made an enemy of Nikola, and he challenged your father as the leader of the Council. Now, we're all bound to this saga and have to see it to its close. Trust me, as a time-walker, I have seen many a grudge played out over the centuries. We need to finish this so that it doesn't breed a legacy of hate."

I made myself a cappuccino and took a seat next to Elsa. "Can I really take this on?" I stared down at my mug.

Elsa reached over and covered my hand with her own before she spoke. "I'm afraid it's too late to be asking that question. All roads lead back to you. So, you can wait here and let Nikola come to you, knowing that he will harm everything he touches along the way, or you can surprise him and make him work harder. You're a woman, so he will not expect you to be capable of committing fiercely brave and, yes, even savage acts. Do not gratify his expectations by giving up before you start. Do you think if you were Gabriel and India's son, you would be questioning what to do next?"

"Probably not," I said.

Elsa spoke again before I could finish my sentence. "Man or woman, it makes no difference," she said. "Many a woman has wrought hell upon her enemies. It's a question of will. Do you think Cleopatra saw her female form as a liability? Did Margaret Thatcher seem timid to you?"

"Of course not," I said, feeling properly chastised.

I was about to say more when the doorbell rang. I walked from the kitchen to let Lily in. My tall friend was standing on the landing looking lovely as usual, in a wool sweater and a pair of black cargo pants, her sexy librarian reading glasses perched on her head.

"Hello," I said.

"Hello, yourself," she replied, stepping into the house. "Boy, I skip one dinner with the clan, and I miss big news."

Elsa, Lily, and I relocated to my mother's studio, now converted into my office, my laptop and other papers on what had once been my mother's drafting table.

"I want to know what you two think about my father's idea," I said as I turned on my laptop.

"I think all of us should go," Lily said. "I did a little research before heading out here, and I think there is a way we can travel with you and actually make your assignment look even more realistic."

"I'm all ears."

"Well," she said. "Election monitoring is usually done in teams. You need more than one person to conduct site visits, examine documents, and maintain all of the data for the official report. There's also a need for security, a driver, and a translator. I think we could make a persuasive team with me as the big data person, Elsa and William managing security, and Josef as driver and translator."

"It's a good plan," Elsa said. "But can you really join us?"

"I'll take a leave of absence," Lily said. "I like my job, but you both are too important to me. I don't want to stay here, again, while you go gallivanting all over the world."

"Gallivanting suggests fun," I said. "We'll be looking for a way to discredit Nikola while we document the preparations these towns are making for free and fair elections. Any hint that he's helped rig an election or pay off a politician would help us discredit him. But it will be dangerous."

"Olivia, I may be a librarian, but I am also a fairy and an Other. I can take care of myself. Besides, who else is going to help you?"

"Lily, your *arm* . . . you just recovered from the last disaster, what if—" I stopped myself. I knew they both understood.

"I'm a fast healer," Lily replied, smiling. "You just focus on learning how to use those skills of yours. I can take care of myself."

I looked at the two women sitting in front of me and said a silent thank you to my grandmother, Bella Rose. Just before her death, she'd summoned Elsa and asked her to look after me. With that single choice, she'd set my destiny in motion—and planted the seeds of a powerful friendship that I knew would be important to me for the rest of my life.

16

WILLIAM WAS NOT SURPRISED, GIVEN THE CONVERSATION over dinner, to receive a text from Gabriel summoning Josef and him to a private meeting, without Olivia.

After he had taken his fear and fury from the dinner table, he'd listened to Josef make his excuses and leave, no doubt driving his motorcycle back across the bridge to San Francisco. Josef had mentioned something earlier about stopping by Lily's to rekindle their romance, but William doubted he would see it through. One would have to be a blind man not to know that Olivia was too much on his mind—on both their minds.

William had watched his brother pass dozens of years without a single meaningful connection to another being. But the ménage à trois in Paris had been a revelation. No words had been uttered, save a few murmurings in French and Olivia's screams as the two vampires had devoured her. The old Josef would have left early, William knew, perhaps even slightly unfulfilled. That is how little he had cared for another's pleasure.

But this time, all three had bonded. Even now, William thought, he could detect the faint smell of the two of them upon his skin, Olivia's sweet taste upon his lips. For days afterward, he had wondered why he had allowed Josef to enjoy such intimacy with the woman he loved. Of course, he'd always known his and his brother's fates were tied to one another, for better or worse. And now, it seemed, the worse would come first.

Standing at the foot of the Council's offices at dusk the next day, William watched as Josef placed his palm on the scanner mounted to the side of the entrance. It only took seconds for the computer to read his hand and unlock the copper door hidden amid the tall ferns at the rear of the de Young Museum in Golden Gate Park. William had been to the building many times and still marveled how one of the most visited museums in the world could also maintain its purpose as headquarters for the Council. It seemed certain that some day such notoriety would work at cross-purposes with the Council's desire to stay hidden.

Josef glanced sideways at William as they strode through the lobby of the museum toward the elevators.

"Any idea what this is about?" he asked.

"I have some idea, yes," William said. "I think you have too."

They rode the car up to the top floor, stepping into a large, open room with a series of cubicles, all of them filled with young, earnest-looking workers typing away on their computers. Gabriel was sitting on the edge of a desk chatting with a young man who also happened to be a werewolf. Olivia's father met William's gaze the minute the vampires exited the elevators, and within seconds he was standing before them.

"Thank you for coming. Let's go to my office," he said.

Josef strolled through the doorway first and took a seat in a large leather chair facing Gabriel's desk. William stood against the wall, not ready to sit. For a moment the three men remained silent, gazing through the museum's large glass windows at a twilight view of the Pacific Ocean churning in the distance.

Then Gabriel took a seat and said, "We are at the edge of the world, no?"

"In more ways than one," Josef replied grimly.

Gabriel nodded. "Yes. Nikola has pushed us to the brink very quickly. Suddenly, I feel the weight of my responsibilities in a way I never have before." He gave Josef a bemused look. "That I should confide my fears in *your* presence should only serve to further demonstrate the place we find ourselves in."

"Why, because I'm a vampire?" Josef asked, sounding mystified.

"No, because you are the *étranger*, the outsider of this group. The one with the least to gain by inserting yourself into this mess—unless, of course, you count the fact that you also love my daughter."

William pretended he didn't see Josef's flinch. "Don't be ridiculous," Josef replied. "I've had no love for anyone or anything since the Nazis took Prague Castle in 1939."

Gabriel looked at William, then back to Josef. "Have it your way," he said. "It doesn't matter. You must see that you, and you alone, are qualified to accompany Olivia to Serbia. You know Eastern and Central Europe. You know the language. She'll need your help to fit in. William, you *must* tell him."

"I will be heading into the country separately," William said grimly. "I assume you realize that by now. You're going to have to take my place."

Josef exhaled, then lifted his head. "I'll keep her safe," he said. "You have my word."

"As much as anyone can make such a promise," Gabriel remarked.

"And the rest?" Josef asked, looking back to Gabriel. "Have you two discussed everything? When she finds out . . ."

William refused to think of it.

"Yes, it is done," Gabriel said, ending the conversation. His eyes were on his folded hands. "Olivia may not forgive me for this. And yet, I see no choice but to upend the world, so that it may be put right again."

THERE WERE NO DIRECT FLIGHTS FROM SAN FRANCISCO TO
Serbia, so Josef and I touched down on a tarmac in Zurich, with two
hours to kill at the airport until our connecting flight to Belgrade.
And really, "killing" sounded about right. At least, I thought I could
stake Josef for how unpleasant he'd been on the journey so far. I
wished for the millionth time that William had been able to travel
with us. But it hadn't worked out. Instead, he'd promised to join us in
a few days after concluding some business affairs.

"All of our traveling has wreaked havoc on my property man-
agement obligations," he'd said while I made flight arrangements in
Bolinas the week before. "I need to stay behind and clean up a few
things."

I offered to wait until he could finish his work, but he insisted
that Josef and I depart first.

"Time is not on our side, darlin'," he said. "You should leave as
soon as possible."

His rush to put me on a plane put my nose out of joint. But I was
the one who'd sent our lives spinning off in this direction. Now I was
living with the consequences.

It was snowing in Zurich. I saw large but delicate-looking
snowflakes falling as we moved through the glass-encased walk-

ways that led to the main terminal. The airport I'd seen through the plane window was new, encased in stainless steel. It shimmered in the winter light like a newly shined teakettle. I was documenting all of these observations wordlessly as Josef had retreated into sullen silence the moment the plane lifted off the ground in California. He wasn't asleep, of course, but he had definitely shut down, putting on headphones and an eye mask for the entire flight. It surprised me to see him so reticent, but then again, I'd never been his direct seat-mate on our prior journeys.

So, I almost jumped in surprise when Josef finally spoke aloud, breaking his eleven-hour silence to address me.

"I need a drink," he said emphatically

"Do vampires suffer from jet lag?" I asked. My voice sounded odd to my own ears after its prolonged absence.

He rewarded me with a heavy sigh and an eye roll. As soon as we took a seat at a small bar, a man came over and greeted us in German, French, and English. Josef responded in French and ordered himself two fingers of Jack Daniel's. Slightly nauseated from straddling the time zones, I asked, in English, for a pot of mint tea. When our drinks arrived, I heckled Josef again.

"You do realize that you didn't speak to me for the entire flight?"

Josef looked down at his glass. "Sorry. I have a lot on my mind. I promise I won't be so gloomy the rest of this journey."

"I thought maybe you were angry at me," I said. "Because you got stuck taking me to Belgrade."

"I could say the same thing," Josef said. "You were more interested in doing this when you thought William would be by your side. But now . . ." He took a large swig of his whiskey.

"Now what?" I asked. I slowly sipped the tea to calm my stomach.

"Now you're stuck with me," he said. "For a while at least."

"And you with me," I said. "I think that makes us even."

Josef regarded me with his dark eyes, all of his wariness showing on his face. For a moment, I thought he was going to confess something terrible, but the cloud passed and he smiled.

"Even it is," he said and signaled for the server to bring him a second round.

I exhaled and settled down in my chair, relieved to have avoided starting the trip off on a sour note. In less than ninety minutes we would be leaving for Serbia. Josef was my sole companion, at least until William, Elsa, and Lily arrived. I knew William would come as soon as he could, but Elsa and Lily wouldn't be arriving for at least a month. For now, Josef was instrumental to my survival.

The rest of our wait passed quietly. When we heard the call to board our flight, Josef settled our bill and we headed toward the gate. Along the way, I was hit with a case of nerves. My breathing quickened, and my hands trembled. Josef noticed my anxiety and stopped.

"Has it hit you finally?" he asked. "Don't worry. It's a good sign that your instincts have kicked in. You're going to need them to get out of this alive."

Josef's honest assessment caused me to burst into laughter. "Sugarcoating things isn't your style, is it?" I said.

Josef stopped in his tracks, grabbed both my hands, and pulled me close to him. "Save your laughter," he whispered roughly in my ear. He was gripping my arm far too tightly. "I have no sense of humor, Olivia. It bled out of my body on the fields of France. What I possess is a heightened sense of survival. It's what you'll need if you intend to live through what we're about to walk into. I need to know you understand that before we board this plane."

I gently pulled my arm free from his grasp. "I understand," I whispered back so as not to make a scene. "But if you're going to be my sole companion, you've got to lighten up. I know you do have a sense of humor. I've seen it. And I need a little lightheartedness in all of this to save my sanity. It will make our jobs a lot easier if we can laugh."

"Laugh in the face of death?"

"Sure, why not? I wouldn't give death the satisfaction of seeing me shed a single tear," I said, though I wondered where my bravado had come from.

"Nikola will love you even more," Josef said, shaking his head. "Your bravery will be like an aphrodisiac."

"I hope you're joking," I said as we boarded the plane.

THERE WAS NOTHING EXTRAORDINARY ABOUT OUR FLIGHT from Zurich to Belgrade, unless you consider the fact that no one on the flight spoke Serbian. The passengers seemed to be conversing in every language *but* Serbian. The flight crew addressed the passengers primarily in German and English. Even the emergency instruction card was printed in English, with not a Cyrillic character to be found.

The landscape changed considerably once we disembarked. Inside the airport, Cyrillic dominated the scene. At first glance I found the language impenetrable. Its characters bore no likeness to the letters I'd grown up with. I paused to stare at the signs, willing myself to see the meaning, until finally Josef came up from behind and gave me a gentle push.

"Come," he said. "Baggage claim is this way."

But first we had to go through passport control, a process that could have been completed on autopilot in the European Union countries I had frequented. Not so in Belgrade. As we stood in line waiting to visit a stern-looking woman sitting behind a glass partition, I glanced at the Cyrillic words for passport control, Пасошка Контрола, printed on a placard above her. When I approached the window, shoved my passport through the small opening, and quietly said "*Dobro vece*," which is Serbian for good evening, the woman glanced up at me. She looked younger close up. Then a mild pressure at the center of my forehead told me she was a vampire.

When a vampire tries to read my thoughts, it registers as a brief tap. Like a woodpecker perched on a tree. I can now say it is definitely less painful than when a demon, say, tries to gain access to my thoughts. The sensation reminded me briefly of my first encounter with William, in the headlands above the Golden Gate Bridge. At first, I'd mistaken his scan as a headache from dehydration.

Well-versed now in shielding myself, I regulated my breath to stay calm, and fervently hoped my entry into Serbia would go smoothly. Josef again picked up on my anxiety. He immediately stepped behind me and bid the woman a firm, but friendly, good evening. She tipped her head ever so slightly in acknowledgment and stamped my passport. We passed through the checkpoint in mere seconds and soon were on the other side of a wall, entering a drab baggage-collection area.

"Do you think Nikola arranged for her to be there?" I asked. Would we be facing a fight before we'd even gotten settled in the city?

"Hard to say," Josef said. "Serbia is a country full of vampires and Others. Finding one at passport control isn't all that shocking. On the other hand, Nikola is practically royalty in this country because of his wealth and celebrity. His reach is extensive. Either way, it won't be long before he knows you're here."

After delivering that fun tidbit of information, Josef decided we should split up. I would gather our luggage, and he would arrange for a taxi. In some cities you can just walk out to the sidewalk and hail a cab. In Belgrade, at the airport at least, you must see the taxi man, who personally selects the car and driver you will use.

We followed this procedure. Before I joined Josef at the curb, I grabbed a hat, gloves, and scarf from my carry-on bag to ward off the evening's brutally cold weather.

After several new Peugeot wagons passed us by for some inexplicable reason, the attendant finally waved us over to an ancient-looking vehicle produced by some Russian car company long ago

abandoned by the rest of the world. Inside was a driver who appeared to be almost a century old. I gave Josef a look, but he shook
his head, gently indicating that we should accept the car the taxi
man had chosen.

"It will be fine," he said, echoing my words one Paris evening
weeks ago. "Get in."

But all was not fine. One of the first things I learned when we
left the airport was that drivers in Belgrade have no fear of death.
They drive at 130 kilometers (80 miles) an hour on the highway
regardless of how close the next car is. Our driver simply sped up
until he was millimeters away from the bumper of the next car. He
never honked, just hovered close enough to make it seem an accident was unavoidable—until the other driver yielded and moved
into the adjacent lane. This happened over and over, until I was so
overcome with raw fear, I grabbed Josef's hand. He looked down,
clearly surprised, but immediately barked at the driver, "*Molim! Da
usporite.*" I deduced that this meant "slow down," because the
speedometer shortly fell to a safer number.

Happily, our cab ride was over in twenty minutes. The driver
dropped us at Square Nine, an exclusive boutique hotel newly built
in historic Belgrade. I watched Josef hand over 1,500 dinars to our
driver, rewarding him handsomely for our near-death experience.

"Don't worry," he said, chuckling. "That was the equivalent of
about fifteen dollars, plus a bit of a tip. It's impolite not to."

Fatigued, I simply nodded and made my way into the lobby
and toward the dark walnut check-in counter. After producing
passports and credit cards, we were given keys to adjoining rooms.
We stood together for a moment in front of the registration desk
eyeing each other awkwardly. I think neither of us was eager to
jump into the elevator together and explore our adjoining quarters.
Instead, I inquired about the gym while Josef wandered off to the
bar. Relieved, I headed up to my room by myself, wondering if I

could muster enough energy to run on the treadmill. It would be a good way to stay up and beat the jet lag.

My body managed to endure thirty minutes of cardio and some stretching, then I returned to my room to shower. I was tempted by the room service menu but decided instead to look for Josef in the bar. As I rode down to the lobby, I steeled myself. Dark, lean, and dangerous, Josef tended to find companions easily. His world was filled with one-night stands and lady friends who, frankly, were none of my business.

I reminded myself of a few facts. *He's not my boyfriend. We're not lovers. He's a vampire. He can do what he likes.* Still, my stomach fluttered when I strolled into the wood-paneled bar and spotted Josef with a stunning woman at his side. Very much his equal, she was tall and thin, with jet-black hair trailing down her back. A cigarette sat perched between fingernails, which were painted the color of midnight.

I suddenly had a vision of them leaving together, and it made me tremendously uncomfortable. Before I could banish the thought from my mind, the glass of wine sitting in front of her tipped over, spilling onto her lap. She gasped and jumped up, a string of curses flying from her lips. At least I guessed they were curses; since she was speaking in Serbian, I had no way of knowing. Josef looked up, his eyes locking onto mine. I turned to leave, but he was at my side within seconds, using vampire speed to thwart my escape.

"Clumsy witch," he said under his breath. "What are you doing here?"

"I'm hungry," I said. "I came to have a bite to eat. I didn't realize you had *company*."

Josef looked back at the bar, but the woman he'd been conversing with was gone.

"I didn't mean to scare your date away," I said, turning to leave.

But Josef was not in the mood to be forgiving. "Where are you off to? You're going to have to join me now, as I seem to be alone."

"I don't know if I want to," I said, lifting up my chin. "You weren't very welcoming just now."

"You spilled that wine on purpose."

"Are you kidding? I can't do anything on purpose. It was an accident," I said. "Go look for her, if you're so smitten. I'm sure you'll find her easily. I'll head back to my room and have a bowl of soup there."

"Oh no, you don't," Josef said. "She's gone, and now you're going to entertain me."

"Sure, I'll entertain you," I replied. "You can watch me eat a bowl of soup. And then you can watch as I get up and leave."

Josef was about to say something rude, I knew. The air around us began to crackle, and a glass sitting on a shelf behind the bar fell off and crashed to the floor. I looked up at Josef, my expression a mix of anger and fear. I honestly didn't know how to control my actions.

Josef gently placed a hand on my arm and escorted me to a set of stools tucked at the bar. "I'm sorry. Let's try not to draw attention to ourselves," he said. "Let's just sit down and get you something to eat."

My stomach rumbled in agreement. Not long after, a bowl of chicken consommé with small egg noodles arrived, along with a glass of Serbian Pinot Noir. Josef, sipping his Jack Daniel's, brooded next to me as I ate my soup.

"Were you going to leave with that woman?" I asked, breaking yet another silent streak.

"Why do you care?"

"I don't," I said. "I'm just trying to make conversation. Remember back in the airport when you promised to be less sullen?"

Josef snorted into his glass. "This isn't sullen. You'll know when I'm being sullen."

Now it was my turn to sulk. All I could think about as I stared at my now-cold broth was that I'd made a mistake agreeing to come to a foreign country with a man I seemed to simultaneously loathe and lust over. If only William had agreed to accompany me.

"No," Josef said finally, a minute into my stormy silence. "I wasn't actually leaving with her. She's a vampire. I was trying to get some information from her. I don't think William would appreciate me leaving you alone in the hotel while I go out and entertain myself."

"You don't have to stay on my account," I said. "I can take care of myself."

"If that were true, I wouldn't be here," Josef replied. "Now, finish your soup."

I slid the spoon into the bowl and finished the last drops of my broth, waving off the bartender's offer of another glass of red wine. I glanced at my watch—almost midnight in Belgrade—and was just folding my napkin on the counter when an enormous figure walked through the doorway of the bar and took a seat at a leather couch against a windowsill. Seconds later, I felt the unmistakable peck of another vampire trying to read my thoughts. Josef was right, Belgrade was crawling with the undead.

Josef turned to look at the source of my discomfort and caught the eye of the vampire, whose green eyes seemed to glow in the candlelight. His long, dark, curly hair was tied back in a ponytail, and when he shed his leather jacket, he revealed bare arms covered in tattoos. A black cat's head with its lips peeled back to reveal sharp feline fangs gazed at us from his right shoulder. But it was his left arm that caught my attention. There on the center of his bicep was the image of a large red heart with three swords thrust through it. The Three of Swords.

Josef leaned in close to speak with me, a gesture I thought useless considering the acute hearing of our companion.

"We're going to get up and go to our room," he said. "Do not look back. Just go along with whatever I do, *da*? Yes?"

"*Da*," I said, nodding.

Josef signaled to the bartender, who appeared with a room-charge slip, allowing us to quickly sign for our food and drink. Then Josef wrapped his arm around me, bringing me in close, all the while smiling as if we hadn't a care in the world. "Kiss me," he said. "Kiss me like we're lovers about to go up to our room."

I thought kissing him seemed unnecessary, but I didn't resist. I was out of my element, and I had just promised to trust Josef and follow his directions. So I played my part. I leaned in and kissed him.

The minute his tongue slipped into my mouth, I was transported back to our night in Paris, my passion for him breaking free from where it always lurked, not far beneath the surface. After what I felt was more than a proper public display, Josef took my hand and pulled me from the room. I did not turn around to see what our late arrival was up to, and neither did he. We walked briskly to the elevator, then waited for what seemed like an eternity for it to arrive. Once we stepped in, I pulled my hand from his and bent over at the waist to catch my breath.

"What the hell was that?" I said.

"I'm guessing he's a member of Nikola's crime syndicate, given the Russian prison tattoo on his shoulder. I've seen a few of those images in my travels over the years. Maybe it was a coincidence that he chose this bar for a drink, or maybe Nikola knows we're here. Either way, he's someone to be avoided," Josef replied.

"I thought maybe you noticed the other tattoo," I said. "He has a tarot card image on his left arm."

"Interesting," Josef said. "What was the image?"

"The Three of Swords," I said. "It's an image of a heart being pierced by three swords. I'm just beginning to understand what all the cards mean, but if I remember correctly, it symbolizes misery and heartbreak—either experiencing it oneself or causing it in others. I'll do some more research. Knowing a few tarot images may help us spot Nikola's henchmen in a crowd."

"Sounds like a plan," Josef said.

"Now, on to another topic," I said, raising my eyebrows at Josef. "Why the kiss? How was that necessary?"

"What, you didn't like it?" Josef smirked. "It was meant to confuse him. Nikola will have told his men to look for a brunette traveling with a red-haired vampire. But William isn't here, I am. So I thought kissing you would help create a mix-up. It's possible he'll report back that it wasn't you after all."

"OK, but I don't think you needed to kiss me in public like *that* to accomplish the ruse."

Just as Josef was about to reply, the elevator doors opened. He put a finger to his lips and peered into the hallway. Seeing no one, he gestured for me to go ahead. Moments later, we were both inside the suite, and I breathed a sigh of relief. I hadn't been scared, exactly, but it had caught me off guard to find Nikola's henchmen already so close on our tail.

"Well, this has been fun," Josef said, leaning against the open doorway to his adjoining room, a look of satisfaction on his face. "I told you I'd have my entertainment one way or another. Welcome to Belgrade. Now try to get some sleep. From the look of things, you're going to need it."

19

SLEEP CAME IN FITS AND STARTS, A COMBINATION OF JET lag, anxiety, and my proximity to Josef conspiring to keep me awake. I dozed off and on and eventually got up to do some research on my computer. Josef paid a visit at about four in the morning, entering my room wordlessly and coming to hover at my shoulder.

"What are you doing?" he asked.

"Looking at tarot cards," I said. "It turns out there are all kinds of variations on the traditional images. I'm creating a folder for you to review."

"How many cards?" he asked.

"There are usually seventy-eight cards in a deck, but my research tonight turned up some with eighty. That's a lot of images to review. The good news is I don't think you need to memorize all of the cards."

"Why not?"

"I'm no expert, but my brief interactions with Nikola make me think he's into mysticism. I'm betting he and his men gravitate toward the more dramatic images," I said, yawning. "I think they'll stick with symbols of heartache, upheaval, and violence. I've prepared the file for you to review with that in mind."

Josef smiled. "Nicely done, Olivia. Let me have your laptop and I'll get started," he said. "Why don't you go back to bed and try to get some rest."

Five hours later, Josef woke me out of a deep slumber to tell me my father was calling from Marseille. I followed Josef to his room, rubbing my eyes and feeling glad I'd brought a T-shirt and yoga pants as pajamas instead of something flimsier. My laptop was sitting on the desk, and my father's face was on the screen.

"*Bonjour, Papa,*" I said, taking a seat. "*Ça va?*"

"Hello, Olivia. I'm fine," he said. "And you? Did you sleep? How do you find Belgrade?"

"I managed to get a few hours of rest. As for Belgrade, it's cold and swarming with vampires."

"Yes, Josef told me you saw one of Nikola's men last night. I have a real estate agent looking for a house for you. You should get a call from her soon. I think we found the perfect place. It's secure, with a gate and cameras."

"Sounds good," I said. "Do you have the name of the person at the OSCE I should contact?"

"Yes," he said. "Madeline Klein, from the Council. Do you remember her? I've arranged for you two to meet off-site, in Slovenia. There is a party for diplomats in Ljubljana in two days. She'll be there with members of the Organization for Security and Co-operation and the European Union. They have some information for you."

I looked up at Josef, who nodded at me and then leaned toward the screen to speak with Gabriel.

"Did you already reserve tickets or should we book a flight?" he asked.

"A friend with a plane will take you," Gabriel said. "I'd like your travel to be as inconspicuous as possible. Josef, check your phone in a few hours for a text with the details."

"*Da,*" Josef said. "I'll take care of it."

We said our good-byes and promised to speak again after our return from Slovenia.

"Let's call William now," I said, realizing with a start that I hadn't heard from him since I'd left San Francisco.

"Later," Josef said. "I spoke to him while you were sleeping, and he told me to tell you he was going to be performing at a club with his band and would try to reach us in a few hours."

"Why didn't he call me?"

"I think he assumed you would be asleep," Josef said. "He does know how to read a world clock."

Shaking off my disappointment, I tried to stay positive, thinking about how nice it would be to hear from him later. In the meantime, just as I finished getting dressed, the real estate agent called to schedule a time to meet at the property Gabriel had in mind. She had to spell the name of the street several times for me, but in the end, I was able to find the address using Google maps on my phone. We agreed to meet around noon at the rental home, which turned out to be walking distance from the hotel.

Josef employed the same security measures to exit our rooms as he had the night before, carefully casing every hallway and room before beckoning me forward. I felt relieved when we finally reached the hotel's dining room and a frothy cappuccino and piece of quiche were set before me.

"Better?" he asked.

"Much," I said. "Did you ever drink coffee, before?"

Josef leaned back in his chair for a moment, clearly thinking about the question. "Before the war, yes, but there was little coffee or sugar to be had in Prague in 1940."

"I don't know how you lived through it," I said, enjoying the warm cup in my hands.

Josef's face took on a look of regret. "You'd be surprised what you can live without in order to survive."

"You're right," I said, feeling foolish. "That was a stupid thing for me to say."

"Forget it," he said. "But if I were you, I would set your mind to coping with difficulty and deprivation. We have no idea what we'll be walking into when we leave Belgrade to work as elections monitors."

Josef's words were prophetic. My first lesson came as we stepped outside the hotel into the windy, freezing cityscape that was Belgrade.

"How cold is it?" I gasped.

"I'd put it at about nine below zero, Celsius," he said. "That's actually ten degrees Fahrenheit. Not so bad, really. To your thin San Francisco skin it probably feels quite frigid, but everyone here is used to it."

I didn't reply, too chilled to bother speaking. But true to his word, the residents of Belgrade seemed unaffected, as elegantly dressed and chic as their European counterparts, albeit draped head-to-toe in down coats or fur.

We headed south from our hotel through Knez Mihailova, the city's beautiful Old World pedestrian plaza. Past the fancy department stores and boutiques, the buildings began to look less elegant and more like massive concrete bunkers. On the flight over, I'd read that the Germans had bombed Belgrade extensively during World War II, clearing the way for the Communists to rebuild the city with the worst in socialist architecture. The result was a cityscape that looked like whiteout conditions, where the eye could barely discern between the sky and the buildings. Still, I craned my neck to peek inside the small bars and restaurants we passed, trying to catch a glimpse of the places that anchored my temporary home.

We arrived on Cara Lazara Street promptly at fifteen minutes before noon and found the broker waiting for us in front of a house set back behind an ornate iron gate designed in the Belle Époque style. The tall, white stucco building looked to be three stories, with well-proportioned windows gracing every floor.

"*Zdravo, dobar dan* . . . Hello, good afternoon, and welcome to Beograd," the agent said. She typed a code into the keypad at the front of the gate. "If you rent this house, it will come with a remote control you can use to open the gate when you drive. Of course, you may reset the code to a number of your choosing. You will also notice that the home is ringed with cameras that can be monitored in the house or by a service."

Josef and I followed the young woman into the house. She looked to be no more than twenty-five and spoke flawless English.

"This home belongs to an American executive with business interests in Eastern Europe," she said. "He has been recalled to the United States and wishes to find a long-term tenant."

For the next hour, we toured a house that was vastly more contemporary and well-appointed than we would have guessed judging from its exterior. A spacious open kitchen and dining room anchored the first floor, while four bedrooms with adjacent bathrooms filled out the second. The master suite on the third floor had stunning panoramic views of the old city. There was even what looked to be a garden outside, although nothing was growing currently. There was also a small outbuilding behind the garden.

"What's that?" I asked, pointing at the structure.

"Forgive me, I forgot to mention it sooner," she said. "It's a personal gym. My client is very health conscious."

Clearly eager to work out himself and no doubt also eager to get me back into training, Josef didn't hesitate. "How quickly can we sign a lease?"

"It's already been completed," the broker said, smiling. "Gabriel Laurent has paid six months rent, plus a deposit. My task was simply to ensure the place was agreeable to you. Seeing that it is, I have been asked to complete one more assignment."

Josef and I looked at her expectantly, then trailed her outside just in time to see a gleaming black Land Rover pull into the drive.

"Your father also asked me to make arrangements to lease a car for you," she said. "Now, if you will come back inside, I have a few papers for you to sign. My associate will show you how to reset the code for the gate and where the feeds for the cameras are located."

Josef left to learn about the operation of the cameras while I signed a few papers, assuming liability for the car and documenting my name on the lease papers. After thanking the broker and her associate, we walked them to the gate and promptly reset the security code. Then we stood inside the compound looking at one another.

"My father can be quite efficient when he wants to be," I remarked.

"Thank God for that," Josef said. "Come on, let's go get our stuff and move in."

"I assume you're giving me the suite," I said, smiling.

"I thought we would share it," he said with a mischievous look. "I've grown used to our adjoining room. I don't know if I can sleep one floor below."

"You *don't* sleep," I said, sighing. Playing house with Josef was going to be even more nerve-wracking than sharing a hotel suite.

20

SURREAL. THAT'S THE WORD THAT KEPT POPPING INTO MY
head an hour later when we moved our suitcases and computers into
the house and arranged through the real estate agent to have a small
amount of food delivered. *I'm living with Josef*, I thought.

After I hung up the last of my clothes in the master bedroom's
closet, I tried calling William on his phone. There was no answer. I
sent him a text for good measure.

I MISS YOU. When are you coming?

There was no response. I sat on the edge of the bed for a minute,
staring at the phone and sulking. Then Josef popped his head in the
doorway and suggested we take advantage of the gray, sunless day to
explore Stari Grad, or old-town Belgrade, together. Novi Beograd, or
the new city, was across the Sava River, over a series of bridges. We'd
decided to save that trip for later in the week, when we returned from
Slovenia.

Our first destination was the historic military fortress located
inside Kalemegdan Park, a vast urban park situated at the confluence
of the Danube and Sava Rivers. I'd already read some of the history:
the fortress's position on two of Europe's most well-traveled waterways
made it an easy target for invading troops, and numerous armies,
most notably the Turks, had overthrown it. The formidable Ottoman
Empire had ruled Belgrade on and off for more than three hundred

years. Josef and I toured the outside of the fortress and examined several wars' worth of military artillery displayed in the courtyard.

"This park is a labyrinth, with a zoo at one end and this fortress at the other," Josef said as we exited the fortress's gates. "If you're ever chased, try not to run farther into the park. Not unless you've memorized how to get out."

"I think I'll make the zoo a part of my running course," I said. "I'll give it all a review tomorrow, before we fly out."

Josef pulled his phone out of his pocket and checked his text messages. "Ahh, the information about our flight," he said. "Your father is as reliable as ever."

"What time is it?" I asked, noticing that dusk was upon us.

"About four o'clock," Josef replied. "The sun sets early in the winter. Let's go get a drink."

Josef led me to one of the main boulevards, where I found myself transfixed by the beauty of the city as it became illuminated by hundreds of small lights. Like Cinderella being turned from an ordinary girl into a princess, Belgrade transformed from a concrete wasteland into a shimmering thing of beauty in the glow of the lights. As we walked, I caught the aroma of popcorn from a kiosk selling the stuff freshly popped to passersby. Our next stop was one of the most remarkable buildings I'd ever seen: an ornate palace with two metal spires climbing high into the night sky. The entire building was bathed in green light.

"The Hotel Moskva," Josef said. "Built in 1908 by Russian architects, and preserved, obviously. And there's a cafe inside," he added, opening the door for me.

My body let off an involuntary sigh of relief as we entered the heated hotel. I immediately removed my winter wrappings and made a beeline for one of the chairs in the café. A sting spread across my nose and cheeks as I defrosted, and I rubbed my hands on my face, hoping to speed up the process.

Josef pulled out the chair directly next to me and sat down, as close to me as a lover would. I realized Josef intended to maintain the ruse of our romance in public. He caught the eye of a waiter, who came over to offer a mouthwatering array of cakes and pastries, along with cocktails and espresso drinks. Josef spoke with the man in Serbian, requesting a cappuccino for me and a shot of vodka for himself.

"Vodka? Are you branching out?"

"When in Rome," Josef said. "You'll have one after your espresso. It's the only thing that can take the edge off the cold."

"Speaking of taking the edge off. Do you need to feed?" I asked. "It's been a while."

"When we get to Slovenia," Josef said. "The hills outside of Ljubljana are perfect."

"*Da*," I said, trying out my beginner's Serbian. There was no reason to draw attention to myself by acting like a loud American.

Our drinks arrived and I leaned back to survey my surroundings, admiring the ornate gold-leaf detail along the upper railings of the room. A never-ending flow of chic patrons made their way across the ground floor and up a set of stairs to the second level of the restaurant.

"What's upstairs?" I asked Josef as he reviewed the email on his phone.

"Smoking section."

"So, who sits down here?"

"Mainly tourists and visiting dignitaries from places where smoking is not as common," Josef said. "Serbians love to smoke. They have one of the lowest life expectancy rates in the world."

"Did you smoke when you were alive?"

"*Da*. Yes . . . of course," Josef said. "Smoking and drinking coffee are two of the main reasons for living."

"Maybe I should take up smoking," I said. "All the great spies from World War II seemed to smoke."

"That's because there was nothing to eat in Europe during the war," Josef scoffed. "Smoking kept your mind off having an empty stomach. One of the great benefits of becoming a vampire was that it marked the end of sifting through the soil of abandoned farms searching for a withered potato or turnip to eat."

"How awful," I said. "What happened to your family? Couldn't you rely on them to help?"

Josef looked down at his shot glass, rolling the remaining drops of vodka in a circle at the bottom.

"Yes, it was awful," he said. "The war was everywhere. Even in this hotel. I'll tell you something you might not read in a guidebook: you're sitting in what was for a time the headquarters of the Gestapo. I hoped many times to blow this building to bits. For the rest, ask me again another time and I'll tell you."

I realized that Josef's life during the war must have involved more suffering than I could imagine. I also knew he had a secret. I could feel the pressure he exerted to keep his feelings from me. I laid my hand on his arm and was about to tell him I was sorry for prying when Josef grabbed my knee under the table.

"We have company again," he said. "Don't look up."

I followed his directions, instead leaning into Josef as if I wished to whisper something important, my lips gently brushing against his ear as I spoke. "Is it the same man?"

Josef leaned back and laughed as if I'd told him a funny joke. Then he grabbed my hand and planted a kiss on the inside of my palm, sending a shiver up my spine. We were getting good at this.

"*Ne, ne*," he said, using the Serbian word for no.

Only then did I look around the room, managing to catch a glimpse of the dark-haired woman who'd been at the bar with Josef the night before. "It's your friend," I said.

Without warning, Josef leaned in and kissed me deeply on the lips, pressing his tongue inside my mouth. My body reacted before my brain, and I kissed him back, sending the temperature in the dining room up a few degrees.

"I never said she was a friend," Josef whispered provocatively as he separated from me. "OK, we've held up our end of the charade *again*. Let's get out of here."

Out of breath, I stayed in my seat a moment longer. Belgrade was a city of surprises, offering no clue what to expect next.

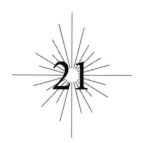

UP EARLY THE NEXT MORNING, I SENT AN EMAIL TO ELSA and Lily describing our temporary home in Belgrade and promising to provide the security entrance code when they arrived. I also dashed off a note to Jason, letting him know I would be in Belgrade until April and requesting that he plan my mother's retrospective for May.

My correspondence completed, I put on a pair of thick running tights, a long-sleeve thermal shirt, and a fleece. I topped that with a Patagonia pullover, a ski hat, and a pair of gloves to stay ahead of the cold on my run. I ran downstairs in my running shoes with a plan to make an espresso before heading out into the wintry world beyond my gates. Josef was sitting at a small table in the kitchen, reading Serbian news on his laptop.

"How did you learn to read Cyrillic?" I asked, bypassing good morning.

Josef looked up at me. "You're going for a run? Hold on, I'll change and come with you."

"Since when do we run together?"

"It's a precaution, Olivia," Josef said. "You're still learning your way around."

"No," I said. "I want to run alone. I need some time to think."

Josef eyed me warily. "OK, but if you see anything suspicious,

turn around and come back to the house. No confrontations, especially with a brute like our tattooed friend from the other night.
Promise me."

"I promise," I said. "What time do we leave today?"

"The car will be here at noon. Although it's overcast, we're expecting to take off no later than one thirty," Josef said. "Once we're on
the ground, we need some time to shop, since neither one of us
brought proper clothing to attend a diplomatic reception."

"Got it," I said. "I'll be back well before noon."

Minutes later, I was out on the sidewalk, too keyed up from my
conversation with Josef to need espresso. A light snow was falling as I
shut the gate behind me and looked around. I saw no one lurking. I
didn't linger either, promptly setting off toward Kalemegdan Park
and the fortress. Small snowflakes nipped at my face as I ran.

I caught a glimpse of the Belgrade Zoo in the distance and headed
that way. I'd read about the zoo, founded in 1936. Another fact I'd
picked up was that the zoo opened at 8:00 a.m., even in the winter. I
paused long enough to pay the woman at the ticket window with a
couple of hundred-dinar notes I'd stuffed into a pocket, then jogged
inside. It was a crazy menagerie, with multiple enclosures filled with
all manner of wildlife. I sped past the birdcages where raptors sat
perched on tree branches and jogged by a lone elephant, walking in
circles in an open pen. Next, I spotted enormous black and white
wolves prowling their cages. Although these looked to be authentic
animals, they reminded me of my visitor in Bolinas and prompted
me to keep my guard up. Next came a parade of big cats—lions,
tigers, panthers, and pumas—all locked behind nothing but a single
chain-link fence that was supposedly electrified. It seemed like an
awfully thin barrier between the animal kingdom and humanity.

I ran out the exit gate, waving to the guard as I sped past and
shouting "*Hvala*," or thank you. From there, I loped down a hill, and
past many city sights, including a large open market and a pedestrian

thoroughfare I later identified on my map as Skadarlija. Finally, I ran north, focused on rapidly closing the loop back to the house. At the entrance, I glanced around again to make sure I hadn't been followed. Though all was clear, I still felt relieved when I entered the security code and walked into our little compound, the gate closing behind me.

Hours later, a set of funicular doors opened at the base of Ljubljana Castle. We took a set of metal stairs to a courtyard surrounded by the castle's massive ramparts. Candle lanterns illuminated a walkway leading to a restaurant. I glanced at Josef and held out my arm, hoping he would escort me through the doorway.

"I dislike politicians," Josef said, taking my arm. "They're always so eager to send other people to do their dirty work."

Josef had purchased a sleek Armani tuxedo that afternoon at a store in historic Ljubljana. I'd chosen a simple, high-collared wool dress with flared sleeves and tried to ignore the way Josef's disposition darkened as the time of the party drew near.

"Well, I'm afraid you picked the wrong assignment, my friend," I said, smiling. "Try not to bite anyone's head off tonight."

"I assure you I will be a model of discretion," he replied.

Inside, our hostess, Madeline Klein, was standing in a far corner, deep in conversation. She was outfitted in a dark pantsuit featuring a three-quarter-length coat and pearls, her signature long gray hair tied back in an elaborate twist. I marveled at my father's Machiavellian plans. To the outside world, Madeline's résumé listed her as the Canadian ambassador to the United States. But she was also a witch and a longtime member of the Council. Highly respected as a diplomat, there was no one outside her sphere of influence. Her introduction of us to the rest of the diplomatic community bestowed a legitimacy that was priceless.

But just as I was about to cross the room to greet her, Josef stopped me and said he would catch up with me later.

"Things will go more smoothly without me," he said.

I nodded my goodbye as I waited to catch Madeline's eye. Acknowledged by a slight tilt of her head, I crossed the room. "Good evening," she said as I came to stand beside her. "Olivia, I'd like to introduce you to United States Secretary of State Diana Chambers and Ambassador Justin Furkhard, head of the OSCE Mission to Serbia."

"It's a pleasure to meet you both," I said. "I'm pleased to be here. The rest of my team will arrive shortly, but I'm prepared to begin work immediately."

"Forgive me for getting down to business," the ambassador said. "Our offices are in Belgrade. Today's Friday. If you come in on Tuesday, our elections team will have your assignment information. I assume you speak Serbian?"

"No, but my driver and security escort do," I said. "They'll ensure I can do my job effectively."

"Excellent," he said. "We need all the help we can get to ensure free, democratic elections in Serbia. Human rights and law enforcement have a long way to go here, in my view. Now, if you will excuse me, I must make the rounds."

"Madam Secretary, it's an honor," I said, extending my hand to Diana Chambers. I was intimidated—and not just because she was secretary of state. She'd also been a corporate CEO, a US senator from California, an ambassador to Germany, and an advisor to powerful leaders around the world. Watching her aura as we spoke was like watching flares from the sun—brilliant streaks of yellow and orange shooting off her body. Here was a confident, happy woman.

"The pleasure is all mine, actually," she said. "I've been friends with Levi Barnes for many years. Your work on his campaign was excellent."

"Thank you," I replied. "Levi is going to make a great congressman."

"Agreed," she said. "In fact, I would go so far as to say his career in politics is just beginning. His future is very bright."

Madeline reviewed our surroundings for a moment, then switched to a radically new topic. "Olivia, I asked Diana to help us gather information from US law enforcement sources about Nikola and his connections to local criminal factions, including the Serbian mafia."

My efforts to maintain a passive expression clearly failed, and Madeline reached out to touch my arm. "Not to worry," she said. "Diana is an ally. We can trust her with our secrets."

Surprised, I focused on Diana. She met my gaze, never once wavering.

"What can you tell me?" I asked, as Madeline walked away to greet other party goers.

"I've arranged for a series of encrypted files to be sent to your computer. You'll receive a separate email with a passkey to access the files," Diana said. "Don't lose the passkey. You won't be able to read the file without it."

"Impressive," I said. "I appreciate your assistance, Madam Secretary."

"You're welcome," she replied. "But I should tell you, it's likely that I will ask for a favor in return in the not-so-distant future."

"Understood," I said, wondering what she had in mind. From her tone, I could tell that whatever her plans, they were significant.

We said good-bye, and when I stepped away, I was struck by how the crowd had multiplied. The dining room was now teeming, diplomats from around the world rubbing shoulders as they sampled bites of duck and venison, polenta cakes and candied cherries. I nibbled, too, on the hunt for my sullen escort. Oddly enough, he was standing next to Madeline at the restaurant's striking cocktail bar, which was carved into one of the castle's rock walls. I threaded my way through the crush of people toward them, only to encounter a wave of apprehension as I got close.

"What's happened?" I asked.

Josef was somehow chosen to be the messenger. He folded his arms as he prepared to deliver what was obviously bad news. "William will not be joining us in Belgrade," he said. "He was asked to take a separate assignment for the Council, tracking Nikola."

"I don't understand," I said. "We made a plan."

"He's not coming," Josef said quietly.

Humiliation stung my cheeks, all the unreturned calls and unexplained silences clicking into place. Had I been sent away as a ruse? If so, this was the second time my father had dealt with me in half-truths—the first being when we'd initially met, and he'd hidden his identity from me.

"What is it with the Council and its secrets?" I asked. "I have a right to know these things before they happen."

"Olivia, it pains me to remind you of this, but you're a witch who is only just coming into her powers," Madeline said, placing her hand on my arm. "The future of our organization is at stake—hundreds of years of striving to keep the world at peace. We had no choice. We couldn't risk having just one plan for Nikola's removal."

"Did my father know all along and keep it from me?" I asked, glancing at the bar with its rows and rows of aperitifs and pristine cocktail glasses. Just for a second, I contemplated trying to bring down the shelves. The glasses quivered ever so slightly.

Josef's voice snapped me out of my building tantrum.

"*Don't*," Josef warned. "Leave it be, Olivia. The sooner we do our jobs, the sooner we can all be together again."

"I take that as a yes. And you?" I asked Josef. "Did you know, too?"

Silence followed. Then, after a moment, he gave me an envelope. A note from William, I assumed. I held the cream-colored missive, aware of the absurd lightness of the paper in comparison to the message it held. The temptation to destroy it burbled up inside as I felt the urge to divorce myself from these people I loved, who so callously planned my life without me.

"Was it really necessary to lie to me?" I asked, tamping down my emotions yet again. "To let me come all this way thinking he would be here?"

"You would never have agreed to let William go alone," Josef said.

"We'll never know, will we?" I said, turning to leave. "Good night."

"Wait," Josef said, grabbing my arm. "You need an escort."

My gaze returned to the well-stocked bar. "Take a step back, or I will rain glass down upon us and these lovely guests," I said. "As Madeline so kindly reminded me, I haven't quite got the hang of this witch thing yet. Unless you want a big mess, remove your hand and let me go."

Josef removed his hand, his mouth open slightly as if words were lurking just behind his lips but could not find the courage to come out.

I whirled around in disgust, William's letter clasped between my fingers and stormed out of the castle. I had no idea what I would do next.

STILL IN A RAGE, I TOOK THE FUNICULAR BACK DOWN THE hill from the castle and decided to explore Ljubljana while I cleared my head. Its legendary metal dragons, bathed in moonlight atop their stone pedestals, lured me into the old city and its cobblestone streets lined with vendors selling arts and crafts, spiced wine, and all manner of sugary delights. While I strolled past the merchants, stewing over my betrayal, William's letter sat in my purse, awaiting an audience. I had little appetite for the series of apologies and excuses I expected to read. Why did men seem to think they could dictate the future? How did they come by this absolute confidence that they could move all of us along like plastic pieces on a game board? Pulling the collar of my coat closer to block the bite of the cold air, I noticed a wine bar ahead, its ornate, arched facade illuminated by candles in bronze sconces mounted to the wall. Despite the temperature outside, the ebony-stained door was left partially open.

I'd avoided drinking at the party to ensure I did my job, but that time had passed. Within a few moments, I had seated myself at the massive wooden bar and been delivered a glass of Pinot Noir. Savoring the cherry-hued liquid, I glanced at my purse, feeling the letter's burning presence. Soon enough, the creamy paper with the deckle edge lay on the counter. It bore no monogram or initials, but William's writing was easily recognized, the familiar black ink of the fountain pen he used for correspondence evident.

Olivia,

When a man leaves his life behind, what else can he say to the woman he loves except that he will be back? I am sorry I could not tell you this in person. For this, I have to rely on Josef, who will no doubt present the facts with little finesse.

You and I have often talked of not being able to outrun our destinies. This is mine: to use my tracking skills to bring this to a close. It is the only way I can see to end this quickly. I will not give you a list of excuses. None of them sound all that good to me. Try to remember that I love you and that I will return and make you my wife. I cannot expect you to forgive me yet. But please, while we are apart, try not to do anything that would make it difficult for you to forgive yourself.

All my love,

W. F.

I grabbed a cocktail napkin and pressed it against the sting in my eyes, trying to maintain my composure. *Damn him for knowing me so well.* I returned William's missive to my purse and tried to get myself under control, staring fixedly at the gray stone wall behind the bar. Absorbed, I did not see my visitor until a shadow crossed my vision.

"This is the second time I've found you by yourself. You should know better than to travel alone. God knows what things could prey upon you," Nikola whispered in my ear.

I stared at him as he slid onto the barstool next to me. Since I was already unnerved, thanks to the revelations about William, Nikola's arrival wasn't as shocking as it should have been. My alleged assassin was now snugly at my side.

"I've been warned about a lot of things, Nikola, but I rarely heed advice," I said, my voice quavering slightly. "I should think by now you'd have noticed I don't like being told what to do."

"Where is William?" Nikola asked, ignoring my remarks. "Or is it his brother whose company you prefer now? I wouldn't blame you. William has always seemed a tad too straitlaced to be a vampire."

"I prefer my own company this evening," I said, trying to stick with some version of the truth.

Nikola smiled as the bartender drew near. "Bring me what the lady is having and refill her glass," he said.

I sensed him, then, curious about me, as he glanced at my wineglass. "Thanks for your concern, but this is my first glass of wine," I said, hazarding a guess. "By the way, how did you find me?"

"Can you hear my thoughts?" Nikola asked. "That's not possible. I, of course, can read humans' thoughts, but the reverse . . . would be positively *unnatural.*"

"You didn't answer my question," I said, avoiding his—and feeling overwhelmingly grateful, for once, that I was a trained empath, and my thoughts could remain private at my choosing. "How did you know where I was?"

"I followed you," he said. "I knew you'd decamped to Slovenia. I knew you would attend the party. I have eyes everywhere. And then, Gabriel is so predictable. How he loves diplomatic affairs and political intrigues. My question to you is, how do you feel about it? He sends you around the world to fight his fight, while he sits back at his desk like a good bureaucrat."

Nikola's words, so close to my own thoughts, pierced my heart. I started on my second glass of wine. Perhaps this conversation would be easier with a little anesthesia.

"I told you once before, you are in no position to judge the living, Nikola," I said. "What do you know about family or honor?"

Nikola swirled the crimson liquid in his glass a moment, bringing it to his nose and inhaling. "This is actually a Serbian Pinot, grown on the banks of the Danube River," he said, abruptly changing topics. "It's complex, a bit smoky, and mysterious, like so many things in the Balkans."

"Very nice. Perhaps you should consider a career as a wine critic," I said, rising from my stool.

Nikola's hand shot out, grabbing mine, pressing me into my seat. "We're not done, Olivia," he said. "Stay and finish your wine."

"What do you want?" I asked, refusing to admit any concern.

"I want you to go back home and stop your snooping," he said. "What do you expect to find with your little investigation? You can't possibly imagine you will catch me in some misdeed. You're playing on my game board now, and I have been at this for years. Do you really think you can beat me?"

"I want you to give up your claim to the Council and stay in Europe," I said in reply. "Let another set of leaders take the helm. You don't care about the Council anyway. It's just a cover for your other . . . *activities*."

His regal chin set high, Nikola dismissed my comments. "Don't be ridiculous," he said. "It's *my* turn to rule the Council. Zoran has never been interested. He's a mere formality, easily disposed of."

"Why are you rushing the succession?" I asked. "And of course there's the troublesome issue of your connection to the Serbian underworld. By the way, the tarot card tattoos are a nice touch. Was it your idea?"

Any satisfaction my sarcasm brought me was immediately replaced with pain. I felt Nikola attempt to use his psychic powers on me, as if he were trying to squeeze my head into a hat two sizes too small. At the ball in Paris, he hadn't seemed to need to use force to feed off another's emotions, but tonight was different. I felt a moment of weakness. Then I redoubled my efforts and shut him out, restoring my equilibrium.

"Another curiosity. Not many humans could withstand me. You are either stronger than I thought, or—no matter," he said, narrowing his eyes. "I will figure out what you are. And I'm not rushing anything."

"What of your criminal friends?" I asked, trying to rub my

temple, which was throbbing slightly, in a casual way. "You know you have no business leading the Council."

"To you, Serbs are heartless butchers, while you like to imagine our Slovenian and Croatian neighbors are so elegant and refined." Nikola sipped his wine. "Well, anyone can invent a necktie, but how many civilizations can say they have the bloodlines of *warriors*? Serbs are maligned, regarded as provincial brutes who haven't the manners to be invited to the table for dinner with their Hapsburg neighbors. How wrong everyone has been about my people. How wrong you are."

"Vampires do love history," I said. "Tell me your story, how you were made."

"Why?" Nikola asked. "I thought you were in a hurry to leave."

"Now I'm not," I said. "Maybe I'll tell you something about me as well."

Nikola closed his eyes as if recalling a long-lost memory. "Very well. I can't see what harm it will do." He raised his glass to me and began.

"I was once the son of a great landowner in Serbia. Our family's holding was in the western part of the country, near the Drina River. In the summer of 1014, there was a great fire in a large valley near my home. My father, whose name was also Nikola, was a stern man, more feared than revered. He ordered me out by horse to search for stray animals and peasants. It was a test of my bravery, you see. But to me, my father's burning stare seemed far worse than riding into the blaze.

"Before leaving, I filled two animal skins with water from our well. I doused a piece of cloth with some of the water and tied it around my nose and mouth as a barrier against the smoke. I rode out of my home following the sun, stained that day from the reddish smoke of the flames.

"I rode for some time," Nikola continued. "After a while, I observed that, thanks to the wind, the fire had changed direction. It was now moving away from our village toward Tara, one of the higher peaks in the Dinaric Alps. The mountains were said to be haunted. Villagers near us were obsessed with rumors of vampires living in the caves that nestled among the mountain's dense forests.

"But I was not one to put any stock in the superstitious tales of peasants. I rode onward into the twilight, conscious of the fact that I was very much alone, for not a creature stirred: not a bird in a tree, not a squirrel on the ground, not a deer in a field. Our land was known for being rich with waterfowl and game; the absence of activity made me uneasy, but I blamed the fire. I decided it must have caused all nearby creatures to seek refuge in the distant meadows.

"I stopped for a moment then to gaze out at the land that would one day be mine. I had grand plans to increase my family's earnings from our holdings—something my father had been unable to do. The snap of a twig woke me out of my daydream, but when I turned, I saw nothing. I then decided to ride back and report to my father that the fire had changed direction, away from our lands. Within seconds, I was knocked from my horse, and something sharp pierced my throat."

"And then what happened?"

"I awoke two days later, clawing my way out of an earthen grave in the grip of a hunger I could not name. There, standing only a few feet away, was my maker: the vampire who'd attacked me." Nikola took a sip of wine, a faraway look in his eyes.

"The man who stole me from my family was no primitive cave dweller, however, but instead a gentleman resplendent in Eastern robes of the finest fabrics. He promised me that under his care I would become wildly wealthy and far more powerful than if I'd stayed with my family."

"And did his prediction come true?"

"You know, it did," Nikola said, smirking. "Which is why I will not let some errand girl for a wealthy French dilettante rob me of my destiny."

"You forget yourself," I said. "Gabriel is a Laurent, a witch from an ancient order. And I'm no errand girl."

"What should I call you, then?"

"His daughter," I said, raising my eyes to meet his gaze.

A hiss escaped Nikola's lips. "Impossible."

"There. I told you something about me."

"So, you *are* a witch," Nikola said. "A human and a witch have successfully mated. It's not supposed to be possible, you know. What other skills do you possess?"

"Wouldn't you like to know," a familiar voice remarked, interrupting our conversation. Josef leaned casually against the bar on the other side of me, his body very close to mine.

"*Dobro vece*, Josef—good evening," Nikola sneered. "Are you enjoying your visit to Eastern Europe? It's been a few years."

"Olivia, it's past your bedtime," Josef said, ignoring Nikola's remarks.

"Yes, and that brings us back to my original question, Olivia," Nikola said. "Which bed are you warming these days?"

I knew better than to be provoked. But Josef—perhaps sensing my mood—grabbed my hand and gently squeezed it in warning. Defiant, I pulled my hand away and answered Nikola with a challenge.

"It's too bad we didn't get a chance to consult our cards a second time," I said. "Fortunes change often, I find."

"Next time, perhaps," he said. "Belgrade is a small city."

"Unlikely," Josef said, wrapping his arm around me.

Silence prevailed as we returned to the hotel. Josef's body was coiled tight, no doubt bracing for confrontation. Fortunately, the journey was uneventful. The minute Josef opened the door to our suite, I sped toward my bathroom and a warm bath as an escape.

"Wait, Olivia," Josef said, in a stern voice. "Come sit with me a moment."

Reluctantly, I grabbed one of the small white chairs from under the table. But I was the only one sitting. My escort delivered his lecture pacing around me like a big cat.

"It may not feel like it, but this is a kind of war," he said, looming in front of me. "War is unsparing in its ruthlessness. It asks all of us to make sacrifices, including William. Try to remember, my brother had left the service of the Council when he met you. It was your presence that drew him back."

"You're blaming me?"

"I'm blaming no one," Josef said. "I'm asking you to do the same."

"No."

"No?" Josef repeated. "And are you willing to get yourself killed while you stew and sulk? You were alone in a bar with Nikola. What if I hadn't found you?"

"I was ready to kill him right there and drink his blood out of one of those fine Slovenian crystal glasses until you stopped me," I said, but instantly regretted my rage-induced sarcasm.

Josef ran his hand across his head, his fingers brushing the short stubble of his closely cropped hair, then turned his back to me.

"Go to bed, Olivia," he said. "Tomorrow we'll be back in Belgrade, and we'll see if you've got what it takes to murder a vampire who's been alive for a millennium."

WILLIAM'S ROOM AT THE HOTEL KATRCA, A PENSION tucked away on the outskirts of Ljubljana, a mile from the center of the city, was small but clean. He sat at the built-in wooden desk along the wall, typing into his sleek laptop and trying to ignore how odd it felt to be writing reports about Olivia. *If you live long enough, anything is possible,* he thought as his fingers clicked away on the keys.

Gabriel,

This is my first dispatch, and likely the briefest, since I've just arrived in Slovenia. I haven't filed a report in years, as you know, and it seems odd to write your name instead of Aidan's. He always received my dispatches when I took assignments from the Council years ago. His death is part of why I accepted this job. Then there's Olivia. From the moment I saw her, I knew she had the potential to become a catalyst. Her energy is extraordinary. It attracts all of us— even before we know why we're looking.

As you well know, my work on behalf of the Council has taken me around the world several times. I've done many things with the goal of helping to protect humanity—tracked fugitive Nazis, jumped from a helicopter into the jungles of Vietnam and Cambodia, slipped into a Russian prison under the cover of night. This mission is different. This time I've got something at stake, something to lose, and if I fail, it will make the next hundred years of my life a misery.

I remind you of this, as well as myself, because I have no one else to communicate with now. These dispatches are my only connection to the life I leave behind. I hope you'll excuse me if you're presented at moments with some sentimentality.

William stopped typing for a moment. He had trailed Olivia from the castle to the bar, seen Nikola arrive—and while waiting outside in the dark, was reminded of the moments before his death in Baton Rouge in 1862.

You've gone and done it now, he'd thought to himself that day as he bled to death from a gunshot wound on the muddy banks of the Mississippi. *You're done for. It's over.* A poor carpenter with little choice but to enlist, he'd joined the Nineteenth Tennessee Infantry in the spring of 1861. He'd survived most of the war, until an enemy bullet had penetrated his leg. Seconds later, he'd known his time was up. He'd lain there, helpless in the muck, listening to the sounds of battle winding down: troops fleeing, cannon fire in the distance, and all the while, the bugs humming in unison in the humid mist of the afternoon.

That's what tonight had been like, he thought. Things happening that you can do nothing to stop.

I can confirm that Olivia and Josef attended the reception at the castle. Madeline was there to meet them and made introductions as planned. Josef, in what was likely his last communication with me before I meet my contact, confirmed that Olivia received my letter. Apparently, she did little to contain her dismay in public. He will have his hands full trying to reason with her.

As for me, I depart tonight for Serbia. As agreed, my first task will be to gain entry into one of the regional criminal networks. Look for my next communication in several days.

His missive uploaded, William reviewed a map of the forests surrounding the historic Ljubljana Castle, hoping to feed before he
began his travels. Then he packed his duffel and prepared to leave,
thinking about his last glimpse of Olivia and the way Josef's arm
had been locked tightly around her body as the two of them had left
the bar. He'd done everything he could to place Olivia into Josef's
arms, knowing it would make the coming hardships easier for her
to endure. He found that didn't lessen the churning in his gut as he
witnessed the success of his efforts.

Memories of prepping for his previous missions came back: *Time
to clear your mind*, he told himself. *No distractions. No thinking about
what Olivia and Josef might be doing now.* Because there was nothing
to be done except leave them behind. So he took the dark stairs out of
the pension and walked onto the shadowy street. He was capable of
making sure nobody saw him.

24

THE NEXT MORNING WE WERE OCCUPIED WITH OUR return to our compound in Belgrade. There was no further discussion of the previous night's events. Nikola's appearance at the bar had been sobering, and I'd decided to postpone my self-pity in lieu of accomplishing goals.

When I came downstairs after unpacking, Josef was waiting for me in workout gear. "It's time to train, Olivia," he said. "I hope you're ready."

Without a word, I went back to my bedroom to change. I paused there for a moment to look at the trio of copper betrothal rings on my finger—a gift from William—before sliding them off. They were a liability while sparring, but more than that, they were a painful reminder. A symbol of something now best left in a drawer.

I was surprised, when I walked into the small gym, to discover that Josef had arranged for new equipment to be delivered. We both donned protective gear, including face masks, and dove right into self-defense training using knives. As usual each time I lunged at Josef with my dagger, he found a way to either knock it out of my hand or toss me to the ground in a heap. My bones ached, and the inside of my suit felt like a sauna.

"Again," Josef said.

As with all my other attempts, this attack ended with me hitting the mat with a thud that made the ornate dagger fly from my fingers and skitter across the wooden floor. I peeled my flattened frame up vertebra by vertebra, trying to unscramble my brain. We'd been at it for hours, and I was still no closer to besting Josef.

"I need a break," I said.

"Not until you can get past my defenses," Josef said.

"A breather first," I said, savoring the rush of cool air against my face as I removed my mask. "Ahh, free at last."

"Not quite," Josef said. "If you don't want the gear on, fine. We'll move on to a different set of drills."

"What do you want me to do?" I asked, shivering as the cold air hit the back of my neck.

"We've been practicing how to keep the blade in your hand," Josef said. "Let's see if you can retrieve the dagger from its position on the floor over there."

"A little advanced, don't you think?"

"No. You've got all kinds of energy in there," Josef said, pointing his finger at me. "Let's see if we can channel it toward something other than breaking wineglasses."

"I'd rather break you," I muttered as I tossed aside the sweaty gear and readjusted myself to sit cross-legged on the mat.

"Do you even know if you could hit a target?" Josef said. "I'm not so sure."

Regrettably, he was right about my newfound telekinesis being a bit wobbly. There was nothing for it but to practice. I closed my eyes, taking deep breaths until my mind was devoid of extraneous thoughts and images. Instinctively, I began massaging my third eye—the spot just above the bridge of my nose—in an effort to remind my sixth sense to wake up. Then, extending my hand out toward the weapon, I urged it toward me. The dagger slid a few millimeters across the floor.

"Good," Josef said. "Again. Remember, it's all a matter of energy. You must be able to control your energy before you can control the object."

Nodding, eyes closed again, I returned to my breathing. This time, I imagined a stream of energy between the dagger and the palm of my hand, and worked between breaths to fill the space, weave a connection. Nothing happened.

I tried once more, pushing hard.

"Don't push," Josef said. "Pull."

Refashioning my thinking worked, and in seconds, I had the dagger in my hand.

As I opened my eyes, I felt a warm trickle of blood below my nose. Unmistakable. And something that hadn't happened since I'd just begun my training with Elsa. In the early days when she's been teaching me to block strong energy with my mind, my nose had bled from the exertion. Clearly, I'd pushed myself in a similar way today.

Josef handed me a heap of tissue.

"Thank you," I said, leaning my head back to staunch the flow.

"That's probably enough training for today," Josef said, coming to kneel at my side. "Why don't you shower and change, and I'll buy you an early dinner."

After showering, I sent an angry email to my father, requesting a time when he could Skype. I expected him to take his time replying, confrontation being one of the things he was least good at. I also read an email from Elsa and Lily, confirming their arrival in a couple of weeks. Foolishly, I looked for signs of William in my inbox too, knowing there'd be nothing.

"He won't try to contact you," Josef said as we wandered through town under a gray, wintry sky. "Too risky."

"That makes it sound like you know what he's up to," I said, my pulse kicking. "Are *you* talking to him?"

Hearing no reply, I turned and found myself alone. Josef had stopped a few feet behind me, his gaze fixed on an old beige stone building. In the evening light, it took me a few moments to recognize it as a Jewish temple. Six-pointed stars featured prominently in the building's ornate stained-glass windows. Josef watched silently as a woman and her small daughter left the building. A guard, who had been standing in the shadows, followed behind, closing a large iron door behind them.

"Do you know those people?" I asked.

Josef stood rock still watching until the three were well out of sight. Only when they'd disappeared from our view did he speak. "I think it's time for us to get a drink," he said, ignoring my question.

"Sure, if you promise to tell me what's going on," I said.

"I'm not sure I know myself," he said, traipsing off toward the Hotel Moskva, which seemed likely to become our regular watering hole.

A few minutes later we were inside the café discarding our winter clothing. Although it was Saturday night, there were still a few tables open. Josef ordered a bottle of vodka and two glasses as soon as we were seated and wasted no time pouring each of us a shot. Up and back, I felt the slow burn as the vodka made its way to my stomach. The minute my glass hit the table, it was refilled.

"Go slow," I said.

"I assure you, I can hold my alcohol," Josef said, refilling his glass as well.

"Yes, but I haven't eaten anything."

Josef's hand went up into the air, signaling a waiter. The man arrived and Josef ordered me a bowl of goulash.

"There, now you can drink," he said, smiling as a napkin and large spoon were placed in front of me.

"Who were those people?" I asked again. "Did you know them?"

"'And thou shalt write them upon the door-posts of thy house, and upon thy gates,'" Josef said. "Do you know what that's from?"

"Old Testament?" I guessed.

"It's a commandment from God to follow his teachings and place a mezuzah—a small talisman with a tiny paper prayer scroll inside—

on the door of your home," Josef said. "We had an old wooden mezuzah on the door of my home in Prague, where I lived with my wife and daughter. The first thing the Nazis did when they came looking for me was to rip it from the wall. They collected them, you see. Along with other artifacts."

I felt all my attention turn with laserlike focus to Josef as I realized that he was about to share his story with me. "Where were your wife and daughter when they came?"

"They'd already left for the country," he said. "I'd sent them there to be safe."

"And were they?"

Josef downed his vodka and poured another, drinking that, too. "No. The Nazis killed everyone in their village to punish those in the Resistance. An informer, you see, told them the town was full of sympathizers. They shot them all, every last man, woman, and child, and then burned their homes. My wife and her entire family perished. I never saw them again."

"That woman and her daughter, tonight . . . did they remind you?"

"This part of the world is drenched in blood. You can't help but remember," he said.

"So you're a Jewish vampire," I said. "I can't recall ever meeting one before."

Josef laughed. "You'd never met *any* vampires until a few months ago," he said. "But I'm not Jewish, not anymore."

I was about to ask him what he meant when the waiter brought my stew. It was just the pause Josef needed. A millisecond later, his veneer of indifference was restored.

"When you're done with your meal, we can go home," he said, straightening up in his chair.

My phone ringing woke me a few hours later from a vodka-infused stupor. I fumbled around on the nightstand trying to locate the source of the sharp pain in my head, my stomach rebelling against the idea of being vertical.

"Hello?"

"Olivia, it's Gabriel."

"*Merde*. What time is it?"

"I don't know," he said. "I got your email and wanted to talk. Are you furious?"

"Yes," I said, my sandpapery tongue making it difficult to speak. "I thought we promised to be honest with one another."

Gabriel sighed. "It proves harder than I imagined," he said.

"That's not reassuring," I said. "It would be good if you could at least *try* to act like a father and stop keeping secrets from me."

"I understand why you would feel that way, *ma chérie*. I did the best I could. William and I went round and round, and in the end, we felt it was better not to tell you."

"I told Nikola I was your daughter."

"*Fais attention*, Olivia," Gabriel said. "You should be more careful. Are you trying to punish me? This is not a game."

"That's funny," I said, trying to manage my temper. "Nikola thinks you view it that way."

"You're keeping your enemy awfully close, that he could issue such an opinion," Gabriel said.

"What do you expect?" I replied. "You sent me straight to him."

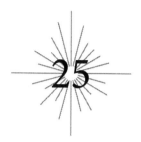

25

THE DAYS THAT FOLLOWED WHIRRED PAST. MY DAILY training sessions in the gym with Josef became more successful. Under his tutelage, objects now flew into my hands on command. I felt accomplished and strong—and increasingly, less human.

Put simply, my new talents could not be achieved by a normal person. Overwhelmed by a feeling of metamorphosis, I often asked myself, *Who is the new Olivia?* In the silence of my solitary nights, I found few answers and wondered whose voice I would trust to define the real me.

I picked up my official paperwork at the OSCE's offices. As the director had promised, an enormous package was waiting for me at the reception desk. Soon we would report for our first official meeting and be given our territory for monitoring. Meanwhile, I needed to memorize the *Election Observation Handbook*, one hundred pages chock-full, from what I'd seen so far, of philosophical and practical information. Teams like mine treated this book as the bible for evaluating local political parties and their ability to conduct free, open elections.

Hours later, the text of the handbook began to blur. A quick glance outside at the gray afternoon sky convinced me that a brisk walk was just the thing to shake off my lethargy. I briefly considered the risks of going out unescorted. Josef was out and had left no word regarding his return. But in the end, my craving to be outside trampled security concerns.

Snow seemed only a vague promise when I left the house. This was the pattern: crisp, monochrome days, with featherlight flurries at sundown and dawn. The weather was expected to turn more severe any day, with a series of massive storms making their way from Western Europe. Belgrade would benefit from a fresh blanket of snow, I thought as I strolled, Etienne Daho belting out a French pop tune through my earbuds. The gritty sidewalks, the massive apartments covered in soot, the muddy ground, beaten down with heavy boot heels—a fresh coat of snow would hide it all beautifully.

I'd meant to walk away from the old city toward the river but instead found myself drawn to the main pedestrian area near the fortress. To say I was under a spell would be too dramatic, but I did feel a compulsion, subtle but convincing, to move in that direction. When I arrived at the north entrance to Knez Mihailova, near the City Library, the cobblestone promenade was full of street merchants. A chestnut vendor got the last of my dinar coins, the aroma of burning coals and the sweet nuttiness of the roasted meats winning me over. I nibbled on the warm nuts as I wandered, spotting a bookseller tucked away at the lip of an alley. Sitting prominently on one of his milk crates was an old, weathered copy of *Dracula* in English.

"*Koliko?*" I asked, wanting to know the price. Like Mina under the spell of the count, I was unable to resist his low price of three dollars and tucked my newfound treasure under my arm.

Continuing on, sticking my nose in the doorways of stores as I passed, I soon came upon a familiar face. Blinking to make sure it wasn't a hallucination, I took in the sight of my fortune-teller Nadia, once again seated at a small table and chairs—just as she had been the last two times, I'd run into her. She glanced up as I approached.

"*Amerikan?*" she asked, using the local pronunciation.

I nodded, for show, tucking my ear buds into my coat pocket.

"Come, child, let me read your fortune," she said.

I glanced around, but no one seemed terribly interested. Nadia was bundled up, her head and face hidden behind a floral scarf.

"*Chuvihani*," she whispered, as I took a seat. "Death is your constant companion here in the White City. How are you holding up?"

"Well enough," I replied. "Are you going to read my cards?"

"Yes, of course," Nadia said. "The spirits demand our attention. To deny them is unwise. Go on, shuffle the deck. We'll do a simple three-card reading, and then I'll take a look at your palm."

I mixed the cards as directed and handed her the deck. She sat for a moment, eyes closed, her left hand resting on the pile of images. After a few seconds, she exhaled a deep breath and selected three cards, placing them on the table. The first image was of a man standing in a chariot with two sphinxes—one black, one white—resting in front of him.

"The Chariot, reversed," Nadia said, pointing out that the card was placed upside down. "This card represents your past. It speaks of being out of control, of anxiety and resentment, struggle. This card is about give and take, light and darkness. You must learn balance and control."

"Go on," I said, silently lamenting how often those themes emerged for me.

"The next card, the Moon, represents the present. It speaks of illusion, obscurity, and unrest. Watch out for children of the moon, Olivia. Your worlds are fated to intersect."

I glanced at the card, with its two wolves howling at the moon, and shivered, reminded of the wolf Nikola sent to spy on me at my mother's house.

"The final card represents your future," Nadia continued. "Another reversal—the High Priestess. You must listen to your inner voice and trust your instincts. You're failing to use your talents, Olivia. What's happening?"

"Nothing is going as expected," I said.

"I can see that," she replied. "Give me your hand."

I did as I was told, then became unnerved by the length of time the time-walker spent scrutinizing my palm.

"Your life line is faded in places," she said. "It means you will be temporarily lost to this world."

"I'll be careful."

"You must be more than careful," she scolded. "You must be prepared to survive."

"What do you mean?"

"You are going to have a brush with death. Perhaps more than one," Nadia said. "But you see here? Your life line continues on, which means you are supposed to survive. You must be ready to save yourself."

"I can't. I don't . . . I can't do this alone," I blurted, my frustration over William's absence surfacing.

"When we first met, I told you that you would experience two great loves," she said. "You must have faith that you won't be alone in this."

I withdrew my hand. "I understand," I said.

"I'm not so sure," Nadia replied. "Don't be reckless. Your life line is not stable."

26

WILLIAM'S DECEPTION WAS A STONE UPON MY HEART.
I found his collusion with my father and Josef difficult to forgive.
After leaving Nadia, I felt restless and found myself once again hoping
William would appear. Everywhere I walked, I searched for him,
and my heart betrayed me by leaping at the sight of anyone with red
hair amid the crowd. For one moment I was certain I'd spotted him,
his lithe body covered in a long wool coat and scarf. I squinted,
wishing it to be so, and then he was gone.

The collapse of the illusion only soured my mood further. And
yet as I trudged along, nursing my grievances, a voice in my head
fought to remind me that William was the most honorable man I'd
ever met. Only something truly important would have separated him
from me. My broken heart wanted justice, but there was no court to
hear my pleas. And worse, the case I'd made in my head seemed more
selfish every day. Everyone seemed to grasp the seriousness of our
mission but me. I was too busy feeling abandoned. I continued to
walk, drowning in anguish. I should have gone home. But I didn't.

Instead, I walked out of the plaza and purchased a pass to ride
the streetcars at a newspaper kiosk. Armed with a small plastic card
printed with a large white Бусплус on the front, I boarded the first
trolley that arrived, following the old women of Belgrade, their hands
grasping ragged plastic shopping bags full of supplies for dinner.

I swiped the card against an electronic reader and lurched for-

ward toward a seat, my body rocking with the movements of the car
as it rolled along its tracks. I really didn't care about the final destination as long as I could sit quietly and let the vibration in the antique
car's wooden frame lull me into a trance. Our route's view mainly
consisted of Soviet-era apartments, their dish antennas protruding
from their concrete sides, faded towels masking partially collapsed
balconies. The streetcar crossed a massive metal bridge suspended
across the Sava River. I was scrutinizing the boats on the riverbank
when I felt a hand come down on my left shoulder, then a sharp prick
at the base of my neck. I turned my head to find the man from the
hotel bar sitting next to me, the one Josef and I had seen the night of
our arrival.

"Hello," he said. "Do you recognize me?"

I did. I immediately tried to get up but found that my body
would not comply. My eyes widened as I sensed a powerful drug
numbing my limbs.

"Animal tranquilizer," he said in a low voice. "Soon you will find
it difficult to speak. At the next stop, we're going to get off. If anyone
asks, I will say you are my girlfriend and you've had too much to
drink."

I tried to wriggle away, willing my body to move toward the
window, but managed only to lurch toward the seat in front of me.
My attacker caught me before I fell. I opened my mouth to scream
but found it impossible to form a sound. *This must be what a stroke
victim experiences,* I thought, *their words trapped and unable to escape.*
Too late, as usual, I regretted my decision to go out alone. As I
slipped away from consciousness, Nadia's pronouncement echoed
inside my head: *You will temporarily be lost to this world.*

A burning sensation on my upper right bicep dragged me awake, and a long-held scream burst from my lips. Remembering my last moments, I tested the muscles of my arms, hoping finally to fight off my attacker.

"Olivia," Josef said. "Open your eyes."

I did as I was told.

"You went out without me?" Josef asked. I inspected myself warily, wondering how I came to be sitting in my bed, clothed in my own pajamas.

Sheepishly, I looked up. "I wanted to get some air. You weren't here."

Silence followed. Josef stared at me as if my words were in a foreign tongue he couldn't comprehend.

"How did I get here?" I asked, steeling myself.

"A better question might be, how long have you been gone?" Josef said, breaking his silence.

Burying my face in my hands and in a voice quieter than I would have liked, I asked. "How long?"

"A day. You've been missing an entire day. When you didn't come home last night, I searched the city for you. I was about to call your father when I heard the bell at the front gate. I saw you, in the security cameras, slumped against the gate," Josef said. He tossed me a note, written in Cyrillic.

"I can't read this," I said, handing the paper back to him.

"It says, 'What's yours is mine,'" Josef said. "It was in your pocket."

I moved to inspect my right shoulder, which was wrapped in a large bandage. Slowly, I peeled off the bandage to see what kind of reminder Nikola had left me with. Under a sea of raw flesh and scabs, I could see an image of the Tower. It was one of the tarot's strongest cards—signaling ruin and chaos. Now I could identify the burning pain that I'd heard made first tattoos so difficult to forget. Nikola had branded me as one of his own.

Of all of the humiliations he could bestow upon me, this . . . was ingenious. I'd forced him to have his tarot cards read in Paris, and now he was leaving me with a lifelong reminder of my hubris and his power.

"Did they, does it look like they . . ." I couldn't finish. The idea of being raped while unconscious was too horrific to verbalize.

"No. Thank God," Josef said. "It doesn't appear they did more than drug you and keep you overnight to give you the tattoo. Nikola is warning you that he's in charge and controls the situation."

"Sneaking up on a woman and drugging her is hardly the act of a leader."

I felt the sting of Josef's palm upon my face before my brain registered what had happened.

"Jesus, why did you do that?" I asked, massaging my cheek.

Josef looked at me coldly. "I'm well aware I have none of my brother's self-control, but neither do you," he said. "I'm sorry I hit you. You know that I would never hurt you. I've sworn an oath to protect you, but I need you to pay attention. This isn't a situation where your sarcasm can save you. You must learn to manage your impulsiveness if you want to keep yourself alive. Now, I'm going to tell you something that just maybe you can learn from. It's the story of the night I was shot.

"I heard the soldiers coming long before I saw them. I was crouched behind a grove of trees waiting for a contact to arrive with information. Unfortunately, he'd been intercepted and led the Nazis directly to me."

Joseph paused. "I didn't know it at the time," he said, "but on the other end of the meadow, William and his father were also hiding, waiting for the same courier, who would of course never arrive. That was life in the Resistance. Every day could be your last, and there was no assurance that the person you were meeting wasn't a spy ready to betray you.

"In any case, I burst into the field from the grove running, praying I would survive and be able to avenge the death of my wife and daughter. I heard the Germans yelling, 'Shoot the filthy Jew,' but nothing happened, so I kept running. For a moment, I really thought I would outrun death."

Josef paused for a moment, then took a seat by my bed. "The bullet from the rifle knocked me facedown in the grass. It pierced my lung. The soldiers turned me over and laughed as they watched me gasp like a fish out of water. One of them was about to reload his gun, but another told him to conserve his ammunition. Instead, he amused himself by giving me a kick, forcing out what little air was left from my lungs. As they walked away, leaving me to die alone in the field, I looked up toward the heavens and renounced God for abandoning me.

"I'm not sure how long I was there before I saw a new face come into focus. 'Welcome to the world of second chances,' he said."

"And?" I said.

Josef lurched to his feet and grabbed me by the shoulders, fingers digging into my newly tattooed flesh.

"Stop!" I yelled.

"Understand: you don't live in a world of second chances!" Josef said. "Witches can't be turned. So, this is *it*. Live or die. The sooner you realize that, the better off you'll be. And maybe, just maybe, you'll still be alive at the end of this."

"That's rich," I said. "I'm supposed to just do what I'm told? Take orders from a group of men who didn't even have the courage to tell me the *real* plan before sending me here?"

Josef frowned. "That's your response?"

Silence would have been the wiser course, but my emotions, as usual, got the better of me. "No," I said. "I should have said that I find it laughable that you, of all people, would lecture me about allegiance and responsibility. You, who confide in no one, love no one. A loner without a connection to another living soul. What do you know about *any* of this?"

Josef's skin paled, and all at once I realized I'd gone too far.

"Josef, I'm sorry . . ."

"You and I, we always say too much," Josef replied, and he turned and left the room, leaving me very much alone.

WILLIAM WAS NO STRANGER TO BOREDOM. WALKING THE
planet for nearly two hundred years, he'd certainly experienced a few
dull moments. Somehow it didn't make his current lifestyle in Serbia
any less excruciating. These criminals he observed, a mix of Others
and humans, *did nothing.*

To call them lazy would be unfair, he thought, because it was
not sloth per se that kept them immobile. It was more a sense of
entitlement and anticipation. They were waiting for the right thing
to come along, the proper score. The big payday. In the interim,
they were content to drink coffee and smoke at the cafés near the
National Assembly Building, which hosted Serbia's version of Congress. A few drank vodka all day, until the evening, when it was
time to go to the discos and drink more vodka or attend a concert
at a nearby stadium. It was a routine only a specific breed of law-
breaker could maintain.

He knew he should be grateful that Patrick "Finn" Murphy had
taken a liking to him, even if that's what had put him in his current,
terribly tedious position. At least he now had a real job alongside
criminals. He'd used his contacts to obtain a few exclusive invitations
and to spread the word on the streets that he was a skilled tracker,
able to find the guy who'd skipped a loan payment or snitched on his
comrades. Before long, he met a vampire who spoke both Serbian
and English—with a thick Irish accent.

At their first meeting, Finn had been coolly friendly. "As long as the work gets done," he said, "I don't care what you do with your free time." At this, he'd glanced over to the provocatively dressed human women populating the back of the bar.

William played coy. It was a mixed bar, meaning humans and Others were comingling, which was a dangerous thing if you wanted to keep your cover. But more importantly, he wasn't interested in sleeping with anyone, unless it meant having Olivia back in his bed. The thought of sharing her again with Josef gave him a momentary pang, but he didn't see much use in brooding. As he'd already reminded himself, he'd been the one to open that Pandora's box.

A long night of drinking with Finn gave way to a text the next day to report to a remote village near the Romanian border. William was using a disposable cell phone he'd bought from a Telekom Srbija kiosk near the main Belgrade bus station. Before leaving town, he fired up his laptop from his room in a youth hostel near Saint Mark's Church and sent a quick note.

Gabriel,

I made my connection, after seeking out Olivia one last time. I watched her from afar in old-town Belgrade—just for a moment. For some reason she was alone. Of course I can't ask Josef why he's allowing her to wander unescorted. Perhaps you should.

I head north tomorrow to rendezvous with an Irish vampire who leads a criminal gang near the Romanian border. There appear to be a few of these houses across Serbia. I suspect they act as satellite locations for various enterprises. Romania, for example, is a gateway for exporting heroin and a preferred route for the human trafficking of young girls into Turkey. All of these are activities I have reason to suspect Nikola is involved in, although there has been no sign of him.

He doesn't seem to mix with the lower-tier criminals, the ones who get their hands dirty. Of course, we always knew he was a bit of a prince.

W. F.

Despite his attempts to stifle his emotions, William keenly felt his separation from Olivia as he repacked his duffel. When he'd watched her wandering the main pedestrian area, alone, her obvious despair had hit him like a body blow; it took everything in his power not to rush to her side. Then he sensed that she might have spotted him, and he'd left immediately. The last thing he wanted was to put her in danger. Now that he was attached to a criminal crew, he needed to remain isolated and unseen by all who knew him.

And he knew he shouldn't blame Josef. He couldn't expect his brother to protect Olivia quite as fiercely as he would have. *He* should have been there to watch over her; that was *his* job. But he'd walked off his post, allowed Gabriel and the Council's executive committee to wear him down with their pleas. There was a time he would have laughed in their faces and gone home to tune his guitars. But that was before *she* walked into the tunnel that day, the first woman to snare his attention in decades. And instead of celebrating his good fortune and binding his lover to him, he'd sent her into the arms of his brother.

William realized, as his tortured thoughts stretched into the dawn hours, that his greatest fear wasn't about Olivia and Josef being together. It was that her heart would harden against William for his subterfuge. That she would grow to hate him for his decision. He'd had little choice in the matter. For the assignment to work, she couldn't follow him. He had to resume his old identity: a solitary figure, with no meaningful connection to another soul.

28

"WHAT ARE YOU DOING?!"

I nearly fell off my chair. I was hunkered down at the kitchen table doing some work and Josef's roar was the first sound I'd heard in hours. Since our argument, we'd maintained a quiet, polite distance—despite the fact that I was effectively under house arrest, forbidden to leave his sight. Not that I would have dared.

Finally, finding my tongue, I said, "I'm just about to review the information Diana Chambers gave me the night of the party in Slovenia." I pivoted my computer so he could see the screen as I used the passkey. Josef narrowed his eyes as he lowered himself into a chair next to me.

"Do vampires use bifocals?" I asked, trying to lighten the mood.

"No. We have perfect vision the minute we're reborn," he said.

We scanned a series of files, including FBI bulletins, confidential Interpol surveillance records, and official reports detailing bribery and corruption in Serbia. Not surprisingly, Nikola's name and photo, along with a list of his vast business enterprises and suspected connections to other major criminals, appeared repeatedly. His dossier also included profiles of Serbian politicians he was suspected of bribing.

"Now I understand why she thinks I owe her a favor," I said, impressed with the level of detail she provided. "There are a few politicians here I expect we'll meet when we begin our monitoring work."

"Why would we have any contact with them?" Josef asked.

"As part of our monitoring responsibilities, we visit party leaders and interview them to obtain information about election plans. Officials need to produce precinct maps, voter guides, and sample ballots— or at least the Serbian version of those items. Any irregularities are reported immediately."

"So you could potentially be interviewing politicians who've been bribed by Nikola?"

"It looks like it," I said. "Knowing this ahead of time is useful. Hopefully, it will cut down on unwanted surprises."

We opened more files. My screen was filled with unfamiliar names and faces. Here were dozens of suspected members of organized crime, men who'd been accused of everything from the brazen jewelry robbery I'd witnessed in San Francisco to illegal organ harvesting, human trafficking, and even the theft of fine art in Europe. It was mind-boggling to see what I'd stumbled onto that day in San Francisco. Silently, I mused about how easily I could have gone in the opposite direction for a coffee and avoided this whole debacle.

"Click on that one," Josef demanded, snapping me out of my daydream. He was pointing to a file labeled BELGRADE. A tap on my track pad brought up a photo of my kidnapper from the trolley, listed as "unidentified." A man named Patrick "Finn" Murphy followed in the next image: an Irish citizen living in Belgrade.

"No name on the man from the bar. That's disappointing," Josef said. "But at least we know these two are connected to Nikola."

"Agreed," I said. "But did you notice? There are no photographs of tarot card tattoos or any mention of them. I'm going to email Diana— let her know." Almost reflexively, I glanced down at my arm, disheartened to think that now I could be pegged as a member of Nikola's gang.

Josef placed his hand on my shoulder, startling me with his tenderness. "Try not to think about it," he said gently. "In time, the memory will fade, and it will get easier."

I nodded, grateful for his comfort. It had been lonely in the house with the two of us not speaking.

Forcing myself to move on, I continued reading, amused to learn that ground zero for criminal gatherings in Belgrade was the lobby bar at Square Nine, the hotel we'd stayed at our first night.

"No wonder we ran into trouble almost the minute we arrived," Josef said. "Somehow, I missed that in my research. I'll have to be more thorough next time."

"*Next time?*" I repeated. "After this is over, I'm going back to more normal pursuits."

Josef sniffed. "We'll see," he said.

Hot spot No. 2, according to the US State Department's notes, was Stadion Crvena Zvezda, or the Red Star Stadium, an arena southeast of the old city used for soccer matches and concerts. Later in the evening, after Josef had excused himself to go out and feed, I researched the stadium on my laptop and noticed that Duran Duran was performing. An absurd idea formed as I read—reckless and foolish a million times over, but still worth it. If ground zero was the Red Star Stadium, then there was hope that some of Nikola's gang would be there, and with them, proof of Nikola's crimes. Emboldened, I waited up for Josef to return.

"No!" he snapped as soon he cleared the doorway of his bedroom and caught sight of me.

"I haven't said a word."

"You don't need to," he replied. "You're here because you have some crazy plan. I can feel it. So, unless I'm wrong and you're here to ravish me, you should get out now—because I've just fed, and I'm feeling very . . . *energized.*"

I sat up straight, feeling myself blushing. I knew from being around William that a vampire's appetite for sex increased after he fed. Somehow, I hadn't remembered that little detail before I'd sprawled out on Josef's bed.

"I think I know how we might get a closer look at some of Nikola's associates," I said, my voice an octave higher than normal.

A set of dark eyebrows furrowed. "Let's just focus on our assignment. The monitoring will be dangerous enough. Why borrow more trouble? After everything that's happened, don't you think we should just stick to our plans?"

"No, I don't," I said, squirming a bit under the heat of his gaze. "Before you cut me off, just listen. We were sent here to help find a link between Nikola and these criminals. I have to think that our work—including the monitoring—is still necessary, even with William's assignment." I took a breath. "I won't lie. What Nikola did to me was humiliating and scary. But I'm not going to give up."

I felt Josef's turmoil, although truth be told, my empath skills were unnecessary: it was written across his face. How was it that the face of a man whose stoicism had been such a mystery now looked readable to me?

"Mind you, I'm not agreeing to anything," he said slowly. "But the price—for me to listen to your idea—is steep. Is it worth it to you?"

"What do I have to do?"

"Take a bath with me," Josef said. "I've wanted to bathe with you since I saw you soaking in my father's tub in Paris."

"*Just* a bath?" I asked, remembering how I'd chastised him for spying on me in the tub that afternoon, the first time we'd stayed in the apartment in Paris.

"If you mean, do you have to sleep with me, no," he replied. "But I want to touch you, and I expect you to reciprocate."

"OK," I said reluctantly. I needed his help to execute my plans. I was also feeling a little bit *energized* myself, although I didn't want to admit it.

Josef filled the large soaking tub in his bathroom. Modesty was a wasted concept with someone who'd seen me undressed in a crowded room, so I simply followed him in and removed my clothes. Then I stood and watched him undress, once again marveling at how different he was from William. Smaller and more compact than his brother, his skin was free of any tattoos to obscure it. His hair was jet black, making it easier to follow as it narrowed from his chest to a thin line running across his abdomen. I had no memory of seeing that on our night in Paris.

"I'm flattered," Josef said, interrupting my admiration. "But remember, I said no sex, so try to control yourself."

Something about his remarks broke the tension, and I let out a small laugh of relief. The warm, bubbly water was instantly soothing. Josef plopped in after me, sending our bath spilling over the tub's edges. The flames of the candles on the counter nearby fluttered in the breeze from his movement.

"May I?" he asked, picking up a washcloth. "Lift your leg."

I nodded, bracing for the sensation of his hand on my body and chagrined at the view it afforded him.

"It's nothing I haven't seen before," he purred, noticing my discomfort.

To distract myself, I decided to ask Josef a question that had been on my mind. "I want to ask you about your maker, the vampire," I said as he ran the cloth across my calf.

"All right," he said.

"What was his name, and where were you when he died?" I asked. "William told me the story, but he didn't mention either of those details."

Instead of answering me, Josef placed his lips against the side of my foot, kissing me gently and nearly launching me out of the tub, the sensation was so erotic.

"His name was Zachary Reed Cooke," Josef said, expertly moving the cloth up my leg toward the inside of my thigh. "He liked to be called Reed. I was away on another mission when he died. We'd agreed that I would go to Belgium and try to link up with some Resistance fighters there. I was caught behind enemy lines for a few weeks. It was too risky for me to travel, even at night. By the time I got back, he was dead."

I couldn't help but notice, despite the matter-of-fact tone, that this was yet another story of Josef being away when someone he loved had been murdered. No wonder he had avoided forming any further attachments.

I kept the thought to myself as Josef rearranged me so that my back was to him. He began to run the cloth across my shoulders and then down my arms. I could feel his hesitation as his fingers came to rest across my collarbone. Aroused but deeply conflicted, I grabbed the cloth out of his hands.

"OK, my turn," I said. "Turn around."

Josef did as he was asked. Instead of the cloth, I grabbed a bar of soap and lathered up my hands. Then I began to massage his back and arms. A sigh escaped his lips, and he leaned against me. I wrapped my arms around him and stopped for a second, guiltily savoring the moment. Josef did, too, closing his eyes as he reclined.

Finally, after several minutes, I returned to our conversation. "How long did you know Reed before he died?" I asked.

"A year and six months," Josef said, still resting against me. "After his death, William and I became inseparable. He helped complete my training as a vampire. I owe him . . ."

I felt Josef's mood turn seconds before he jumped out of the tub, out of my arms.

"That's enough soaking for one night," he said gruffly. "We can talk about your idea tomorrow."

Confused, I stayed in the tub a few minutes longer, alone. Somehow, I'd managed to insert William right between us. While the logical part of my brain knew it was for the best, other parts were decidedly disappointed..

29

IT TOOK SOME CONVINCING, BUT EVENTUALLY, JOSEF SAW
the wisdom of me dressing like a man to attend the Duran Duran
concert. To read people's emotions, I needed to get close. To get close,
I needed a disguise. Nikola's men were looking for a woman, one with
a prominent tattoo on her bicep. My ability to move freely in that
crowd would be limited at best, but if Olivia could become Oliver—
voilà.

We discussed my idea in the morning. As usual, Josef made no
mention of our previous night's activities. He simply sauntered into
the kitchen as I was making coffee and asked me to explain. I'd expected to have to work harder for his assistance, but surprisingly,
after asking a few probing questions, he signed on.

The hard work, it turned out, lay in my transformation. Josef and
I eventually realized we'd have to cut my hair. With reluctance, using
scissors and then a razor, he made my curly brown locks disappear.
Next it was time to erase any outward signs of femininity, removing
earrings and nail polish. The final stage of the disguise involved
wrapping my breasts tightly to my chest with an Ace bandage, flatten-
ing things enough to pass inspection in the darkened arena. For the
finale, I pulled on a pair of motorcycle boots along with some dark
jeans and a sweater. My dagger, which I could now summon from a

few feet across the room, had to stay behind at the house. It wouldn't make it through security at the arena.

"What do you think?" I asked, walking into his room for inspection.

"Lower your voice, or let me do the talking," he said, the muscles in his throat tight.

"Good point," I said, pulling on a black wool ski hat Josef had laid out for me. I had no facial hair, and my body was slight, but as long as I kept a low profile, it seemed likely I would simply go unnoticed amid the thousands of concertgoers.

"Let's review the ground rules," Josef said as he put on his own coat and hat.

"No need; I remember," I said. "Are you ready?"

"Not really," he replied, shutting off the lights as we left the room.

Ninety minutes later, after I'd inhaled a quick dinner and Joseph had imbibed numerous shots of vodka, we arrived at the stadium.

"They have a VIP lounge," I said as we approached the main entrance. "I arranged for passes, and there are tickets waiting for us at the will call window."

"Can anyone use the lounge?" Josef asked.

"Anyone willing to pay the five-hundred-dollar admission fee."

As soon as the bouncer for the lounge opened the padded red doors, I knew we'd come to the right place. A burst of psychic energy pressed against my head as we walked inside, and I quickly locked down my mind to avoid being detected by the vampires in the room. I scanned the room, noticing a few demons sitting in the corner of the lounge—the lack of color in their aura a dead giveaway to empaths like me. As we strolled toward our reserved booth, I reminded myself to stay in character: Oliver strolling with his friend. For my male impersonation, I thrust my shoulders slightly forward and slowed my gait.

The crowd was drunk, or well on their way. No one seemed to

notice our arrival. I could have pulled a handgun out and shot Josef in the head and no one would have been the wiser. Instead, all of the lounge's patrons were obsessively staring at their cell phones. After a few minutes, a young woman came to take our order. Josef asked her to bring us a bottle of Stoli Elit and some *frites* and punctuated his request with a flirtatious wink. The waitress cooed and giggled as she left, smitten by Josef's deadly charm.

Trying to look bored, I pulled out my phone, hoping to blend in.

"So, *Romeo*, what do you see out there?"

"Sadly, no one we know," Josef replied, leaning back into the worn black leather of our booth. "The man who kidnapped you isn't here."

My reply was delayed by the arrival of our food and drink. Josef poured us each a generous shot. "*Santé!*"

We tossed back the fiery alcohol. Josef refilled our glasses.

"Go slow," I said, as usual worried that my liquor consumption would outpace my food intake. I left my glass, filled to the rim, untouched in front of me, and leaned back to survey the room. I recognized no one. It was just as well since my kidnapper might very well recognize me—disguise or not. I shuddered involuntarily as I contemplated the hours he'd been alone with me, while I was unconscious. Josef, noticing my distress, tapped my arm.

"You OK?"

"*Da*," I said, using Serbian to reply.

"There are a lot of Others in this room tonight," Josef said, leaning in to speak to me as if we were two friends trying to hear each other above the din of the club. "Oddly, it's mostly werewolves."

I recalled Nadia's prediction—"*Watch out for children of the moon*," she'd said—and wondered if we were in for more trouble. "We should go to the main hall," I said, suddenly feeling superstitious. "The band will come on soon."

Josef paid our tab, leaving a generous tip and what appeared to be the impression that the waitress might get lucky later. I tried to play a shy boy unable to hit it off with the ladies, unlike his more confident friend. Josef caught up with me, his eyes brimming with mischief.

"And you were worried I was going to get us into trouble," I said.

THE TEMPERATURE ROSE TEN DEGREES AS WE ENTERED the concourse, and the crowd quickly swallowed us into its undulating center. We shuffled along with the rest of the concertgoers into the main hall. The house lights were still on, but soon dimmed as the stagehands arranged the instruments in preparation for the main act. A haze of smoke, mostly from cigarettes, filled the hall. Josef and I strolled the outside ring of the room, secretly looking for familiar faces or sensations. When we came upon a crowd of tough-looking men congregating in one of the far corners, I spotted a few with tarot card images on their arms right away. I paused, pretending to search my jacket for something.

"In the far corner," I said as I rifled through my pockets.

"Can you detect anything?" Josef asked.

"Nothing useful," I replied. "There's a mix of Others in that mob, all seething in their skin—restless, but nothing significant."

Just as I finished speaking, the lights went out, and the sound of a camera's shutter rapidly clicking came through the speakers, sending the crowd into a frenzy as they realized "Girls on Film" would be the first song in the set.

We should have anticipated the surge of people trying to get closer to the stage, but all of our planning had been focused on a confrontation with our enemies, not a fluke encounter triggered by plain old bad luck. The crowd became unruly as the audience in front of the stage tried to hold their positions against those in the rear who were trying to move closer to the band. Resistance seemed futile to me, considering that the men pushing from behind were some of Belgrade's most notorious criminals—men I could feel were in no mood to be refused. Josef and I had just agreed to leave when the fight broke out. Blows began to fly, and I pushed back to make some space for myself. It was then that I saw the two men with knives, drunk and teetering on their feet like skittish Bolshoi dancers.

So much for security.

It should have been easy to stay out of their way, except for the fact that the audience was rocking back and forth like a ship tossed at sea. A shove sent me straight into the path of one of the blades. The knife tore open the skin above my collarbone, leaving a wide gash. I fell to the ground and made myself disappear. Then I watched, my eyes adjusted to the darkness, as my attacker stopped swinging to search for the body he'd hit. Arms dragging on the ground like an orangutan, he swept his blade across the floor as if he *knew* he should look for me. I tried to open my mind to test out my theory, but the pain from my wound made it difficult to think straight. I was scurrying backward on the floor, trying to avoid another injury—not to mention being trampled—when I felt someone grab me from behind and pull me out of the fray.

"Don't say a word," Josef growled in my ear as he pushed us through the crowd and out of the stadium. Outside in the frigid night, he wrapped his coat around me to hide the bloodstain blooming on the front of my clothing and hailed a taxi. Not a word was uttered as we sped toward the house. Once inside, he clamped onto my good arm and dragged me through the hallway to the kitchen, threw me into a chair, and grabbed a knife from a drawer. Making a small incision on his right hand, he thrust the open wound to my lips. "Drink," he said, eyeing me angrily.

"Why?" I asked. "My injury isn't that bad."

"You fool," he replied. "You were almost killed. I want you to drink so I can find you more easily if you ever disappear like that again. You're lucky my sense of smell is so good, or you'd be dead."

"That's how you found me? My scent?"

"Drink first. Answers later," he replied, never moving his hand from my face.

I complied. As I closed my mouth around the gash, I remembered the night William saved my life with his blood, when I was bleeding to death after the bombing that killed Aidan. Tears threatened, and after a minute, I pushed Josef's hand away. "Enough."

Josef licked his wound, using his saliva to close the cut. He stood for a moment, his gaze searing. "Take off your shirt," he said, and turned to pull a plastic first aid kit from a nearby drawer.

"Funny, whenever I'm around, we seem to need medical supplies," I remarked nervously.

"Just take off your shirt so I can see how badly you're injured," he said. "I could smell your blood; that's what helped me find you. After all of our training, I know your scent. Although locating you in the dark, when you're invisible, on the floor of a sold-out Duran Duran concert is pretty amazing, even for me."

"I didn't see that coming," I said as I pulled my bloodstained T-shirt off with one arm.

Josef was staring at me, my chest really, which was still bound in an Ace bandage.

"Stand up and let me unwrap you," he said, slowly unraveling the cloth. It was a relief to be unbound, to breathe freely again. I sat back in my chair dressed from the waist up in nothing but a black running bra. Exposed to the air, the cut at my collarbone stung like hell.

"Take off the bra," he said. "The strap is sitting in the wound I need to clean."

I tried and found that my right arm was too sore to remove

something so snug to my body. I stopped midway and eyed Josef warily.

"You'll have to help."

"Damn fool," he muttered, as he cut the bra away with the knife he'd used earlier on himself. "How did I ever let you talk me into this?"

"I thought we might locate some of Nikola's gang, maybe be able to follow someone out of the concert," I said, stammering from the pain. "We could have discovered something important. There were so many criminals there . . ."

"But we didn't. And we won't. The fates are against you, against *us*," he said.

"I don't believe that," I said, wincing as he wiped the wound with alcohol and pulled the first suture through my skin. He pulled the next stitch even more tightly. "Ouch! I thought you were supposed to look after me."

"True, but that doesn't mean I have to make it easy," he said, closing the wound and fishing around in the first aid kit for a large bandage and some tape. "Hold this," he continued, handing me the gauze pad.

I placed the square over the gash and held it there while he cut several pieces of surgical tape. Carefully, he placed the bandage over the cut, running his fingers along the adhesive to seal it to my skin. Despite his attempt to be gentle, the pain was excruciating, the area around the wound throbbing. As Josef's fingertip reached the last millimeter of tape, he hit a tender spot. Agitated from my injury, adrenaline coursing through my veins, my survival instincts took over, and I lashed out at Josef with all my might.

"Enough!" I shrieked, leaping up and pushing him backward. My body was on overload, all of my energy spilling out into the room. All around me, cabinets opened, and glasses flew out, crashing to the floor. Josef came toward me, his eyes ablaze.

"Olivia!" he bellowed. "Look at me. You're safe. Calm down. Now."

It took a few seconds, but his words snapped me out of my frenzy, and I froze. I stood stock-still, surveying the damage I'd caused—and realizing once again that I was more skilled at losing control than at mastering my gifts.

"OK then," I said, awkwardly. "I'll just clean up and go to bed."

"Wait, let me wash you," Josef said, jumping up for a cloth. "We can clean this mess up afterward." He ran the towel under the faucet and returned with a warm compress. Then, slowly, he wiped the blood and grime from my face and injured arm. The warm water cooled, giving me a chill, and I shivered, my arms covered in goose bumps.

Josef's fingertips were hesitant at first, lightly skimming the surface of my breasts. I pulled back a bit as a mix of desire and guilt flooded my system. Josef began to whisper, words pouring out under his breath. I strained to listen, eventually realizing he wasn't speaking to me.

"I touch, but never feel. I look, but never see. I'm so bloody tired. Just once I want—"

"We shouldn't," I said, cutting him off.

Josef leaned in and placed a searing kiss upon my lips. "I don't care," he whispered, pulling back just enough to look into my eyes. "We've been at war with each other and the world since we arrived. Please, just for one night, I want some peace."

I should have said no, that there would be no peace for us. But in my heart I knew Josef was asking for something that part of me wanted to give. My moment of hesitation passed and was replaced by raw desire. I kissed Josef back, setting off an explosion of passion. One moment I was in his arms, the next, sprawled across the table that had been our makeshift emergency room moments before. With one arm, Josef sent the bandages flying, placing me underneath him while he teased and prodded me with his kisses. All of the anger and pain of the last few weeks resurfaced, and I pulled Josef close, nipping and biting the tender skin around his neck until he cried out in ecstasy.

"Come. Upstairs to my bed," he said, rising from the table and extending a hand. I stared into Josef's face trying to read his expression—relief, desire? It wasn't predatory, and for once in my life, I had no fear that he might devour me. Wordlessly, he took my hand and led me to his room.

Then we were standing inside his doorway, eyeing each other like awkward teenagers. Finally, Josef stepped forward and took my face into his hands, this time kissing me more gently, like a man courting his lover. His kiss was less tender than William's, his body more muscular. Had I been allowed to continue with the comparisons, a renewed sense of guilt might have stopped me, but Josef, perhaps detecting my hesitation, pressed on with his seduction. Eased out of my remaining clothing, now lying on his bed, I arched toward him as he caressed my breasts, fastened his mouth on one nipple, then moved his hands down my body with one intention. I moaned, only partly because my wound ached with my writhing. Josef smiled, delighted to see my reaction.

"*C'est rien*," he said, repeating his words from our night in Paris.

In the end, that was the only similarity between the two evenings. As part of a threesome, Josef had been the rogue, intent on pushing my boundaries. But tonight, as he slid inside me and held me in his arms, he was simply a man wanting to please a woman, needing her touch. And he loved me intently, as if his life depended on my reaction. Not a word was uttered, nothing I can remember anyway. Darkness faded to daylight, and then to darkness again before we reluctantly emerged from our cocoon. I lay next to Josef, our hands intertwined, glancing down at my body, bruised and marked by wounds—both his and my attacker's.

"I look a mess," I said, sitting up. "What will Lily and Elsa say when they see me?"

Josef frowned. "Will you tell them?"

Would I? Not likely. It seemed to me that I was entitled to my own secrets. Telling them wouldn't help any of us, especially if Josef wanted to bring Lily back to his bed.

"No," I said. "This time belongs to us. Besides, you might want to . . . pick up with Lily once she's here tomorrow."

Instead of offering a hint of his intentions, Josef posed another question. "Will you tell William?"

I crawled back into bed, pulling his hand into mine. "Yes. He predicted this . . . at least, I think he was trying to say he knew it might happen. He told me you would save my life, and that you . . ." I paused, hesitant to say the words aloud.

"What?" Josef asked warily.

"That you loved me."

"William is a sentimental old fool," Josef said, turning away from me.

I exhaled the breath I hadn't realized I was holding, relieved to have the old Josef back, knowing it would make everything easier.

"I told him the very same thing," I said, giving Josef a sly smile before leaving the room.

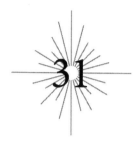

WILLIAM HOPED THAT HIS HEAVY WINTER GEAR WOULD provide a bit of anonymity. He had never enjoyed being the lone stranger in a small town. But that was what the job required, so every time he went out, he piled on a coat, scarf, and hat—despite being immune to the cold.

He'd managed to spend the first few days on the outskirts of the village without attracting attention. It was actually better to be out and about, since being "at home" was hardly relaxing: he was now staying at one of the safe houses used by Nikola's criminal network. Luckily, on his third night in town, he returned from an outing to find the house empty.

He was expected in town for a drink with Finn later, but he wanted to get a few words to Gabriel before. William powered up his laptop and began typing.

Gabriel,

Arrived by car a few days ago. I'm staying at an old farmhouse just outside of Veliko Središte, a small village near the Romanian border. It's a safe house for Finn and his crew, and a good place to stay out of sight, complete with a tractor parked in the driveway.

The weather has been terrible. Temperatures have plummeted. I managed to travel in between storms. My Serbian is rusty at best, but I've picked up enough to know this winter is the cruelest the village residents can remember. Weeks of punishing snowstorms have delayed heating oil deliveries, driving up the price. The ground here in the northeast froze early, ruining potato and onion crops. Supplies are meager and tempers are running high among the town's twelve hundred inhabitants. Although I would say deprivation and poverty are no strangers to this area. It breeds a darkness that lurks in the hearts of some of these villagers; a potent tool used by kings and generals since the dawn of the Hapsburg Empire.

Although I have no proof, I sense Nikola knows how to exploit this anger to power his criminal enterprise. Between Olivia and I, we must find a way to convert our instincts into hard proof. As you can imagine, the conditions are ripe for locals to feel embittered, intent on making their own black-market economy strong enough to heat their homes and feed their families. From the look of things, the whole village seems to help with the criminal endeavors. One mother is rumored to have burned a priceless painting allegedly stolen in Denmark in the fireplace of the town's Orthodox church, hoping to destroy evidence implicating her son in the robbery . . .

※

William stopped there, realizing it was time to go. There was no honor among thieves, and the odds were good someone would go through his belongings while he was away, so he hid his laptop before departing. He'd been traveling with essentials only. His passport and identification were locked in a safety deposit box in Belgrade. If the Serbian police stopped him he would be a nonentity with no identification and no record with Interpol or any other law enforcement organization.

Pulling on his hat and coat, he shut the door behind him, not bothering to lock it. Then he walked along the narrow road into town, observing in the low, late-afternoon light how the snow clung to the crevices of the village's stately old trees. It was beautiful now, he thought to himself, but any more, and the branches would break.

Finn was already seated at a table inside the bar when William arrived. The bartender, without a word, brought a bottle of Jack Daniel's and a glass.

"You know me well," William said, pouring himself a generous serving. "What are you having?"

"Vodka," Finn said. "Although I'd prefer blood. I'm starving."

William glanced around the bar, the look on his face telegraphing his concern.

"Don't bother," Finn said. "This place is ours. It only serves our kind."

"How do you manage to keep humans out?" William asked. "Aren't they curious?"

"This isn't like America. Let me show you something," Finn said, pulling a folded piece of paper from his pocket.

William unfolded the flyer, which was printed in Cyrillic, an official-looking seal at the top of the page.

"A magistrate from the town council handed out this paper in the main square today. It contains a warning that there is a vampire on the loose," Finn said. "The man implored the villagers to 'place the holy cross in each room and run garlic along the windowsills.' This is a country of superstitious people. According to the newspapers, the townspeople think an ancient circus performer named Sava, rumored to be Serbia's first vampire, has risen from the grave. Little do these poor, primitive people know that the vampires of Serbia actually drive Range Rovers and serve in the National Assembly. The only thing lurking in the countryside is the wild imagination of a gullible people."

"So what keeps the townspeople from coming in here?" William asked.

"Fear, of course," Finn replied. "Notice they didn't ask people to assemble to kill the brute? This is the way it has been in Europe for centuries. It reminds me of home. People here understand darkness and light, good and evil. They have no interest in anything but keeping things in their proper place. They know we walk among them, but they foolishly think a little garlic on the windowsill will keep us away."

"Is that why you like this area?" William asked, hoping he wasn't pressing his luck. He'd seen people punished for less invasive questions.

"You'll find out for yourself starting tomorrow," Finn said. "We leave at dawn to run a few errands. I know I don't have to ask you to get some sleep, so you might as well stay here and drink."

True to his word, Finn whisked William away at dawn and plunged him into the crew's enterprises. Three weeks later, William returned to the farmhouse. Back for what was supposed to be a short stay, William fished his laptop from the barn next door to complete his note to Gabriel.

I write this next part of my report several weeks after beginning the note. I'm rarely alone and may not be able to communicate with you regularly.

As I was mentioning, the town is shrouded in gloom and rife with superstition. When I first arrived, a local magistrate came and warned the townspeople to stuff garlic in their pockets to avoid a vampire on the loose.

I tell you this as a prelude to a greater story, but honestly, Nikola, being one of Serbia's oldest vampires, must howl with glee at these fabulous diversions. These rural towns near the border are brilliant base camps for criminal activities. While the villagers all race to douse holy water on their doorsteps, he can traffic their daughters in Turkey, where they favor the pale glow of preteen girls above all else. While the town councils issue warnings to locals not to go out at night, Nikola can smuggle in heroin, assured that the villagers are too distracted to notice. There is a part of me that admires Nikola for his elegant ruthlessness—and his choice of henchmen. My travels these last few weeks with Finn reveal that his gang dabbles in virtually every criminal enterprise. I have no proof, but I know Nikola is behind it all. He is the rapacious force behind this vast empire of human trafficking, drug smuggling, money laundering, and weapons transport into war-torn territories in the Middle East and Africa. Finn is not capable of masterminding what I've seen.

To my everlasting shame, I've witnessed a string of crimes against society since I took up with these thieves and sociopaths, including the delivery of a van of young girls to a brothel in Turkey. The situation was intolerable, of course, and I sent word—at great risk—to some distant associates to remedy the situation immediately. The owner of the house, which is located in an otherwise unremarkable suburb in Istanbul, has disappeared, and the victims were all sent home to their families. Finn, of course, will simply find more girls to sell. He oversees much of this with an efficiency that American CEOs would admire.

If only I could identify the direct connection to Nikola. In the criminal underworld, Finn is known for being Nikola's crew boss—that's why I targeted him all those weeks ago at the nightclub in Belgrade—but I'm still empty-handed. Nikola has never appeared. And of course, I cannot ask directly who we work for when I collect my earnings at the end of a job. There is a hierarchy within our group of Others. Werewolves seem to do more of the physical work, which includes fighting, and occasionally murder. The vampires tend to be the managers, planning the jobs and, like me, serving as couriers. Somehow, I have to find a connection to Nikola, without being discovered. It will not be easy.

ELSA AND LILY ARRIVED LADEN WITH EQUIPMENT: CAMERAS, laptops, and a satellite phone that would allow us to make calls from remote locations. Seeing them was a delight after my month alone with Josef.

"You've cut your hair," said Elsa, fingering my short locks suspiciously as I greeted her at the airport.

"I like it," Lily said. "But you look tired. We're both anxious to hear what you've been up to." It was good to see them, but a part of me dreaded telling them about my misadventures.

Soon we were seated in the living room amid piles of supplies, cataloging our possessions. I'd stopped by the OSCE offices the day before to collect our final assignment packet. The elections would take place in April, and most of the other teams had already left the city. We were one of the last groups to depart, a fact I'd learned from the scheduling manager on duty.

"OK, before we dive into the details about locations, let's review our assignments," I said.

Lily jumped in first. "Before I left San Francisco I created a template to log all of the information we'll need to gather," she said. "The nice thing about taking a leave of absence is that it gave me time to experiment with different computer programs."

"And you, Elsa? What did you do to prepare?" I asked, my

tongue firmly in my cheek. I thought she'd probably been cleaning her knives and practicing yoga.

"I consulted with Nadia about portals in the region," she replied, throwing me for a loop. "I thought we might like to know how to escape quickly."

"Good idea," I replied solemnly, reminded once again not to underestimate her. "But I thought the portals' locations were supposed to show up on my arm—that's what the spell Nadia helped apply to my arm in San Francisco was supposed to do, right?"

"Magic can be interrupted," Elsa replied cryptically.

"Or disrupted," Josef added, coming into the room. "I overheard your conversation. I'm set as driver, translator, and part of the security team. Elsa is my backup."

"And I'm responsible for the face-to-face interviews with officials. Lily and I will both manage photography," I said. "So, on to our schedule. First on our itinerary are two small villages located in the wine region along the Danube River." Although I tried not to show it, our assignment actually sent a shiver up my spine. I remembered Nikola, in Slovenia, giving me wine-tasting notes. "Mysterious," he'd said. Was this another sign of fate working against us, or just a coincidence? One way or another, we were going to find out. Novi Sad, the second-largest city in Serbia, was nearby, but we would bypass it—at least for now—and head northwest toward Croatia.

"The weather is turning brutal up there," Josef said. "I better take the car out now to get some gas and other supplies. Why don't you three walk into Old Town and have some dinner?"

Three heads nodded in unison, knowing smirks on our faces. Josef was outnumbered and ready for a break.

As we were preparing to go out, my cell phone rang, Gabriel's name flashing on the screen.

"Did everyone arrive safely?" he said, bypassing hello.

"We're all here."

"When do you leave?"

"There's a storm coming," I said. "Josef wants to be out tomorrow at first light."

"Good plan. The car I leased has new tires and was recently serviced," Gabriel said. "You should be able to travel through most areas, even in bad conditions."

"You sound like a concerned father," I said, still angry at his deceptions, "but I know it's politics on your mind."

"I *am* a concerned father, Olivia," he said. "Perhaps one day you'll understand the difficulty of satisfying more than one master—occasionally there are conflicts. *Je suis désolé.*"

"A fault confessed is half forgiven," I said, repeating an old French saying.

"*Bon!* Half is better than nothing," he said, perking up. "Now put me on speaker, I want to talk to everyone."

I did as he asked, setting my iPhone on the coffee table.

"*Bonsoir*," Gabriel said. "I'll cut to the chase: Nikola sent me an email earlier in the day informing me he intends to seek the votes to amend the Council's bylaws to allow for an early transition. He's also put forward a proposal to limit the Council's intervention in human affairs, claiming the organization has to conserve its resources. He's pressing for a vote no later than May, and of course, he's doing this while most of my core team is away, leaving me with fewer resources to lobby members. Despite my good standing with my colleagues, I think it's possible he could collect enough votes—especially if China and Russia align with him. I worry that some of our members will agree with his central argument, which is that that our methods are outdated. In our digital age when information can be shared and meetings can be virtual, why do we need a year to transition our leadership?"

"Do you want us to come home?" I asked.

"No," Gabriel said. "Madeline will help me prolong discussions, but it would be good if you could return no later than mid-April, after the elections. That's probably as long as I can stall things. We must obtain evidence to discredit Nikola."

"Frankly, it's not as easy as we thought to uncover evidence," I said. "The intelligence files we were given are limited and reveal no connection between Nikola and any criminal activity. In fact, we discovered something they haven't, but it doesn't get us very far."

"*Vraiment?* Tell me."

"Most of his gang bear the mark of *le tarot*, images from tarot cards," Josef replied, inserting himself into the discussion. "Olivia discovered that Nikola likes to have his fortune read. Even the un-dead can be superstitious, it seems. When we arrived at our hotel in Belgrade, one of his men was there, a prominent tattoo on his bicep. We've seen several more images since."

"*Merde*, even for an Other, he is a bit bizarre," Gabriel sighed. "Olivia, pick up. I want to speak to you."

I picked up my phone and wandered out of the living room, turning off the speaker as I looked for a private space to talk. Gabriel's intense concern was pulsing through the phone lines, giving me an idea of what was coming next in our conversation. "I'm here."

"Josef called me earlier to tell me you were injured in a knife fight," he said. "I suspect that's not the half of it. Please tell me you are trying to use your skills."

"There was no time," I said. "I left my dagger at home because it was a concert. Next time I'll be prepared."

"You have more at your disposal than a blade, Olivia," Gabriel said. "Your mind is a force no weapon can match. Ask Elsa to work with you now that she is there."

"And do what, bend people to my will? Isn't that your job?"

"Think of it more as friendly persuasion," Gabriel said. "The human mind is . . . *malleable*. Be safe. I want you to come home alive."

I laid my head against the doorjamb at the kitchen. "Why did you ask me to do this? Did you really believe I could help?"

"*Oui, bien sûr*," Gabriel replied. "Of course. The prophecies . . . the more I think about them, the more I believe them to be true. You are special, Olivia. One day you will lead the Council. You will master your skills and become a foe few will dare to cross."

"It doesn't feel that way now," I said.

"Never fear, one day soon it will," he said.

I hung up with my father just as Elsa came through the doorway. "Ready?"

I agreed and led my friends to the restaurant I'd had in mind. It was a traditional spot where all the waiters wore dark suits and wouldn't allow you to begin a meal without a bowl of soup. Slowed by the chill wind and snow blowing on our faces, it took us a bit longer to get there than I anticipated. Once seated, we complied with tradition, ordering consommé and plates of pickled vegetables and roasted meats. There was kasha on the side, and a basket of dark bread to soak up the luscious sauces laden with paprika and garlic.

"I don't know about you two, but the cold really makes me hungry," I remarked, noticing for the first time that my companions were sitting rather close to one another. My mind focused on a fresh energy emerging from our threesome as I reclined to digest my dinner and observe. In all the tumult of their arrival, my empathic skills had been unfocused. Now, with no distractions, I was able to detect what I'd missed before. My two friends were in love—presumably with each other.

"Lily," Elsa said, observing my scrutiny. "She's finally noticed."

"Well, you two have come a long way since the day I first introduced you," I said. "Care to fill me in?"

"We've had a lot of time alone together since you left," Lily said, taking Elsa's hand. "I don't think either one of us realized it at first, but eventually . . . well, as you can see, we're together."

"That was fast," I said, before I could stop myself. "I thought you both . . ."

"Liked men?" Lily asked. "We do. You and I never really had reason to discuss our sexual preferences, but as it happens, both Elsa and I are bisexual. Not that we would put a label on it. The heart simply chooses who it wants."

A pang of jealousy hit me directly in my sternum as I picked up on the unadulterated devotion these two had for each other. Lily was right; the heart did pick who we loved, often to our everlasting surprise.

"I'm happy for you both. And you can work together . . ." I said, knowing they could finish my thought. "I only wish . . ."

"William is trying to help us," Lily said. "Please don't hold a grudge."

The Serbian Pinot Noir in my glass swirled round and round as I fidgeted.

"I know you're right. It's just hard. I resent being misled. And being here alone with Josef has been . . . *difficult*. He's got his own ghosts to deal with, plus we've run into all kinds of trouble."

For the next thirty minutes I tried as best I could to describe my weeks in Belgrade: my kidnapping, cutting my hair, the wound from the concert. I also told them of Nadia's new reading and her warning about my safety. At the end of my tale, my friends exchanged worried glances.

"It's a good thing I'm here," Elsa said. "Josef can't kill a vampire, but I can. From now on, you'll not leave my sight."

Elsa's words reminded me of Josef, who'd used the same phrase the night after I'd been kidnapped. Something must have registered on my face, because Lily and Elsa both perked up.

"Olivia," Elsa asked. "What's on your mind?"

"Nothing," I said. "I was just thinking about Josef again. Despite what I said a few minutes ago, it hasn't been all bad. There have been moments when he's been really good to me. It's been lonely here and he's . . ."

Elsa and Lily exchanged knowing glances. "When fate throws people together, you never know what will happen," Lily said knowingly.

33

AT JUST PAST DAWN, JOSEF BACKED THE LAND ROVER out of the driveway with me in the passenger seat and a huge load of equipment in the back. Elsa and Lily were cozied up together in the backseat.

"Coffee, please," I said, looking over at my taciturn driver. Josef silently complied, pulling into a parking space outside the storefront of a popular Belgrade coffee chain. Elsa opted for tea; Josef stayed behind, no doubt lamenting his luck at being responsible for a car full of semimortal women.

Soon we were on the A1, the main highway out of Belgrade. It was a slick affair, impeccably paved with well-marked by signs in both English and Cyrillic, but a storm had moved in, bringing poor road conditions. Josef was no nervous driver, vampires being blessed with an oversupply of confidence, so with infinite patience, he simply took us through the freezing fog banks, allowing the car's GPS to guide us toward our first destination. I gazed out the front window, straining to catch a glimpse of anything, but all that registered was the outline of an endless forest, its trees half-obscured. Once, just once, I thought I saw something else, a group of animals gathered in a field, but when I looked up again, they were gone.

The next morning, Lily quizzed me about some of the information necessary for my interviews while the rest of our team picked up supplies in the village. Our family-run pension perched near the banks of the Danube River was cozy but empty, the deep winter being an unpopular time for travel.

"Ask me again," I said. "All these three-letter abbreviations for Serbia's political parties are so similar. How does anyone keep them straight, I wonder?"

"You're almost there. Let's go through it again," Lily said. "What is the SNS?"

"Serbian Progressive Party," I replied. "Not to be confused with the SRS, which is the Serbian Radical Party."

"Exactly," Lily said. "Now, what about the local elected officials? Did you read the information I left for you this morning? I rearranged the files from Diana Chambers, filtering by name, region, and political party. Knowing who we're dealing with will make the site visits easier."

I glanced over at my best friend, so luminescent, with a mixture of admiration and sadness. I was grateful for her help but regretted dragging her into my intrigues. "Thanks, Lily. It's so good to have you here with me."

"But?" she asked, knowing me too well.

"I'm just sorry I dragged you into this mess," I said. "You should be back in Bolinas frolicking with the brownies in the fields or something. Or helping San Franciscans find good books to read. Not trying to track down clues to a vampire tycoon who misuses public contracts to pay off political parties."

"I see my research is helping you already," Lily replied. "I gave serious thought to what you're saying before I left, but my place is here with you and Elsa. So tell me what's *really* on your mind. There was a time I wouldn't have had to ask."

"That was before the explosion," I said. "Before . . ."

Lily gave me a knowing smile. "Our friendship is strong enough to survive all of this, Olivia," she said, cutting off any further protests. "And for the record, I detest brownies; they are mischievous little devils, known to steal the shoes off your feet. I think we'll all be glad when your father returns to his apartment in the city. It will send most of those extra creatures back to the sea, or wherever they came from. Now let's get back to work."

I was still reviewing my notes the next day as Josef pulled our car into the first village on our assignment list for a meeting with Aleksandar Kostunica, the local mayor and a rising member of the Serbian Progressive Party. After several days of snow, a hazy, partially blue sky had emerged, albeit with subzero temperatures. My mood was anything but sunny, though, as I contemplated how to get what we needed from my interview with a man who was rumored to be on Nikola's payroll. We'd agreed to meet at the local party offices, located near the village's post office, where voting would take place when elections were held a month from now. The proximity meant we could conduct a site visit after our interview.

"Promise to be nice," I said as Josef held the door for me.

"*Da*, Olivia, *da*," he said, alerted to the sea of eyes that focused on us when we entered the lobby of the building.

"*Hvala*," I replied, thanking him. We walked straight to a clerk at a counter and asked for Aleksandar. Moments later, we were led into an opulent office, ridiculously out of scale for the post-Soviet style, four-story concrete building we'd just entered.

"Mayor Kostunica, it's a pleasure to meet you. What a lovely office," I said, waiting for Josef to translate.

"It's OK, I speak English," the mayor replied, startling us both.

"What a nice surprise," I said. "Let's begin then, shall we?"

"English is the language of business, is it not? As I am a businessman, it makes sense for me to speak English."

"Yes, I read that you own a large construction company that has many contracts to build roads in the region," I said.

"That's one of many projects," he said. "We also build hotels and municipal buildings. I'm a lucky man."

"I understand you've built hotels for Nikola Pajovic," I said, trying to remain impassive.

"Of course," Aleksandar replied. "He's one of the richest men in Serbia. Who wouldn't want a contract with him? But what does this have to do with elections in my tiny little village?"

"Well, I'm wondering about something I noticed in my research," I replied. "According to our records, you and the local SNS chapter have both outspent what's listed in your party's bank accounts. Perhaps Nikola has been a generous donor as well."

"I'm sure it's just a simple accounting error," Aleksandar replied, a thin smile appearing. "After all, free elections are a relatively new concept in my country. And we only just established campaign finance laws. Sloppy record keeping is no doubt to blame."

"Perhaps," I said. "I understand three other people have filed to run against you. I'm sure extra funds would be useful to run a persuasive campaign."

"I've been a good mayor," he said. "The people in this town have jobs with the government, they don't have to wait in long lines for their services, and their children can attend the colleges they choose, do you see? Things here run smoothly."

"I *do* see," I replied. "Well, thank you for your time. Is the village clerk here? I need to collect copies of the sample ballot and your posters for marking the polling place."

"Of course. My secretary will show you the way. Before you leave, may I ask you a question?"

I could sense his loathing now. He, like me, had done a good job of hiding his feelings until the end.

"Why don't you like Nikola?" Aleksandar asked. "He is a good man and friend of the party. He's made sure our people work and have food on the table. Do you doubt his motives?"

In a subtle show of two against one, Josef, who'd been lurking in the back of the room, came to stand by me. "I don't know what you're talking about Mr. Kostunica," I said. "I have no feelings about Mr. Pajovic. I'm here as an impartial monitor to ensure free elections take place, nothing more."

"I see," the mayor replied. "My mistake."

Forty minutes later, the frozen ground crunched beneath our feet as we walked back to the car from the post office. I pulled the memory card from the digital camera I was holding and slipped it into my pocket. I would include images of the building and the documents we'd requested in the final report I emailed to the OSCE's Belgrade office.

"What do you make of things?" I asked Josef as he opened my car door.

"The election side of things looks to be running smoothly," he said, turning the key in the ignition. "In this village at least, all of the political parties, even the fringe ones, are being allowed to distribute their information freely. But I think we need to ratchet up our security measures."

"Why?"

"It's obvious to me that Nikola warned the mayor we were coming," he said.

"How could he?" I said. "Our work is supposed to be confidential."

"Knowing Nikola, he probably warned all of his colleagues to expect a visit," he said. "We may have less time than we thought to figure this whole thing out."

34

FALLING ASLEEP THAT NIGHT WAS NO EASY FEAT, BUT I managed, eventually, only to be pulled out of a deep slumber by a painfully erotic dream.

When I opened my eyes, Josef was lying next to me. I'm not sure how long he'd been there, but his proximity caused my body to suddenly feel overheated. I lay still, fighting with myself. I didn't want to turn him away. I was coming to understand that as much as I loved William, I was also drawn to Josef. Our attraction was much more than some cheap physical thrill; our impulsive natures called to one another.

"I know it was supposed to be a one-time thing, but I miss you," Josef said, shocking me with his honesty. "I need you, Olivia. Please don't turn me away."

I answered by pulling his lips to mine. The kiss started out gentle but soon Josef took over, pouring all his urgency into his task. Our tongues tangled as a set of knowing fingers removed my pajamas. Josef quickly removed his T-shirt and jeans and rejoined me in bed. I felt his sharp fangs along my neck as Josef worked me into a state of ecstasy.

"Your breasts are beautiful when your body is arched like this," he said, taking one of my nipples into his mouth. I gasped loudly, Josef muffling my response with a kiss.

"We're going to wake the innkeeper if we're not careful," I said when he finished kissing me. "I'm worried she keeps a stake under her bed."

The elderly proprietors were efficient but practically invisible. The walls of the pension definitely had ears, though, and I thought I'd seen our landlady cross herself once or twice as Josef was walking by. Their superstition wasn't surprising since Serbia was the place where vampires were allegedly invented. Our innkeeper had probably been in the business of spotting the supernatural for too long to be fooled by us. Luckily, she appeared inclined to leave us alone.

Josef's eyes seemed to gleam in the darkness. "You wouldn't let them drag your poor lover into the town square, would you? They'd stuff garlic in my mouth and set me aflame."

"I could be persuaded to spare your life," I said, laughing as Josef pulled me into an embrace.

"Well then, let me get busy persuading," Josef replied, filling my mouth with a kiss.

Just before dawn, as we lay in bed, my conscience returned with the sun. I was drawn to two men, but I'd already made a commitment to William. I knew Josef saw the change in my demeanor as I rolled over and took his face in my hands.

"I'll never regret our time together, but I'm not sure if we can continue like this. It's confusing for me to share two beds; without William here, it feels like I'm being disloyal."

"I admire your loyalty to my brother, even if it stings," Josef said, jumping out of bed and heading for the door as he pulled on his clothes.

"You have my loyalty too," I said.

"I'll probably do my best to make you regret it," he said and disappeared into the hallway.

My bed stayed empty after that, and although there were times I was lonely and tempted to seek him out, I didn't. Why I remained steadfast when I was so angry with William, I couldn't say, but Josef never approached me again—and that made it easier to maintain my resolve.

We were much too busy for nocturnal interludes anyway—at least I was. Despite Josef's concerns about security, the next two weeks went smoothly. Our days were filled to the brim with candidate interviews, field visits to party offices, and other tasks necessary to document the environment leading up to an election. We encountered a few examples of interference, such as polling places that didn't seem to carry information about one candidate or another. Our travels also introduced us to one local candidate for town council who liked to give away free dinners at his restaurant in exchange for a promise to vote. Overall, though, our work went smoothly.

I sensed our last day, in the one remaining city on our list, would not go so easily. Josef and I rose early to pay a visit to a local party boss with deep ties to Nikola. Dragan Thaci, successful real estate agent turned public relations executive, was meeting us for coffee at his office. Somehow, despite being headquartered one hundred miles from Serbia's capital city of Belgrade, he'd managed to secure lucrative contracts for marketing and advertising on behalf of the Ministry of Health and other national agencies. Thaci, according to my research, was also said to enjoy generous donations to his party from a known drug smuggler. He also managed PR for Nikola's newest casino on the Adriatic coast. The two had been photographed at a number of events together. My gut told me there was something to be found in the troika of drugs, gambling, and a high-flying PR maven. I was certain it would be an unpleasant interview, and my instincts proved to be spot-on.

"Well, that went poorly," I said as we were driving back to our guesthouse after our meeting.

"Had you expected something different?" Josef asked. "I told you Nikola was warning his cronies."

"I thought he would at least pretend to be civil for the first half of the interview. To keep up appearances," I said. "Accusing me of being a spy for the CIA and 'part of a vast conspiracy' along with the Vatican and Germany seemed a little dramatic, even for him."

"I liked the part where he accused you of spreading fear and defeatism," Josef said. "He tested my translation skills, talking so fast."

"You know, I think that may actually be a crime in Serbia at the moment," I replied.

"While he was browbeating you, I caught a glimpse of the papers on his desk," Josef replied. "Thaci runs a security company with Nikola. There was an invoice for providing overnight security to the Port of Belgrade. Can you imagine? Provide the surveillance for the docks, and you can smuggle anything in or out of the country."

"And the customs officials are members of your political party," I said. "Jesus. We may have just found something we can use. It's too bad we couldn't take a photo."

"What if I told you I stole it?" Josef asked sheepishly.

I was glad I wasn't the one driving, or I would have veered off the road. "I'd say you are a mad genius, intent on getting us killed," I replied. "Nikola will come for us now for certain. We need to get that document out of our hands immediately."

"It might take him a few days to notice the invoice is gone," Josef replied.

"Or he left it there hoping we would steal it," I replied, knowing that with Nikola involved, we might never know the truth.

The sky was a familiar gray, much like our mood. By the time we arrived at the guesthouse, Lily and Elsa were huddled by the fire in the parlor, studying their computer screens. I pulled up a chair and grabbed a late-morning cup of tea and a snack the proprietors had set out on a table, waiting mere seconds before spilling the news.

"Stop the presses," I said. "Josef found something we may be able to use to prove Nikola's criminal activities. We need to scan it quickly, destroy or hide the original, and leave town as soon as possible."

"That would be advisable for a number of reasons," Elsa said, pointing at a weather map on her laptop. "There's a large storm coming our way. We should leave as soon as possible anyway."

"It's messing with my Wi-Fi," Lily said, frowning. "I can't upload to our Dropbox account right now. We'll have to do it later."

"How big is the storm?" I asked.

"If I didn't know better, I would suggest it was conjured by witches," Elsa said. "It's several miles wide and moving rapidly."

"How do we know it's not conjured?" Josef asked.

"We didn't ask for any kind of intervention from the Council," Elsa said. "And I don't sense any black magic. It's possible Nikola could have a few dark witches in his employ, but we would have seen them by now. Vampires don't normally consort with witches of *any* kind."

"I can confirm that fact," Josef said.

"Regardless, we need to pack up," Elsa said. "I have a bad feeling."

I felt it too, a powerful shudder working its way up my spine. Trying to shake off the sensation, I ran my hand along the shirtsleeve covering my tattoo, only to grow ever more certain that something wicked was headed our way.

THE SNOW CAME SOONER THAN EXPECTED, DROPPING IN faint, soft flakes that spun themselves into a great white wave, wreaking havoc on visibility. Lily sat up front with Josef, scrutinizing a map as he drove. Our goal of reaching a major highway, crossing the river, and then doubling back to the smaller roads to reach our next village had been thwarted, the fast-moving storm demanding a change in our itinerary.

"I know it's crazy, but our best bet may be a car barge a few miles ahead that crosses the river. I read about it in our Michelin Guide," said Lily.

"Honestly?" I asked.

"Yes, I still read actual books," Lily said. "And Michelin still makes the most reliable guides."

I smiled in the darkness of the car, but in the driver's seat, Josef was not amused.

"You want to cross the river in this snow?" he asked.

"No, but we don't want to get stuck on a two-lane road in the middle of nowhere," Lily said. "We've hardly got any food or water."

In the backseat next to me, Elsa gave me a nudge in the ribs. When I looked over, I could see she understood that trouble lay ahead regardless of our route.

"What's on the other side?" Elsa asked.

"According to the book, the road on that side of the river is part of the Danube Wine Route," said Lily. "We should be able to find rooms in an inn or guesthouse."

"Should?" Josef asked.

"Nothing in life comes with a guarantee," Elsa said, her tone decisive. "Josef, this is the best plan we have at the moment."

"Take the next turn," Lily said. "Go left and follow the road to the river."

Josef did as he was told, the Rover thumping and bumping down a narrow, unplowed road in the near-blinding snow. The road ended abruptly at a small cement shack next to a large metal platform tied to a set of posts. I squinted, trying to figure out how this so-called "barge" worked. It appeared that once we drove our car onto the platform, a system of pulleys and cables attached to the raft would pull us across the river.

"Oh dear," Lily said, when she saw what awaited us. "Even the hobbits had a bit more than that to carry them out of the Shire."

"Doesn't matter," Elsa said. "We need to get across the river. Josef, see if there's an attendant inside, otherwise we'll have to pull ourselves."

Josef turned around in his seat to look at me, wondering, I suppose, if I was going to sanction the trip. I nodded grimly, realizing that any more attractive options were lost to us. Getting the message, he reached into his parka for his wallet. Confident he had enough cash to make a convincing request, he disappeared into the storm. In silence, the three of us contemplated floating across the dark river, where one mishap would mean our deaths.

Thankfully, Josef returned promptly, his coat and face covered with snow. "OK," he said. "There is a bargeman. He took our money and told me he's pulled cars across in worse weather than this. Everyone unbuckle your seat belts. If something goes wrong, I want you to be able to escape quickly."

After that upbeat advice, there was nothing left but to sit white-knuckled in the vehicle as we traversed the Danube. Time seemed suspended for the endless minutes we floated, the barge pushed and tugged relentlessly by the river's currents. All of us kept a singular focus on the view out the front windshield, waiting for signs of a nearing shoreline. At times, visibility was so limited from the snow it seemed we weren't moving; only the constant whir of the towropes overhead signaled that we continued to move. Finally, we reached the other side. When Josef drove the car onto solid ground, his achievement elicited yelps of delight from the passengers.

"Lily, can you direct us to a place to stay?" Josef asked. "I think we've had enough adventure for one day."

"Done," she replied. "If we stay on this road, we should come to a series of wineries and guesthouses in about thirty minutes."

"That long?" Elsa asked.

"Maybe longer in this snow," Lily replied apologetically.

"Damn," Elsa muttered under her breath.

I looked out the window, my unease growing. Somehow, I knew the barge trip had been only our first adventure and that something far worse was lurking.

We had been driving for less than ten minutes when Josef stopped the car abruptly, issuing a swear word as he slammed on the brakes.

"Wolves?" he said aloud, as if testing the word.

"Werewolves, actually," I said, eyeing the three beasts standing on the road in front of us. "Can you run them over?"

"This is supernatural magic in front of us, not a wild creature in a national park." Josef said. "Have you ever seen a car after it's hit a mature deer? That's nothing compared to a werewolf. If I try to hit them, they'll send our car tumbling over like a toy. We have to get out and fight."

I felt my breath coming faster, panic closing in. I looked at Elsa. "Does anyone besides me have a knife?"

"There's a small metal container behind you that looks like a toolbox," Josef said. "Reach over and grab it."

Just as I began to search for the weapons, one of the animals, much larger than a normal wolf, jumped up against the driver's side window, snarling and drooling at Josef. The creature began to beat on the window with its head, intent on breaking the glass.

"Olivia, any luck with the weapons?" Josef asked, his voice taut. A second wolf now perched upon the hood of the car, giving us a perfect view of its bared fangs.

"Yes, I've got them," I said, handing Elsa and Josef a large hunting knife each.

"What about me?" Lily asked.

"Stay inside," I said. "Someone has to drive if we're wounded."

Despite the banging of massive wolf skull on glass and metal, Josef managed to stay calm, pulling us into a quick huddle to discuss strategy: "Elsa, open your door first and draw them away from the car. Olivia and I will follow and kill them as they give chase. Olivia, remember that you can move objects with your mind. Throw things into their path. Pull down tree branches, move rocks, blow snow, I don't care, but don't rely solely on your blade. These creatures are enormous. They'll wear you out if you simply try to fight them."

Elsa did as she was told, jumping out of the car with great speed. She uttered a few words at the wolves that I couldn't make out, then bolted toward the forest, luring the beasts to run after her.

"Go!" Josef yelled, and I did, saying nothing to Lily as I opened the door and intentionally tumbled onto the frozen pavement.

I rolled low and came back up, gripping the knife in my left hand. Josef was beside me in a moment. Running toward the forest, my pace was slowed by all the fresh powder on the ground, while Josef's steps, with his vampire speed, seemed to skim the top of the snow. Soon enough, though, I caught up with my friends—surrounded by the wolves, their weapons drawn against the snarling beasts in a deadly standoff.

Frantic, I looked around for loose stones and logs, but the forest floor was obscured by snow. I remember Josef's advice to use every tool at my disposal and extended my hand, willing the snow to move. At first, it was just a light swirling of flakes, but soon my efforts were producing miniature tornadoes that covered the wolves' dark pelts with white, the snow beating against their eyes so relentlessly that they began to back away. Elsa lunged forward upon their retreat and plunged her blade into one of the animals. It let out a furious howl and then collapsed, eventually materializing into a naked human form. I recognized the tarot card image of the Devil on the man's arm immediately, but his face was not familiar.

I then discovered that in order for my witchcraft to work, I had to concentrate. Watching Elsa had caused my snow blowing to stop. As a result, it was easy for the second wolf to leap and knock me backward. I managed to hold onto my knife, but getting a clean swing proved difficult with almost two hundred pounds of beastly canine standing on my chest. Too fearful to try to harness telepathy—not that I'd really tried it with werewolves—I felt myself panicking. Just in time, Josef appeared. He grabbed the wolf by the scruff of its neck and cut its head clean off. I rolled out of the way, avoiding most of the gore, and then sprang up, keenly aware there was a third wolf somewhere nearby.

"Olivia, behind you!" Elsa yelled, and foolishly I turned, following the sound of her voice to find her perched high up on a tree branch. Too late, I whirled back around—just in time for a collision with one last attack. The impact knocked me to the ground again, my head taking the brunt of the fall. My vision darkened, and an explosion of pain ripped through my ear. As I made myself disappear, I feared that as Josef had discovered back in Belgrade, my scent—which more than likely reeked of fresh blood—could not be camouflaged.

Whatever had happened to my head, it blurred the vision in my left eye. I fumbled around for a weapon, hoping by some miracle that I hadn't lost my dagger. If I was going to die out in this frozen wilderness, I wanted to have some connection to William in my hands. I heard the thunder of bodies moving toward me and pivoted in time to see the wolf coming in for another pass, followed closely by Josef and Elsa. The creature was barreling toward me, no doubt using his keen sense of smell. Lying wounded and weaponless, I braced for my death.

By some miracle, the moment never came. Instead, Josef grabbed the beast by the tail and Elsa, not far behind him, plunged not one, but two knives into its body, killing the wolf instantly. She had my dagger. As the wolf morphed into another tattooed human body, my protectors collapsed on the ground near me. I crawled on my hands and knees to join them and realized I'd reappeared only as Elsa reached out a hand to me. She looked limp herself, Josef too, all of us overcome with exhaustion.

"You saved my life," I said, just before passing out.

A FLURRY OF WHISPERS WOKE ME, ALONG WITH THE
sensation that someone had screwed a clamp over my left eye socket.
I lay still, listening, while my body adjusted to the excruciating pain
on the side of my face.

"She's been out for a few hours," Lily said. "What if she has a
concussion? She shouldn't be allowed to sleep."

"If you'd been clocked in the head by a werewolf, you'd sleep like
the dead too," Josef said.

"But the dead don't actually sleep, do they?" Elsa replied tartly,
bringing a faint smile to my lips. At least I was among friends.

"I'm awake," I murmured, "But my left eye won't open."

"You collided with one of them," Elsa said.

"I remember," I said, trying to raise myself up.

"Bad idea," Josef snapped, arriving just in time to help ease me
back down onto the couch as a wave of sickness washed over me.
"Stay still."

"*Mmmm*" was the only sound I could emit at first, my head
throbbing. Then finally, "Where are we?"

"Nowhere near the village we intended to reach," Lily said. "We
had to find a place to stay immediately, so we stopped at the first house
we saw from the road. Elsa rang the bell. When no one answered, Josef
broke the back window and let us in. We've been riding out the storm
here for the last few hours."

The next thing I knew, I awoke to find the room empty except for Josef, who was sitting, his eyes closed, in an armchair next to me. I watched him through my one good eye, noticing how dark and thick his eyelashes were, wondering if his wife used to stare at him in her quiet moments before the war came. As if he'd heard me, Josef opened his eyes, looking directly into mine.

"I just woke up," I said, admitting the obvious.

Now it was his turn to stare.

"Is it that bad?" I asked.

Josef rose from his chair and sat next to me, pulling my hand into his. Gently, he placed his lips on the back of my palm, sending me reeling. His gentleness could mean only one thing: I was a mess.

"Tell me."

"You've been unconscious for the better part of a day, and you look like hell," he said, keeping my hand in his. "The cut above your eye required ten stitches, but that's not what caused the swelling. The wolf's muzzle hit you directly in your eye socket, full bone-to-bone impact. That swelled your eye shut. And there was a small tear at the corner of your eyelid that needed two small sutures. That's just the insult to the injury, but I think it will leave a little scar."

"But?" I asked. "What's worrying you?"

"I can't see your pupil, so I don't know what's been damaged. You need to see a doctor, but we can't travel until the snow stops."

"When will that be?"

"This storm has made the roads impassible," he said. "The Serbian government declared a state of emergency. It will be a day or more before we can leave, assuming no one shows up to kick us out."

Snow, snow, snow . . . Comically, the harmony chorus to "White Christmas" began to play in my head. We were hiding out in a stolen house. I could only imagine the OSCE's official comment if we were caught. Fleeing from the storm was a plausible argument; we could offer to pay full restitution for the supplies we'd consumed. "We were attacked by werewolves and needed a place to stay until we could figure out if I'd been permanently blinded in one eye" was probably not on the agenda.

"Were any of you hurt?" I looked at Josef with my good eye, assessing his injuries.

"Just small cuts and scratches," Elsa said, coming into the room alongside Lily, who was carrying a tray of steaming mugs.

"And the bodies?" I asked.

"Left deep in the forest to rot," Elsa said. "I enchanted the ground around them; it will be next spring before anyone can get close."

"Part of Nikola's crew?"

"Yes," Josef said. "They all had the telltale tattoos on their arms. We photographed the entire crime scene, including your injuries."

"Do you think Nikola tracked us here?"

"We thought about that," Josef said. "Lily sent us on a road in the opposite direction of our next village. Our car is parked at the back of the house. I doubt even his minions can patrol in this blizzard."

"Your last visit must have hit too close to home," Elsa said. "That invoice may be as important as you thought. As soon as we can get Wi-Fi, I will send it to Madeline for safekeeping."

"He was watching us. It's the only explanation. That's why we need to just pack up and go home, before someone else loses an eye— or something worse," I said. "Let William finish this. He's probably farther along in this quest than we are anyway."

To my surprise, my companions shook their heads in unison.

"No," Lily said, speaking for the group. "We thought you might suggest that, but we can't. Nikola is expecting us to give up. If we run now, we'll play into his hands *and* damage Gabriel's credibility by walking off our posts so close to the elections. We have proof, now. Or at least Nikola thinks we do. We can't just bolt and run. We have to play this through to the end."

My dear librarian, the peaceful fairy who'd always wanted a life of service, was now a hard-boiled team player.

"What about my eye?" I asked.

"If anyone asks, we'll say you slipped on the ice," Josef said. "It's plausible in this weather."

I managed to right myself and swallow a few Advil. The mugs were full of soup, and I gratefully sipped mine, my stomach reminding me that I'd neglected to eat for more than a day. Elsa and Lily sat on the couch next to me; Josef was back in his chair, scanning the headlines on his laptop. We were stuck here for hours, possibly days. It seemed like a good opportunity to ask a question that had been nagging at me.

"Why do you think Nikola is so determined to destroy me . . . us?"

"He's always been this way," Elsa said. "From the moment I met him. At the time, his country was embroiled in the Balkan War. Nikola was bitter at how, as he saw it, the West was vilifying Serbia. He made all kinds of threats, but no one ever took him seriously. When you connected him to the robbery, Aidan was compelled to investigate—something the Council had never done before. You shined a bright light on him and now possibly have collected proof that he's not fit to serve as director of the Council. It's made him angry."

"Nikola is a prince, or close to it," Josef said, joining the conversation. "He's not used to being accountable. He was Serbian aristocracy, raised by a cruel father, turned into a vampire by chance. For most of us, becoming a vampire takes decades of adjustment, but for him, it was natural. As if he'd been born to it. It suited his ambitious nature."

"He told me the story of how he was made," I said. "The night he cornered me at the bar in Ljubljana."

Josef grimaced. "Imagine a vampire telling a witch his life story."

"Why not?" Lily asked.

"Because vampires need their secrets," he said.

"Vampires or you?" Elsa asked.

"Both," Josef replied. "We're talking about him though. Some of us are born evil, and some of us become damaged along the way. Nikola relishes suffering the way a bad little boy loves torturing cats. He does what he does because he can."

We all sat in silence with our mugs of soup for several minutes.

I was the first to speak. "So, what of your secrets, Josef? Will you tell us more about your wife? We are a captive audience, and I have a feeling your secrets want out."

I stared at him for a moment, silently transmitting a simple request that he let go and give back to the ghosts lurking in the shadows of his ancient mind their names and identities. I felt strongly that Josef's secrets wanted to be released; he was holding them captive, not wanting to let them go. Finally, though, he gave in.

"Very well," he said, adjusting his body in the chair. "I met my wife, Anna, in Prague. I'd moved there from a country village, determined to find a job at a hotel or café. My father had been a successful baker and had passed all of his skills on to me, so I found work quickly, at one of the grand hotels near the Charles Bridge. I reported to the ovens well before dawn each day to bake pastries and breads for the hotel's guests. My social life was limited—I had to be in bed very early—but one day as I was walking home, I saw a girl selling flowers.

"She had dark brown hair and eyes . . ." Josef looked away. "She was beautiful. I began to make excuses to pass by her stall whenever I could, and then I introduced myself. One day I asked her to coffee. We began to spend time together. I was alone in Prague, and my family visited rarely, so Anna's company was the warmth that had been missing in my life. Eventually, we married, and a year later our daughter, Rebecca, was born. She was a beautiful baby."

Josef paused long enough to accept a glass of scotch from Elsa.

"Our life was happy until the Nazis arrived. Once they invaded Czechoslovakia, things became unbearable. I sent Anna and Rebecca away, to Anna's father's village, where I thought they would be safe. Anna didn't want to go. She said we should die together, if that was God's will. But we didn't."

I broke the silence, because I wanted to know. "Did you blame yourself?"

"No. At the time, I blamed God," Josef said, finishing off his drink. "I blamed him for abandoning my family, for letting us all be hunted down like dogs by the Germans . . . but I lost my interest in God years ago."

"So you joined the Resistance," Elsa said, speaking with the authority of the time-walker. I felt certain she'd seen some of the horrors of World War II herself.

"After the hotel fired all of its Jewish employees, I knew I had to do something," he said. "Sitting around waiting to be arrested and sent to a work camp was not appealing. I'd been trained to work hard as a baker, and I was young and fit, used to long days and heavy lifting. So I decided to try to help liberate my country. But you know how that ended."

"And after?" I asked.

"After I was turned, I continued to work in the Resistance," he said. "It was different, being more than human. I devoted my new life to becoming a better saboteur and assassin. William was more of a medic and a tracker, although he did his share of other tasks. We enjoyed working together. Being a vampire means staring down the long face of a clock, and the war kept us busy, filled our days with something meaningful. Otherwise, it would have just been time on our hands with nothing to do but remember."

"It's late," Elsa said, saving us from falling into melancholy. "We should get some rest in case the snow clears. We need to be prepared to leave as soon as we're able."

Elsa and Lily stood and left the room first, leaving me alone with Josef. "Are you angry with me?" I asked.

"Since the day I met you," he said, smirking. "But thank you. It's been a long time since I spoke of Anna. She deserves to be remembered."

"And you? What do you deserve?"

Josef left his chair to sit next to me, leaning in to kiss me gently on the lips. I let him, happy for a little bit of comfort as the bones around my eye began to throb. And I kissed him back.

"I know you want to fix me, Olivia," he said when we separated. "But I'm not William. I'm not an honorable man, willing to make sacrifices for others. Not anymore."

He was a hero, of course, having saved my life and Elsa's and Lily's with his strength and courage. But I knew there was no point in telling him.

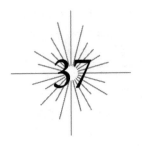

THE BARTENDER LINED UP SIX SHOTS, THREE FILLED WITH blood and vodka, and a companion set filled with blood and Jack Daniel's. Finn drank first, pouring one glass after another into his mouth. William followed, slightly more deliberately. Excess made him uneasy, and that was making his extended sojourn into the criminal underworld more and more uncomfortable. Worse, he didn't know where exactly the blood was from.

Unable to protest, he plastered a lazy smile on his face, working hard, as usual, to impart an aura of passive interest in his surroundings. They were in yet another bar filled with Others, this time in a village outside of Novi Sad. They moved around so much now, William hardly had time to register the names. And maybe it was European tradition, but outside the Mission District in San Francisco, William couldn't think of any specific cities in the United States that had Other-only bars. New Orleans maybe? New York? In general, he thought, America was indeed a melting pot, and the Others just mixed right in.

Finn eventually departed, interested, he said, in moving on to a human nightclub to find some female entertainment. William declined, saying he had little interest in humans. After Finn left, he thought about the enormity of the lie. The *only* thing he wanted was to be with a human female: *his*. Well, *partially* human, he reminded himself. Instead, he was miles apart from Olivia and beginning to forget things. The way she smelled when he climbed into bed next to her at the end of the day. The taste of her skin after she'd visited the gym. Even her cries of pleasure when they made love seemed like murky memories he could hardly recall. That was his punishment for this assignment. He sighed. There was nothing left to do but signal to the bartender for another round.

Later, he sent an update to Gabriel, caring little, by that time, if the dispatch made sense or not.

Gabriel,

I am no closer to connecting Nikola to these crimes. The only constant is Finn. I should describe him, in case the information is important later. Like most vampires, he is slender and quite pale. He accentuates the look with his devotion to black jeans and T-shirts. He is never without a black motorcycle jacket, although the weather calls for heavier gear. His arms and torso are covered in tattoos, and oddly, some of them are symbols from tarot cards. The most prominent shows the image called the Hermit, or so he told me. It's inked on his right bicep. Olivia would probably understand the meaning of the card, but even without knowing details, I believe "hermit" is a good way to describe him. He was turned during the plague epidemic in Ireland in 1339, saved by his maker after he'd barricaded the doors and hidden in his own home from a riot among the townspeople. Whoever the vampire was, he convinced Finn that he'd never survive the epidemic and would be better off joining the undead.

Finn lives in a series of half-abandoned houses off of quiet rural lanes in small Serbian villages. Inside these ramshackle buildings, he executes plans and carries out orders —but there is no trace of Nikola. He never comes. He doesn't use email. They're using encrypted message apps, but I'm not able to gain access. The teams of Others he uses to commit crimes always vary, and they seem to know little about their assignments until the last minute.

The lack of information is smart. No permanent connection is made between the crews and the people, places, or tasks they are assigned, making it nearly impossible for the authorities to identify a pattern to guide an investigation. And those who are interrogated have little to offer the detectives.

Finn has collected a terrible cadre of criminals, immortal beasts, whose lives were surely marginal at best before joining his crew. Late at night, when they've gone out for their evening's entertainment, I sit alone wondering how these two parallel worlds can exist: the Council and its devotion to furthering humanity, and these infernal creatures so happy to inflict suffering and dwell in the social chaos it creates. Since the day I was turned in 1862, I've been fighting to maintain my sense of humanity. Admittedly, it has ebbed and flowed over time. For the most part, after I passed my youth as a vampire, I have forgone feeding on humans and devoted my life to helping others. I have not avoided violence, far from it. But I have tried to steer myself toward a common good. I told myself that the blood I spilled was for a greater cause—for freedom, to end fascism, to maintain civilization.

As you well know, when I first met Olivia, I had become skeptical that the Council's work remained relevant. Now, locked inside this lunatic asylum, I am reminded why the organization was founded. This is also why I feel I cannot continue this assignment for much longer. My time here feels fruitless. I suspect that Olivia is right, and that killing Nikola is the only way to rid the world of him. He will not leave a trail of rope for us to hang him with.

Of course, I can't kill a vampire, and neither can Josef,

which means all this upheaval of our lives has been for nothing. I had hoped to spare Olivia the blood on her hands. Now it seems as if that is inevitable.

A SIGH OF RELIEF ESCAPED FROM MY LIPS WHEN I BLINKED in reaction to the bright beam of light penetrating my pupil. This reaction, mercifully, meant no permanent damage to my eyes.

"*Da*," I replied, acknowledging the physician's test.

Thirty minutes later, I walked out of a nearby pharmacy carrying a small bottle of antibiotic eyedrops to ward off infection. My face still looked as if I'd been jumped in a back alley, but at least my vision was back to normal.

The day had dawned under more dark storm clouds, and Josef was able to join me for the venture. He'd actually played the role of my *brother*, telling the skeptical emergency room doctor, in Serbian, that I'd slipped on some ice and banged my face on the rearview mirror of a parked car while falling. I just smiled, put my hands up as if to say "Oops!" and collected my prescription.

The two of us returned to the house where we'd ridden out the storm to pick up Lily and Elsa. We packed the Land Rover, all of us beyond ready to move on to more civilized digs. The weather remained grimly overcast, and by afternoon we reached the second village on our task sheet. Our arrival was almost a week later than planned, but no one seemed to mind back in Belgrade—the entire country was doing its best to dig out from the worst snowstorm in memory.

At our new hotel, Lily and Elsa were still trying to upload the last of our documents—including our precious evidence against Nikola. Once finished, they intended to visit the town's post office and ship our paper files back to the United States. Our plan was to regroup at the end of the day, with our smoking gun safely transported out of the country.

"I think this calls for a drink," I said. "What do you think?"

Josef shook his head. "It's late afternoon," he said. "The only people who drink at this time of day are disgruntled veterans and war criminals."

"Or individuals who've just regained their sight," I pleaded. "One drink and then straight back to the hotel."

Josef relented and escorted me to a local café and bar. We strolled in through a haze of cigarette smoke and found two seats at a small table in the back.

"Stay here. I'll order," he said, returning a few minutes later with a shot of Jack Daniel's for himself and a beer for me. "Try to keep your head down," Josef said. "The bartender seems overly curious. I think he's wondering how you got those bruises on your face."

I nodded, sipping my beer. The door to the café opened and two men walked in. One had spiky, jet-black hair and wore a motorcycle jacket, which I thought an absurd choice for this winter. I was about to go back to drinking when something about his companion grabbed my attention. Under a navy wool ski cap, I caught a glimpse of fiery red hair, tied in a ponytail. My heart raced, and I looked up directly into William's eyes, which flitted past me coldly, as if my chair were empty.

Josef reached over and grabbed my hand. Almost imperceptibly, he shook his head, warning me not to speak. My legs vibrated with the effort it took to remain still. We were all in danger if I made a scene. But my body didn't care—it wanted to leap out of the chair and attach itself to William.

I watched as he walked up to the bar and greeted the bartender with a hearty handshake and a brief embrace, three kisses on the cheek. Clearly a regular, he ordered not one, but two shots, for himself and his companion. Meanwhile the bartender continued to stare at us, then pulled William and his companion into a whispered conversation.

"I told you this was a mistake," Josef muttered. "Let's go."

By the time we stood up, though, the bartender, who as near as I could tell was asking Josef in loud tones how my face came to be so chewed up, had blocked our path. In the confrontation, I recognized the word *sister* in Josef's diatribe, and realized he was still trying to maintain our ruse as siblings. He turned to me. "This man wants to know how you hurt your face. He thinks I beat you."

"*Ne, ne,*" I said, reassuringly. "I slipped on the ice and hit my face on the car. It was an accident, but I'm OK." In case the bartender didn't understand English, I mimed the motion of falling.

The man seemed unsure, and then William walked over. His companion was still at the bar, watching us. I looked up into his green eyes, tears brimming. I assumed the bartender would think I was afraid, perhaps upset. And he would have been right, of course, but not for the reasons he suspected.

"I had an accident," I said, addressing William in a choked voice. "But my brother brought me to town today to see a doctor," I said, pulling out my eyedrops with the prescription instructions.

William whispered something to the bartender, who backed off and returned to his post. We didn't wait a moment longer but slipped out the door as soon as our path was clear.

"Don't look back," Josef said under his breath. "They'll think you lied."

He might as well have asked me to swallow a sword. At that moment, I wished I'd been blinded in the werewolf attack—it would have spared me the pain of seeing William. I heard the café door open behind us, and I was certain he was there, standing outside to watch us walk away.

Why did you do this to us, you bastard? I thought to myself, knowing he probably heard me. Hoping he would.

Back at the hotel, I retreated to my bedroom and eased myself into a chair, rigid with grief. Elsa came in and, noticing my catatonic state, fetched Lily. The two of them did their best to soothe me, assuring me that his indifference was necessary to save our lives. Neither of them tried to tell me we'd be home soon or even that they knew William and I would see each other again. They didn't actually know if any of that were true. Later, after I'd cried all of my tears and Josef had given up on speaking to me and left the room, I began to form a plan, a way to end all of this once and for all so we could go home.

Days passed, but I never saw him again. On autopilot, I continued cataloging and documenting my last remaining notes for the OSCE. Subverting my feelings to ensure a successful election was one of the first skills I mastered as a political consultant. No matter how depressed I was, I had an obligation to complete my work. Meanwhile, Elsa and Lily waited for word from Gabriel that he'd received our evidence.

Eventually, the bruises on my face retreated, black to blue, blue to green, green to yellow, until finally, a week after the attack, I looked less like a crime victim and more like an insomniac, the skin around my eye discolored as if from lack of sleep.

The drive to Novi Sad took longer than normal because of icy roads. The storm cleared and the days were bright again, not that the sunshine warmed things up. With the windchill, the temperature hovered just below zero as we loaded up the car.

Still, when we arrived on city streets that evening, we all felt a bit relieved at leaving the smaller villages and rural roads behind. Walking in the cold was painful, but we dragged ourselves out for some sightseeing, happy for a diversion. Our group strolled into an old Eastern Orthodox Church whose doors had been left open, to admire the religious art and paintings. Just as I was about to cross the threshold, I saw a para, the Serbian version of the penny, on the ground, scratched and covered in grime. Superstitious, I picked it up and placed it in my coat pocket. I needed all the luck I could get. Then, when we were too chilled to tour any longer, we chose a restaurant for dinner, Josef keeping us company while we filled up on rich food to warm our bones.

"You three remind me of my wife," Josef said. "She loved to eat. It was a good thing I was a baker."

"Did she work after you were married?" I asked.

"Yes, she was like all of you," he said. "Determined to be independent and help with money for the family."

"She sounds like our kind of woman," Elsa said.

Josef smiled. "She was," he said, suddenly looking lost in a happy memory.

"Here's to strong women," Lily said, raising her glass of wine.

"To strong women," we all replied.

"And the men who love them," Josef added.

39

WHEN WILLIAM SAW OLIVIA, HER FACE SO DEEPLY BRUISED,
only his many years of training as a spy in the Resistance saved him
from giving himself away. The anguish in her eyes almost brought
him to his knees. He wanted nothing more than to snatch her away to
safety. Instead, he'd maintained his impassiveness and managed to
pretend she was a total stranger, even as she'd flown out of the door in
Josef's protective embrace. *Again.*

After the two fled, Finn and William returned to the bar to finish
their drinks.

"What was that all about?" Finn asked.

"Not sure," William replied. "The bartender seemed to think
they were trouble. Thought it was odd the vampire was traveling with
a witch. But we don't need the trouble. This bar is a mixed crowd,
after all."

Finn eyed William like a dog sizing up a threat.

"Seemed like you knew her," Finn said. "Your face had this odd
look for a second."

"I was just shocked at how beaten up she was," William replied
calmly, shaken that Finn had seen through his mask. "Reminded me
of that girl in Turkey. I wondered what she did, that's all."

"I didn't pick up on her being a witch," Finn said. "I think Alexi
was mistaken. She seemed pretty ordinary to me."

William wondered if this was Finn's way of testing him. "Don't know, don't care," he said. "I thought it was better to avoid a scene. We want to leave here tomorrow without attracting too much attention."

"That's why I like you, William," Finn said. "You're all business. I never have to worry about you having another agenda. A few more vampires like you and I could run my own crew."

"Why would you want to do that?" William asked. "Seems like you've got a pretty sweet setup. I've never seen anyone come around to tell you how to run the show."

"True, our boss is very hands-off," Finn said cautiously. "But like all good capitalists, I dream of the day I take orders only from myself."

"Not me," William said. "Too much trouble."

Finn glanced at William again. "Don't bullshit me," he said. "You're ten times smarter than all of us. What I can't figure out is why you're hanging around."

"Just trying to keep busy," William drawled. "I'm really not that ambitious."

He was, of course. He just coveted different things. William wanted his life back, the one where he enjoyed all the finer things the world had to offer, with Olivia in his life and in his bed. What were the odds? *Of all the bars in Serbia, she had to walk into mine?* The dangerous converging of their worlds was a sign. A bad omen. Instead of uncovering evidence to discredit Nikola, he'd run smack-dab into Olivia, bringing unwanted scrutiny on them both. He'd been on enough failed missions over the years to be honest with himself; perhaps the whole idea of him going undercover like this had been a dead end from the start.

Later, after Finn had once again gone looking for entertainment in town, William—against his better judgment—went in search of Olivia. He tracked her back to her hotel and lurked beneath her windowsill. He stood there for some time, her thoughts, as usual, as clear to him as if she were speaking to him directly. He normally relished the sensation—however impossible their connection might seem in the supernatural world, he was happy for such transparency with his lover. But tonight, the clarity chilled his already cold blood: Olivia was plotting to kill Nikola.

Her nocturnal planning confirmed his growing inclination to leave Finn's crew. Nikola had to be removed, and building a case against him was taking far too long. A power player like Nikola did not abide by any rules. Why should they play fair? It was time to go back to Belgrade.

Besides, he was certain that Finn suspected his deceit. The vampire didn't know why William had a secret, but he knew one existed. Finn might also know more about Olivia then he let on, although William couldn't prove it. He should have known his love for Olivia couldn't be hidden away. *Poor besotted vampire, your heart is high on your sleeve.* Oh well. The signs were there: it was time to evaporate.

The usual vampire rules applied: he couldn't kill Finn. As he saw it, William's job now was to disappear so completely that searching for him would be pointless. He assumed that after Nikola was dead, Finn would assume control of the syndicate, and given that, he'd forget all about William's appearance and subsequent betrayal.

He had no idea how Nikola's death might unfold, but he knew that Olivia would be involved. And she was definitely going to need his help.

40

THE CLICK OF THE SECURITY GATE LOCKING BEHIND US AS we pulled into our compound in Belgrade was a welcome relief. During the ninety-minute drive back to the city from Novi Sad, as I kept watch for werewolves, vampires, or any other kind of damnable plague Nikola could rain down upon us—I half expected locusts— the throbbing beat of my pulse in my throat was so great I could barely swallow. I knew he was expecting me.

It was my father, though, who found us first. Not long after we'd tossed our suitcases on the floor and collapsed on the furniture to rest, Gabriel called from Marseille.

"Why do I have to read about your injuries in official reports addressed to other people?" he asked. "You should have called me."

I wanted to say, "We were busy, having broken into a house to hide during the blizzard to stay alive." Or possibly, "For forty-eight hours, it seemed I might go blind in my left eye." And then there was my favorite: "We accidentally encountered William, and at enduring his indifference, my heart has grown brittle, its beat a useful reminder that the organ still functions."

Instead, I replied simply. "There was too much happening. I was about to get in touch. Beyond sending you and Madeline the documents, this is the first chance we've had to contact anyone from a secure location."

A sigh escaped Gabriel's lips, hurling itself across the miles, its distress undiminished despite its travel. "The director of the Council is pleased with your work," he said. "But your father simply wants you to come home before something worse happens."

Before this trip, I might have succumbed to his melancholy and lamented the complexity of our relationship. But that time had passed. His needs were unimportant; my focus was solely on how to kill Nikola. It was the only task left for me, and I planned to complete it, whether I'd be alive to depart Belgrade or not.

"You should be happy," I said. "You've got a strong piece of evidence to discredit him. I expect this will all be over soon."

"Olivia, what do you have planned?" Gabriel said. "Don't forget you inherited your telepathy from me. Please just pack up and come home."

"It's not that simple," I replied, trying to shield my thoughts. "I'm still under contract with the OSCE. I have to wait for my final orders." I ended our call abruptly. The last thing I needed was Gabriel's concern. It was too little, too late as far as I was concerned.

The next day, during a late-afternoon lunch at Mala Fabrika Ukusa, a chic Belgrade restaurant near the landmark Cathedral of Saint Sava, Elsa, Lily, and I sampled a series of traditional Serbian dishes delivered in petite copper pots. Midway through our gastronomic tour, I noticed an email in my in-box from the OSCE. It confirmed receipt of our reports and assigned us new villages to monitor on Election Day in April. Updated itineraries and other information would be available in a few days, the note said.

"Will you accept the work, or go home?" Elsa asked, spearing a miniature sausage out of one of the pots.

"Accept, of course," I said. "If we leave too soon, it will confirm Nikola's suspicions. But we do need a plan to end this, so we can all go home."

"Before the elections?" Lily asked.

"If necessary," I said self-consciously, knowing her penchant for orderly systems. Leaving early meant incomplete information; it meant tasks undone, none of which suited Lily. "With enough notice, they could send a replacement team."

"Won't your father put an end to Nikola now that he has evidence?" Lily asked. "We can finish our assignment and protect his reputation."

I glanced around at the nearby tables, relieved that most were empty due to the late hour. "Nothing will happen until *we* do something," I said. "I'm not sure if I can kill Nikola, but I have enough hate in my heart to try."

"You'll need more than hate," Elsa said. "To kill a vampire, you must remove its head cleanly and burn the body or stab it through the heart with a wooden stake. To get close enough to do either of those things takes planning and skill, especially when the target is someone who's been dead as long as Nikola.

"When I was a young girl," Elsa said, "I used to watch the warriors in my village train in their compound for hours. First, they would clean their weapons, and then they would play complicated sparring games. Only when the sun was about to set would they stop. It seemed like such a waste of time, all of their games and athletics, but then one day a marauding party rode into our village. I was coming home from the well with water for dinner. I watched, frightened, as the men smashed and stole things. They were riding straight for me.

"Just as I thought I was about to be snatched and carried off into the forest, one of the warriors appeared, galloping in on his horse, his sword in his hand. In a matter of seconds he'd felled two of the gang, bringing both man and horse to the ground. Other warriors from the village joined him. They killed all of the intruders. The next time I passed by the men training, I watched closely, realizing that every move they made, every swing of their sword, every tilt of their body, was practiced and repeated until it became instinct. If you really want to survive the confrontation you're seeking, then we should go home and practice—and with something bigger than a dagger."

"What do you have in mind? I asked. "Guns?"

"They would be useless against him," Elsa said. "I have something larger and heavier in mind."

"A sword?" Lily asked.

"Precisely," Elsa said. "I've collected a few in my travels."

"And did you check these items with your luggage for your flight to Belgrade?"

"It's nice to see your sarcasm return," Elsa said. "I like you better when you're surly. You, my friend, have not been using the portal system here in the city. I told you I researched the locations. Give me a day and I'll bring you a few items."

"I should have used them," I said. "I could have visited San Francisco at least once by now, even if just to meet with Gabriel."

"It's better you didn't," Elsa said. "Your focus was needed here."

I nodded. "I know you're right. But do you really have to travel to find a sword? Can't we just break into one of the museums and steal something from the Ottoman Empire?" I asked. "The Turks left a lot of weapons behind."

"I did consider it," Elsa said. "I think it would draw too much attention."

The next day Elsa left, returning as promised a day later with two wooden crates. We carried the boxes to the gym and opened them, burrowing beneath the reams of straw to pull out two steel swords that were neither razor thin like a gentleman's rapier nor massive and wide like a highlander's broadsword.

"Infantry sword," Elsa said, gesturing for me to pick one up. "Very sparse design, light and easy for you to practice with. Later, if you like, we can use a Turkish saber, complete with inlaid prayers from the Koran."

"Where did these come from?"

"Here and there," Elsa said. "It's one advantage of being a time-walker; you can travel just about anywhere as necessary."

"OK, but where do you store them?"

"The Council has a weapons vault," Elsa said.

"Of course it does," I said.

It was just the two of us in the gym. Josef was resting, and Lily was off tending to her own errands. A halfhearted late-winter sun hung in the sky as we began to work. The fundamentals, as usual, felt backbreaking. Wielding a two-pound sword in one hand for hours was like weight training and required strength and balance. I'd been working on those skills with Josef, but Elsa was introducing new elements to the lesson as we practiced. In our heavy fencing gear, we rotated in and out of stances, extending, swinging, and lunging. Over and over, I swung two feet of steel above my head and low at my feet.

I had expected to feel awkward, to move with a tentativeness born of trepidation or embarrassment. Instead, the moment my fingers gripped the sword, I felt a surge of electricity. A humming began in my ears—a sensation of convergence that brought certainty to my swing. The more I worked, the harder the blood pumped through my veins, revealing something primordial, some inkling of an instinct.

"You did that whole last progression with your eyes closed," Elsa said. "Did you notice?"

"How is that possible?" I asked.

"You know the stories about the prophecies," Josef said. I hadn't heard him come in. "It must be true. You're imprinted with the instincts to do this, Olivia. No one else could be so fluid without practice."

"You look horrified," I said.

"In awe, actually," Josef replied. "When you wield that sword above your head, you look like a real woman king."

"She's a king in need of more training," Elsa said. "Josef, stand in for me."

Josef picked up a sword, not bothering with padding since his wounds would heal easily. As we stood toe-to-toe, I was transported back to the first time we met, at his studio in San Francisco, where he taunted me into fighting him. This time, I needed no invitation, and I began my attack without warning. The clank of our swords rang through the room. Elsa moved back into a corner, now a mere observer as Josef and I battled. Not unlike in our boxing matches, he swung at my face, reminding me to keep my guard up. Objects flew through the air—barbells, yoga blocks—just missing Josef. Back and forth we went until finally I felt the moment was mine and I knocked the sword from his hand. Josef watched as the blade slid across the floor and then he faced me, bowing at the waist.

"I believe we're done here," he said. "So much for the girl who wouldn't fight. Well, done."

Elsa hugged me and departed, and on impulse, I walked straight up to Josef. With one hand carrying my sword, I used the other to caress his face as I kissed him. He leaned into me, his demanding mouth extending our kiss. Later, I tried to blame my momentary weakness on too much adrenaline. As I sat in bed later that night, though, I knew that the kiss had been a thank-you, and perhaps, knowing what I intended to do, even a good-bye.

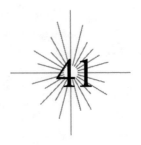

MAIL FINALLY ARRIVED FROM SAN FRANCISCO THE NEXT DAY, a copy of *Campaigns and Elections* magazine sliding out of the DHL pouch onto my lap as I sat in the kitchen enjoying breakfast.

"Jesus, Stoner Halbert made the cover," I said, holding it up so Elsa and Lily could see. "He's been hired by the Republican National Committee to manage field operations for the presidential election next year."

"He managed to recover nicely," Lily said, sipping her coffee.

"I'll say," I agreed. "The last time I saw him, he was teetering off into the sunset in Palo Alto with a landslide loss to his name."

"He's been busy," Elsa said. "I've made a point of keeping track of him. He was picked up for another race right away, out of state. Losing as a Republican in Northern California is not viewed all that dimly in North Carolina or Kentucky. He's been doing a lot of work for the Foxx brothers."

"Wow, it really does pay to make a deal with the devil. He's aligned with some serious conservative industrialist money," I said, setting the magazine aside. "It will be interesting to see what happens."

"Speaking of men with black marks against them," Elsa said. "Have you given any thought to what you're going to do when William returns?"

"No."

"Because of Josef?" Lily asked.

"No."

"Olivia," Elsa said. "We're your friends. Talk to us."

"I don't really know," I said. "I love William, but I'm so angry. I can't get past the fact that this is the second time since we met that he's kept things hidden from me. How can we have a life together when he treats me like that?"

"And Josef," Lily asked again. "Are you in love with him?"

"You make my life sound like a soap opera," I said. "It's embarrassing."

"Stop," Lily scolded. "You think you're the first woman to love more than one person? It's not a weakness. It's an acknowledgment of how complex we all are. I told you, the heart does the choosing."

"There is so much betrayal. How do we ever get beyond it?"

"You have to learn to forgive," Elsa said.

"So you think what William did was OK?"

"I think that William loves you so much that he could be persuaded to do just about anything to save your life," she said.

"I'll think about it," I said. "Can we change the subject?"

"OK," Elsa said, raising her hands in mock surrender. "What's on your agenda for today?"

"I need to sit down with my laptop and review the new elections files from the OSCE for our next assignment," I said. "We should split up: you two should hit the drug store and replenish our first aid kit that was, um, *depleted* after the wolf attack. I asked Josef to take the car to the garage for servicing after the sun goes down. We need to be out of here in one week."

"Let's meet up later, at the Hotel Moskva," Lily said. "That place is growing on me."

Of course, wandering alone in Belgrade was a bad idea, but we had a lot to accomplish and only a few days to finish up. It was easy to distract Elsa and Lily with our laundry list of tasks, and it freed me up to orchestrate a confrontation I'd been planning since my ill-fated sighting of William. Having sent werewolves who failed to kill me in the middle of the blizzard, Nikola was no doubt as eager as I was to meet again. Walking around unescorted would give him the perfect window to arrange a rendezvous.

And that was how I came to find myself standing outside Square Nine, the hotel Josef and I had stayed at when we first arrived in the city. Inside was the bar where we'd seen the first of Nikola's henchmen, the vampire with the Three of Swords tattoo.

I got what I wanted—and quickly. I paused on the sidewalk for only a moment before the gorgeous black-haired woman I'd seen Josef with was at my side. She gripped my arm in an unfriendly fashion and escorted me into the hotel. I sat down at a small table in the empty bar, noticing that the curtains had been drawn. To keep out prying eyes? After a few moments, Nikola came strolling in. I sent a large vase in the direction of his head. It missed by millimeters, crashing to the floor.

"Impressive," he said. "But I'm afraid I'll have to ask you to stop or I'll be obliged to call one of my associates in to drug you, and we all know how that ended last time."

"No drugs," I said.

"Very well," Nikola said, smiling. "Now that we've gotten that settled. How do you like my hotel?"

"Is it yours? I should have known," I said. "It's nice, but a bit modern for my taste. I prefer something with more history."

"That would explain your love of vampires," he said. "But don't you find the older hotels boring? Trying to preserve history is so dull."

"History is how society learns, Nikola," I said.

"You're not that naive," he said. "If anything, history is what compels me to leave the past behind. It hangs around my neck like an albatross."

"No wonder you love the tarot," I said. "It reveals the endless possibilities of the future."

Nikola smiled. "Exactly," he said. "I thought I would give you a reading before we begin our evening. You did mention it, last time we spoke."

"How nice of you to remember, but I already have plans for dinner with my friends," I said.

"I'm afraid they'll be dining without you," Nikola said, walking over to the bar to pick up an ornate wooden box. "Can I get you a drink? You might as well."

"Maybe later," I replied. "What's the box?"

"Tarot cards of course," he said. "Let's see what the cards say when you don't have magic at your disposal."

"Since I'm staying for dinner, I guess I have time," I said, sounding bolder than I felt. "Why don't you shuffle the cards?"

"All in good time," Nikola replied, leaning against the bar. "First, I want to ask you a question. Will you tell me the truth?"

"Maybe," I said. "It depends on what you ask."

"Do you regret meeting your father and joining the Council?"

"No."

"No?" he prodded. "Even after everything that's happened?"

"It wasn't the Council that killed my mother," I said.

"True, but if Gabriel hadn't engineered your arrival, none of this would have happened."

"Maybe it was destiny," I said. "Did you ever think about that?"

"You're determined to avoid saying an ill word about him?" Nikola asked. "Even after he separated you from William?"

The grief his comment elicited made me drop my guard for a moment, and instantly I felt the sharp, piercing jolt of Nikola trying to get into my head. I steeled myself against him.

"Your loyalty is admirable," Nikola continued. "He doesn't deserve you. And William the Pilgrim, he's no match for you either. Frankly, I'd rather see you with Josef. At least he acts like a vampire."

"If I were a man, would you be giving me relationship advice?" I asked.

"If you were a man, you'd be dead already," Nikola replied. "I've been nipping round the edges of your life because it suits me. I'm intrigued." He paused for a moment. "If it's true, and you really are the child of the prophecies, then you are destined to be quite powerful. When I killed your mother, I thought you were just a meddling human who needed to be scared off. Obviously I underestimated you. You're much more than I imagined. With your father out of the way, we could rule the Council quite effectively."

"No."

"Why not? You owe that meddling old fool nothing," he said. "I've come to respect you. You're more of a warrior than some of my men."

"This isn't about my father or William," I said. "It's about the Council and its purpose. You want the organization to turn its back on humanity at the very moment when they need our help the most. You'd have the world stew in its own blood so you can continue to run your criminal empire and make money. You have the connections in Serbia to continue your efforts indefinitely. I know. I handed over the evidence."

"I am chagrined you got your hands on that invoice," Nikola said. "I'm afraid not everyone I deal with is as careful as they should be."

"Or trustworthy," I said. "Why don't you just leave the Council? Why do you need to be the director so badly?"

"Because I believe in the survival of my species, Olivia," Nikola said. "The era of humans is over. They've overpopulated the planet and squandered their natural resources. Why should we, as superior beings, have to clean up their mess?"

"Because we can," I replied.

"Ridiculous," Nikola said. "There's no return on the investment. My enterprises, on the other hand, earn a nice revenue."

"The good of the few at the expense of the many? You've got it all backward."

"Not at all, my pet," Nikola said. "I'm just more honest about how the world really works." He smiled. "Maybe I should just drain you of your blood and make you mine. When I orchestrate your father's ouster, he'll have to watch as you stand by my side."

"Drink from a witch?" I asked. "I'm no expert, but I'm not certain it would even work. Remember, I'm not *entirely* human. And I'd rather you just kill me than spend eternity as your lover, human or otherwise."

"You wound me," Nikola said. "Don't you find me attractive?"

"Pretty is as pretty does," I said. "You've kidnapped me, twice. Had me tattooed and stalked by wolves. Killed my mother. Committed heinous acts of hate and violence with your crime syndicate. And you're currently trying to humiliate my father and subvert the mission of a venerable organization. I'm afraid your good looks don't factor in."

Nikola let out a sigh. "Very well. At least you find me attractive. I am vain in that way, you see. And now, on to our evening's entertainment: I'm going to read your cards before we play a little game. I thought we'd see if the odds are in your favor."

"A game?"

"Yes, it's something I made up just for you," he said, coming to sit next to me at my table. Nikola opened the box and removed his set of tarot cards, which were tattered and dog-eared from repeated use. He shuffled the deck. "We're going to take a look at what fate has in store for you. Then I'm going to send you out on an adventure."

He was doing his best to keep his thoughts guarded, but I heard the word *zoo* clear as day in my head. I felt a sense of relief that at least I'd have a chance to get out in the open to fight with him. His men hadn't removed my dagger yet. It didn't mean they wouldn't, but I was betting on Nikola being too confident to bother.

"Are you choosing the cards, or am I?"

"I'll deal," Nikola said, turning the cards over once more for good measure. "In the interest of time, we'll do a three-card reading."

I nodded and watched him pull the first image from the deck.

"Three of Swords," he said. "How apt: something to cry about in your past. Separation from loved ones."

"Go on," I said, trying to stay focused. Nikola's attempts to feed on my anxiety were draining. I had to work overtime to keep him at bay. "Can I ask you something?" I said. "Do you need human emotions to live or is it just for fun?"

"Impressive," he said. "Few people ever notice."

"How would they? Psychic vampires are not supposed to even exist."

"Well, that makes us even," he said. "You're the stuff of myths as well. Your mother must have known. Is that why she kept you a secret from your father?"

"You should have asked her," I said.

"That would have been difficult," Nikola said. "She was so drunk, she barely registered my presence. It made my task easy."

Nikola's proclivity for cruelty had been well established, but I was already raw and weary from so many weeks of heartache and injury. That's the only excuse I had for breaking my promise and sending objects flying across the room.

"Remember, I warned you," Nikola said as the door to the bar opened. "You'll have to see what the cards say another time."

My friend with the jet-black nails returned, this time carrying a small syringe, which she plunged into my neck.

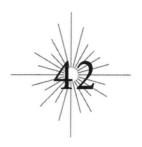

42

COLD, DAMP CEMENT RUBBED AGAINST MY LIPS, THEN I felt a searing pain on the side of my head. It took a few seconds before I recalled conversing with Nikola, and then that wretched woman drugging me into unconsciousness. Gingerly, I searched for the source of my discomfort. My fingers returned wet and sticky from a gash above my ear.

As my senses rebooted, I traded one discomfort for another. I'd only just become accustomed to the throbbing when the urine-soaked scent of the ground registered.

I willed my body upright so I could get a better look at my surroundings. My head swam but recognition came quickly. I'd jogged through the Belgrade Zoo many times. And always, I passed by the wolves. I understood right away that I was *inside* their pen. *More wolves—hurray*, I thought.

My musings were interrupted by the sound of a chain rotating on its flywheel, a signal that the animals were being let into their compound. I rummaged around and found my dagger, still hidden in the inside pocket of my coat. Then I looked for the front of the cage, hoping there was some kind of simple padlock I could open. I set my mind to undoing the lock's mechanism as I crawled toward the main gate, but my senses were heavily dulled by the sedative I'd been given. Then I ran out of time. In front of me stood an enormous male, his glowing white teeth bared in a fierce snarl.

Despite my fear, I tried to gather my wits, knowing my life depended on developing a battle plan. Keeping one eye on the wolf, I scanned the area for a place I might be able to climb up out of its reach or a structure I could hide behind, but there was nothing. The pen was barren, save a water bowl in the corner. There was not so much as scrap of paper I could send swirling into an attacker's eyes.

Seeming to understand that my search had yielded nothing, the jet-black beast lunged at me, sinking his teeth into my left forearm. The pain was immediate, and I felt my stomach lurch as his teeth hit my bone. Fortunately, my right hand remained free, and I swung around and plunged the blade of my dagger into the creature's shoulder. He recoiled with a shrill yelp. I pulled out the blade, and as he trotted to the back of his den to lick his wounds, I heard a familiar voice call my name.

"Olivia!" Elsa exclaimed from outside the cages. A set of keys dangled in her hands. "Are you *mad*? Why did you go after Nikola alone?"

I had no answer for her, so I changed the subject. "What took you so long?" I asked, knowing full well that she'd probably burned Belgrade to the ground looking for me.

"We divided the city up into three parts," Elsa said as she unlocked the cage door. "I got the zoo as part of my search area, and I asked the animals if they'd seen anything unusual. The elephant told me you were here."

Coming from a woman who could turn into a panther in my dreams, this did not sound like an odd answer. "How did you get in?" I asked, realizing the zoo was closed for the night.

"I scaled the fence, searched out the night watchman, and borrowed his keys."

"Is he alive?"

"Yes, but tomorrow will be painful," Elsa said, watching me walk through the cage door, my wounded arm tucked against my body. "Stay in the shadows and wait for me. I'm going to make sure we're alone before I look for an exit."

"OK," I whispered.

I was pressing myself further into the darkness of an enclosure when a familiar purr set my pulse racing.

"Olivia," Nikola said. "You managed to break free before I could get here. I wanted to be here when you woke up."

"So you could watch me fight with a pack of wolves?"

"I know," Nikola sniffed. "You do seem to bring out the worst in me. Now then, I think it's time we begin our adventure."

I waited for him to make a move toward me, but instead, he raised his hand and signaled to several henchmen, who moved in unison to open the enclosures of several lions, an albino tiger, and of course more wolves. Most of Nikola's crew were carrying guns, but it seemed unlikely they would shoot me. There'd be no sport in it. My chances of outrunning a lion were limited at best, I thought, but then I saw something Nikola did not: Elsa barreling toward me on an enormous elephant. His back turned to bark orders at his men, Nikola never saw the large foot of the beast as it reared up and came down upon his head, knocking him unconscious.

I would've liked to stay behind to see what the gash on the side of his head looked like, but I knew better than to dawdle. I grabbed Elsa's outstretched hand and jumped up onto the elephant. Now we were in a race to see if our magnificent host could withstand the attacks of its natural predators long enough to get through the zoo's gates. I did what I could to help, sending debris and objects flying into our attackers' paths, and feeling a jolt of success when I managed to uproot a bench and hurl it at a wolf.

As we broke through one of the chain-link fences at the front of the park, I thought I caught a glimpse of someone following us. Friend or foe, I couldn't determine amid the chaos that ensued as we galloped across the street into Kalemegdan Park, with the military fortress looming in the distance.

"Listen to me," Elsa said. "I hid several swords inside the main walkway to the fort. No matter what happens, we need to make our way to the weapons. Once you get a sword in your hand, this will all be easier."

Elephants at full pace are fast creatures. Before we knew it, we were in the middle of the park, surrounded by darkness, although I sensed assassins of every variety awaiting our moment of weakness.

"We need to dismount," hissed Elsa. "Now." She seized my hand, and together we slid off the creature. The elephant loped away, probably at Elsa's command, hopefully to a place where he'd be spared from harm. I felt relieved to be on the ground—sitting atop an enormous animal had made us vastly more visible to our enemies. Ironically, we were both more comfortable running through the darkness while avoiding foes; it was an exercise Elsa had taken me through countless times back in San Francisco.

We sped through the park together, avoiding trees and brush, looking for signs of predators. Meanwhile, I continued to feel the presence of a third party trailing me. My adrenaline was running too high to make sense of my impressions, but I did notice that we'd not yet encountered a single werewolf from Nikola's posse.

The sound of footsteps warned me that my observation was out-of-date, and I whirled just in time to be knocked to the ground with a painful thud, my dagger skittering away into the night. A vampire, and an angry one at that, slid his hands toward my throat. Instinctively, I concentrated and pushed a thought out to him: *You're blind and cannot see.* Seconds later he brought his hands up to his face and cried out in anguish.

Using his moment of confusion, I brought my knee to his groin—not an easy gesture when lying flat on the cold ground. He was re-pelled momentarily but renewed his attack with a fierce gleam in his eye when my magical suggestion wore off. Fortunately, he'd failed to notice that I was traveling with Elsa—who appeared from behind with feline agility, grabbed my attacker by his hair, and removed his head, which landed with a thud next to me. Elsa extended a hand. Wincing, I rose, my hips and back aching from the fall, and we continued toward the fort.

Elsa ran ahead over the Fort's gangplank, determined to retrieve our weapons. I glanced over my shoulder, certain once again that someone was watching from afar. There was no one behind me, but as I turned, intending to intercept Elsa and the sword grasped in her hand, Nikola stepped from the shadows and kicked the weapon out of her fingers. No sound escaped her lips as Nikola grabbed her by her long black hair and dragged her toward the bridge and the shadows I stood in, retrieving the sword along the way.

"How is it that you two managed to kill most of my men but didn't see me coming for the sword?"

It was a good question, since we'd killed only one of his cohorts, but I wasn't about to admit anything.

"Let Elsa go and I'll tell you the whole story," I said. "This is between us after all."

Nikola's head was still open and bloody from the elephant attack; it would heal, of course, but right now it added to his menacing presence.

"I don't think so," he replied. "Not until you come here where I can see you."

I didn't step forward. Instead, I began to search the area for objects to aim at his head.

"*Tsk, tsk*, Olivia," Nikola said. "I'm holding the point of this sword at her throat. If I were you, I'd resist the urge to pummel me with garbage."

"Release her now and I'll agree to your terms," I suggested, attempting for a second time to wield my newly perfected skill of mental persuasion.

"Just like your father, I see," Nikola replied. "Your power of suggestion won't work on me, but it does give me a fuller understanding of your skills. I really must insist you become my companion. You're much too rare to kill."

Nikola's words came with a terrible pain in my head as he exerted tremendous effort to mine my emotions. I found my ability to block him out greatly diminished from exhaustion. Blood still flowed from the wolf bite on my arm. I had to create a diversion before I ran out of energy completely.

As if it had heard my thoughts, someone or something lurking farther back in the shadows heaved a large metal trash can at Nikola's head. The attack narrowly missed him, but it did provide Elsa with an opportunity to break free and run back inside the fort. I hadn't the time to investigate the identity of my guardian angel. Nikola didn't give chase; I knew he was waiting for me, so I stepped into sight, determined to end our confrontation.

"It's time we completed our business," I said. "I'm growing weary of our association."

"That's too bad," he said. "I'm beginning to enjoy your company. You're far more intrepid than I imagined. Are you sure you won't reconsider my offer? I'd certainly never leave you alone to defend yourself like this. You'd live a life of luxury and privilege with me."

"It's tempting," I said, "But quite impossible after everything that's happened."

"That's too bad," Nikola said. "I've seen women forgive much worse."

"You do attract a certain type," I said. I focused on Elsa's sword, lying on the ground in the distance, then put my thoughts into action to bring it to my hands with its sharp point toward Nikola's chest. He stared blankly for a moment, clearly taken aback to be at the wrong end of an ancient Turkish saber. But his surprise lasted only a second before he ramped up his psychic vampirism, straining my nervous system with his probing.

"Let's see if you can make a move before I break your resolve and claim you as one of my possessions," Nikola said. "In the end, there really is no choice."

"We all have a choice," Elsa said, appearing behind him suddenly and driving her blade directly through his heart. Nikola's eyes widened in surprise. Elsa withdrew her sword, giving me a simple order.

"Finish it," she said. "Remove his head."

But battling Nikola had drained me to the point of oblivion. Despair flooded me. I was depleted and, growing weaker by the moment, worried I would fail to summon the strength to finish my quest. Then I heard a voice very strongly in my head—my own. "Swing," it said. Mustering the very last drops of strength I had, I lifted my weapon and swung, landing my sword at just the right height to remove Nikola's head from his shoulders.

I had no last words, no final gloating phrase at besting him. Not a single word escaped his lips either. Perhaps he was too shocked to grasp that a bastard witch child and her time-walking companion had thwarted his best-laid plans. Then, when I looked up, I found William standing before me, and I knew instantly that he had killed the other men in the park.

"You're just in time," I said, picking up Nikola's head from the ground and walking to the far edge of the courtyard, my companions following, to toss it over the embankment into the fast-moving waters below. "*Adieu*, you bastard," I said.

"Olivia!" William exclaimed as I dropped my sword and fell to my knees. "Darlin', let's get you out of here."

43

ONLY HALF AWARE, I FELT WILLIAM'S ARMS LIFT ME AND CARRY me away from the fortress. A series of voices briefly registered: Josef and Lily discussing plans to burn Nikola's body and erase any trace of our battle; Elsa directing William to a portal at the entrance of the park. His strong arms supported me as he walked for a few minutes, and then he uttered the ancient word used by Others to make the jump through time and space: *Aperio.*

Darkness enveloped us, and I had the sensation of falling, like Alice down the rabbit hole. Then I registered nothing further from the outside world, simply hovered between destinations, too weary to live, not ready to die. I was content to linger in the empty space between time and memory. But my retreat was short-lived. Elsa's stern voice interrupted my peaceful in-between, insistent for attention.

"Get up and live," she demanded. "It's not your time yet."

Finally, her badgering too great, I relented, climbing painfully into consciousness.

"Thank God," William said as I opened my eyes. "We weren't sure Elsa would reach you."

"I was tired," I said with some effort, my lips stiff from disuse. "I wanted some peace." Then, because I could, I added, "You left without telling me."

William rose from the chair he was sitting in and knelt before me, his red hair hiding his face as he leaned forward to take one of my hands.

"It is a decision I will always regret," he said. "I hope one day you will forgive me."

"Where are we?" I asked, unwilling to give him a reply.

"Lake Bled, Slovenia," he said. "Castle Bled, to be more precise. Part tourist attraction, part private residence of a trusted Council member. The castle is now closed for repairs to allow you to recuperate."

"He's dead?" I asked.

"Nikola? Yes. Sent back to the mighty rivers of Serbia," William said. "But at great cost to you, darlin'. You've been unconscious for four days. The first two, you fought a fever from an infected wolf bite. After that healed, we realized your wounds were more psychic than physical. That's when Elsa decided to visit."

"Where is everyone?"

"Lily and Josef are in Belgrade finishing the OSCE assignment," William said. "Keeping up appearances seemed important, and thanks to your work plan, they were able to stay on track. Elsa is on her way back to San Francisco, to help Gabriel prepare to brief the Council. Here, it's just the two of us."

For some reason, his words triggered an unexpected surge of emotions. Now, finally, we were alone. How many times had I wished for that very thing? Regret and anguish spilled out in a torrent of tears. William, for his part, said nothing, only holding me tightly as I spent myself.

When I finished, he lifted me from my sickbed and carried me to a stately bathroom with an enormous soak tub. The water running, he undressed me, then drizzled various oils and scents into the bath. The tattoo on my arm loomed suddenly. Strangely shy, I lifted my fingers to obscure the image, but William caught my hand midway.

"There's no need," he said. "I bathed you when we arrived. You were covered in the muck of battle. It's fortunate for me that you killed Nikola, or I might have broken the covenants and done it myself. But you should not be ashamed, Olivia. You survived."

"I wonder," I said as I slipped into the perfumed waters. A murmur of relief escaped my lips. William picked up a cloth and began to wash me, a gesture so similar to Josef's that that it almost undid me. Guilt stained my cheeks; confusion reigned. An internal voice I did not recognize suddenly spoke to me, warned me to be cautious, to not be seduced by his overtures. It was a new voice, perhaps born from a broken heart, one that did not have the capacity for such great disappointment again. Mired in emotional turmoil, I tired quickly. William helped me back to my bed, where, under his wary gaze, I fell into a deep, restful sleep.

I awoke at sunset the next day, feeling restored. I grabbed a robe and walked into the hallway to investigate my lodgings. Out a window was a view that confirmed we were indeed in a castle, perched high on a hill overlooking the ancient spa town of Bled. Majestic white swans floated in the water below, like a scene from some great Eastern European ballet.

As I continued, I found the hallway opened into a large dining room where dozens of candelabras burned, the glow of the candles accentuating the red of William's hair as he stood facing away from me. I was afraid it was a mirage, an image that would evaporate, leaving me alone. The voice of caution inside me shouted, but I muted it, my desire to be near William too great. We had plenty to discuss, serious grievances to air, but I wanted my lover back.

Sensing my presence, he turned but made no move toward me.

"How do you like the castle? I've told you before that you belong in a castle," William said. "It's in your blood."

"I've seen a great deal of blood spilled—mine and others'—these last few weeks," I said. "I wonder if it was worth it."

"Don't try to put a price on this," William said. "We're alive, and we're the same people we were before."

"No," I said, shaking my head. "Not quite." I caught myself. "I don't want to talk about that right now."

"Of course," William said. "What would you like? Are you hungry? I had the kitchen prepare a meal in case you woke up."

Hungry? Yes, but the kind of sustenance I needed wasn't on any menu. It couldn't be raised in a pen or grown in a field. It was elemental, as old as time, and more important to me than any delicacy on earth.

"I'm hungry, but not for food," I said, closing the gap between us. While my thoughts and emotions were a jumble, my body knew exactly what it wanted. Without waiting for an invitation, I leaned in and kissed him. The minute our lips touched, I felt the familiar jolt of our connection to one another.

"I have been dreaming of this moment for months," William said, breaking our kiss. "Leaving you was one of the most difficult things I have done in my long, lonely, immortal life."

I could feel the question hanging in the air, so I answered. "I missed you too," I said. "Sometimes, more than I wanted to."

That was all the encouragement he needed. William untied my robe, running his hands over my body. The first flick of his tongue against my nipple caused my body to arch deeply into his arms like metal to a magnet.

We separated for a moment so William could remove his clothing. The sight of him unclothed brought tears to my eyes. Part of me was embarrassed at my neediness in the face of his betrayal. But then all was lost in a sensuous haze as I ran my hands across him, relearning every curve and dimple. I caught a glimpse of the massive angel tattoo inked on his back, its wings outstretched seemingly to shelter its beloved, and I paused for a moment, suddenly hungry for a taste of William. I leaned in, a hair's breadth from his neck, feeling my teeth clench, my desire so great.

"Have a taste, Olivia," he murmured. "I intend to have mine."

We lived in the eye of the storm for a little while. When the tempest passed, William led me to his room. This time he removed my robe and studied me as I stood naked before him.

"I like your short hair. I can kiss your neck more easily," he said as he ran his fingers through my cropped locks. He issued small kisses at the base of my neck. But his advances were sharp, tinged with the edge of his fangs. I shuddered as he traced a path, pressing on until his hands met the skin on my arm where the tattoo sat. I froze for a moment, unable to get over my embarrassment.

"You're beautiful to me," William said. "Every scar, every mark, I accept as a part of you. I love you, Olivia, and that will never change."

His words were an igniter switch, setting our bodies aflame once more as we tumbled toward the bed and once again loved each other in a violent frenzy, all of our pent-up desire and regret coming to a head. This was lovemaking far wilder and more dangerous than we'd ever experienced. I was ravenous, consumed with a desire to mark every part of him with my mouth. William watched as I made my way down his chest, biting and sucking with enough enthusiasm to make him wince with delight. His reaction was obvious, and when I took him into my mouth, he closed his eyes and shuddered, lost in our passion. William reciprocated, his fingers testing inside me and then teasing until it became unbearable, then finally using his tongue to coax me into complete ecstasy. Then, for a moment, he stopped, lifting his eyes to mine.

"This is it, darlin'," he said, repeating a phrase he'd used at the beginning of our romance. "With this, everything else will be the past; this will be our future. Do you understand?"

I nodded and opened my arms, inviting him inside me, because I thought I did understand. But William had more than just the joining of our bodies in mind. Our reunion was intoxicating, and my arousal so intense that I didn't foresee him biting into my jugular until he was there. I froze as I felt him penetrate my neck, startled by the pain, the strange sensation. I realized in that moment what his words had meant. He was formally taking me as his mate. I'd consumed so much of his blood to survive previous injuries that once this was done, ours would be an unbreakable bond. The moment of conscious recognition passed quickly, reticence morphing into rapture. My climax was so consuming that my powers went haywire. A lamp fell off a nearby dresser and smashed on the floor. When we were done, William ran his tongue across the puncture wound in my neck, using his saliva to heal it.

As we sat in bed, both of us trying to recover, William leaned off to the side and plucked a small velvet bag from his nightstand. He poured the contents into his palm, opening his hand to reveal the set of copper betrothal rings he'd given me.

"Josef sent these to me when he packed up your things. He found them in a drawer," William said. He lifted my hand and slipped the rings back on my finger. "You may have noticed, out the windows, that there's a small chapel on the island in the lake. It sits atop one hundred steps—it's said that the groom who can carry his bride to the top will have a successful marriage. We can go there, tomorrow if you like. We'd have to stand outside, but—"

"No," I said abruptly, surprising myself. Confusion and despair washed over me. Isn't this what I'd fantasized about in my endless hours alone? Apparently, not. I'd been hurt too badly to dive into commitment with ease. The voice of caution had returned with a vengeance. "If you'd asked me before you mated us, I would have told you to wait."

"I don't understand," William said. "You didn't seem hesitant when we were making love. I thought . . ."

My stomach began to churn, and I sought to find the right words. "Making love to you is something my body *needed* after all these months," I said. "There were times when I thought I would go mad without you. At first, all I did was long for you. Then I got angry; then I grew numb from despair. I couldn't help but want to be with you tonight, William. *I love you.* But I need some time to sort things out, to start making decisions because *I want to*—not because of circumstances, or because someone forced my hand. Marrying you would confuse things."

"We're mated," William said, a bit of steel to his voice. "It's done."

"I'm not so sure," I said, remembering what I'd said to Nikola about drinking the blood of a witch. "I thought I would feel your pull more dramatically. Me being a witch may have weakened the bond."

"Olivia, I don't need control over your mind to claim you as my wife," William said. "I repeat. We're *mated*. I will not give you up."

"I'm not ready to trust you yet," I said, fighting back tears. "You deceived me. You let me leave for Belgrade believing you would follow."

"Josef was there. He took care of you, he . . ."

"Slept with me? Yes, we did, more than once." I didn't need to probe his mind to understand his thoughts; it was clear from his expression that he'd expected as much. "So, you *knew* it would happen. You practically set it up. You could have warned me."

"I can't prepare you for everything, Olivia," William said. "You want to be independent, but you don't like surprises."

"A surprise is learning I have the strength to cut a man's head off with a sword," I said. "Expecting my lover to arrive, when he's actually conspired with my father and made other plans, is something else."

"I have apologized," William said. "It's not in my nature to grovel."

"I'm not asking you to," I said.

"What do you want, then?"

"I want to go home and get my life back in order," I said. "I want to learn to live with you on my terms. Then we'll see. I need a break from my father as well. I'm tired of everyone else deciding the path my life takes."

"What about Josef?" William asked. "Will you be taking a hiatus from him as well?"

"Yes," I said. "The truth is, I love Josef, but our attraction comes out of strange circumstances. If you'd been by my side the whole time, would Josef and I have made love?"

"I wanted to be there. Believe me. I want to hear about everything that happened to you, every moment that I missed." He paused. "Will you tell me?"

"Yes," I said. "In my own time."

"So, what happens now?" William asked.

"We go home," I said. 'The rest we will figure out. I'm not sending you away, William. I'm asking you to give me some space."

I did love William, and my father, but my wounds were more than skin-deep. I'd lost faith in the people I held dear, and Josef was a distraction I didn't want or need at the moment.

William and I had two more weeks at the castle together. As the days passed, my physical injuries healed. I relished being with him, but I also yearned to go home. Home to my little house near Golden Gate Park, home to put some distance between us so I could sort out my thoughts and feelings in private. Returning to San Francisco would also make it possible for me to help plan the retrospective of my mother's paintings with Jason.

As I had suspected, the blood bond between William and I didn't work quite the way it would have between human and vampire. I could feel William's presence more keenly, but he held no special sway over my feelings or desires. He did his best to woo me with fantastic lovemaking, outrageous gifts, and gestures of devotion, but my jaded heart refused to yield.

Just as we were preparing to leave, I received word from my father that he'd called for a meeting of the General Assembly of the Council. Not since World War II, William said, had such a meeting been ordered, summoning senior staff and their deputies from around the globe. Being sucked into my father's bureaucracy was something I'd hoped to avoid—yet a part of me was curious to see how these powerful people would respond to the report of Nikola's death. Would anyone mourn his departure from this world?

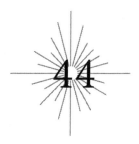

44

SPRING IN SAN FRANCISCO IS BRILLIANT. THE WEATHER is mild, and the flowering trees bloom madly. It was the perfect time of year to go home—and I tried to get outside as much as I could.

That's how, not long after my return, I found myself swinging my sword in slow, languid movements along with the rest of the tai chi enthusiasts in Golden Gate Park. The practice had become part of the routine I'd established now that I was back. I got up at dawn for a run, my sword slung over my back, and followed up with martial arts in the park and then home for whatever the day held in store. The park's cool air, spring blooms, and mossy tree limbs helped ground me each morning.

This day was no different, except that I found Josef sitting on my landing as I walked toward my doorstep.

"Hello," I said, suddenly feeling guilty that it had been a few weeks since we'd seen each other.

"You're training without me?" he asked, eying my sword.

"For now," I replied, leading us up the stairs and inside so I could make coffee. "I like practicing in the park. It's peaceful."

"That's a word that can't be used to describe me, I'm afraid," he said, offering me a rare smile.

I laughed. "No, but you've got other good qualities," I said.

"Like what?"

"You're loyal," I said, suddenly feeling serious. "And you saved my life, more than once."

"Then why are you avoiding me?"

"I'm not avoiding you," I said. "I'm focusing on me for a while. When you're around, I can't think."

"I know how you feel," Josef said, coming to stand near me. He picked up my hand and held it gently in his. "Do you regret what happened?"

"On some days, I regret all of it, the whole damn thing, especially the parts where I threw myself in Nikola's path," I said. "I nearly got us all killed. But my time with you? No. What we did was for each other, and it belongs to us." I walked over to my fridge to pull out a bottle of sparkling water. "But *we* don't belong together," I continued. "What we have is like an unstable element, ready to explode at any time."

Josef lifted my hand, kissed it, and let it go. "I do love your fighting spirit and your fierceness," he said. "But I'm not William. I can't offer you that kind of attention or devotion."

We were both lying of course, but it seems like the prudent thing to do. "So, we're friends?"

"Don't be ridiculous," Josef said. "We'll never be just friends, but our business is settled. Now on to William."

"What do you mean?"

"Are you going to forgive him?"

"Eventually," I said. "He lied to me and let me leave for Belgrade without saying a word. The three of you . . ." I broke off, still not sure what to say.

"Your father knew he was brewing up a disaster, but he believed there was no other choice," Josef said. "Would you have agreed to let William go if you'd been told?"

"I don't know. No one gave me a chance to decide," I said, earnestly. "I'm just trying to restore some order to my life. To be in control of things."

"What is it you're looking for that will convince you to forgive him?"

"I don't know," I said.

"And you expect William to wait while you have long lunches with your art dealer?"

Josef's remark hit close to home. A few days after I'd returned to the city, Jason had invited me out to discuss India's show. Lunch with him had been a pleasure, and we'd followed it up with other get-togethers. I'd started looking forward to our meetings at Café de la Presse, finding his warmth and humor a welcome diversion from the turmoil in my private life. Our mutual attraction was more than evident, and I had let it play out, feeling guilty but also curious if I could make a go with someone less complicated than William—or at least more *human*.

So far, we'd shared nothing more than a little bit of handholding and a few heated looks. Intelligent and more than attentive to my moods, Jason should have been the perfect companion. More than once, I'd contemplated leaving William for him. In the end, though, I'd confirmed what my heart had understood long ago: I was deeply in love with William and Josef; unable to trust one brother and afraid of my feelings for the other. I knew our fates were tied together, I just needed more time to figure it all out.

"Olivia!" Josef scolded. "Stop daydreaming and pay attention to me. You are playing with fire. When I walked into this room, I smelled the bond on you. William is the gentlest soul I know. He has given himself to you. Please don't torment him like this."

"Giving yourself is a matter of trust," I replied crisply. "It's about having no secrets, about putting yourself in another's hands. William has yet to do that, and until then, there can be no bond. Not the kind he wants. In any case, it was his bad luck to fall in love with someone half-witch. The blood bond doesn't work on me, not the way it's intended to."

Josef shook his head. "Just think about what I've said, Olivia," he said. "It seems to me William *has* put his future in your hands. I just hope you know what you're doing."

45

THE NIGHT BEFORE THE GENERAL ASSEMBLY MET, A terrible nightmare plagued my sleep. William woke me, and I emerged from the dream with a shout.

"Do you want to tell me about it?" he asked.

I nodded, trying to catch my breath. Damn Nikola and his long shadow. I had been back on the streetcar, drugged and unable to speak or move as something unknown closed in on me. Only in the dream, my muted state lasted for an eternity. Since we'd been home, William hadn't asked me about my experiences, for which I'd been grateful. Unburdening myself now, though, seemed like a good idea.

"It was a dream about the night I got my tattoo," I said. "I was restless, so I left the house alone, without Josef. I ran into Nadia in the main square and she read my cards, lectured me about how I should be careful. I complained about you being gone and she scolded me for not having faith. I should have gone home right then, but instead I began to sulk and hopped on one of the streetcars to brood. One of Nikola's men followed me on board and drugged me. I woke up a day later, with no memory and this on my arm. The dream was similar, only this time I couldn't see who was coming after me."

"How did you get home after they drugged you?" William asked.

I looked away, feeling ashamed. I'd been so focused on being angry with William, I'd hardly noticed how furious I was at myself.

"One of Nikola's henchmen left me on the doorstep and rang

the bell," I said. "Like I was the mail. Didn't Josef tell you any of this?"

"No," William said. "He told me they were your war stories, yours to tell."

"It was like war, as much as I know about things like that. It's not the word I would have chosen before," I said, exhaling a long, shuddering breath. "But now, when I think back, I can barely allow myself to acknowledge the details. I don't want to see those images again, or be reminded of the horrible things I did, to others or myself."

William pulled me close. "I would gladly erase every one of those ugly moments from your memories if I could," he said. "I'm not sure there was a way to spare you from a confrontation with Nikola. It was almost certain from the moment you met. Something in the stars, I suppose. Try to forgive yourself, Olivia. It's the only way any reluctant soldier survives."

"Reluctant? I don't know," I said. "I asked for this to happen. In fact, I insisted. It's my fault."

"The fault lies with us all," William said. "Not that it matters, but you had no idea what you were asking for."

"All the worse," I said, resting my head on his shoulder. "I feel like I should have known better."

"We all do, even me, and I've been at this for a while," he replied. "Go back to sleep, love, and try to dream of better times ahead."

I did manage to fall back asleep, and woke in time to dress and walk through the park to the de Young Museum for the meeting. The fog rolled in that morning and stayed for three days, allowing all of the Others on the General Assembly to come and go. My father had been working overtime to prepare the building, concocting extra enchantments and spells to expand the borders around our headquarters. Walking toward the museum's entrance, I realized that the fire alarm had been triggered: a loudspeaker implored all personnel to immediately exit the building. Another trick to keep humans from getting too close.

William was with me, the rest of our group set to meet us inside. When we exited the elevators, I smiled, in awe of what magic could accomplish. Just as my father had conjured new conference rooms out of thin air in the early days of my work with the Council, now the top floor of the museum had been converted into an enormous conference hall, hundreds of chairs neatly placed in rows leading up to a podium complete with more chairs and a microphone. Large royal-blue banners featuring an image of the Guardian, the mythical panther dueling the serpent from the fountain sculpture that stood below in the Music Concourse, hung on the few solid walls of the room. I spotted my father looking serious in conversation with an aide. Elsa and Lily were standing by the windows, looking out toward the rough-and-tumble waves of the Pacific Ocean.

"Is Josef coming?" I asked when I reached them.

"I don't think so," Elsa replied. "He said he would be at the dinner tomorrow at your mom's house in Bolinas."

I would have liked to discuss the dinner and our plans to place a marker in the meadow to honor her memory, but my father arrived at my elbow, gently signaling that he wanted to speak with me. As usual, the first few seconds between us were awkward. I could read his thoughts and he mine, but like all families, we didn't want to discuss any of it.

"Olivia, I'd like it if you'd sit on the dais with me, please," he said. "I have some important announcements, and I'd like you by my side."

"Of course," I said. Whatever our differences, this was not the time or place to display our family's dirty laundry. If there was one lesson I'd learned since joining the world of the Others, it was to keep my emotional turmoil private—not to let it spill over and control my behavior. Looking back, I could see that feeling out of control had always been my greatest fear. I worried my skills would own me instead of the other way around. That's what my mother's life had been like.

Gabriel's aide caught my attention, signaling that it was time for us to take our places. I stepped up onto the dais by my father's side and looked over the crowd, relieved to see William, Lily, and Elsa take seats in the row directly in front of us. As I took my seat on stage next to my father and several other leaders, including Madeline, I suddenly felt self-conscious, separated from the rest of my pack.

There were opening speeches, tributes to those who had traveled great distances to attend, and then my father got down to the business of trying to discredit Nikola, describing his criminal activities and using the invoice we'd stolen as one piece of evidence, along with many of the reports from Diana Chambers.

"I submit," my father said, "that this invoice and the accompanying reports demonstrate a clear tie between Nikola and individuals engaged in criminal activities that have not only been sanctioned by elected officials, but perhaps even initiated by them and made possible by magical intervention. Obviously, this kind of behavior is antithetical to the mission of the Council. If Nikola were here, he would no doubt raise a spirited defense, but he's not. He's dead. His death is directly related to the kidnapping of my daughter, Olivia."

A gasp whispered through the audience when Gabriel acknowledged me in front of two hundred people.

"Realizing that Olivia and her investigators were about to incriminate him, he arranged for her abduction and murder," he continued. "She and her team were forced to kill him to survive."

The room erupted into a series of side conversation and rumblings.

"If I could have your attention," Gabriel shouted, breaking through the din to continue. "Please, I would like to conclude my remarks.

"The responsibility for all of this rests solely with me," he said. "The world is changing, and so are our members. The drive we once shared for a common good is diminishing; we are succumbing to the same cynicism that plagues our human counterparts. If we do not redouble our efforts to be true to our mission, then the fate of humanity is in jeopardy. I believed I could manage this myself. I thought that it was something that could be fixed internally. But I was wrong, terribly wrong. So today I announce a proposal to create a new department, to be called the Division for Council Internal Security. This new entity will be responsible for monitoring the activities of our members and routing out any criminal behavior or corruption. We can ill afford to have the police brought to our doorstep."

Gabriel gave himself a brief pause before he dropped the bombshell.

"I'd like to nominate my daughter to be the inaugural director of the DCIS," he said. "Her skills and background are ideal to lead this new enterprise."

Surprise glued me to my seat at the same instant I realized I was supposed to get up and say something, but what? As usual, my father, in all of his grandiosity, hadn't consulted with me before offering up the job. But I knew that to refuse him in public would be disastrous, so I stood up and put on my game face.

"Thank you," I said, from the podium.

All eyes were on me now: the daughter, the reluctant half-witch who had somehow bested a thousand-year-old vampire. I could sense the skepticism in the room, the curiosity emanating from the audience, as I contemplated what to say. And then it came to me.

"When Nikola was preparing to kill me, he told me that the time of humans was over," I said. "That they had squandered their natural resources and run their countries ragged. Better, he said, to profit on their misery than to waste energy trying to save a group of people who don't appreciate it."

I watched a few heads in the audience nod in agreement and realized that Nikola still had his supporters.

"I don't share that viewpoint—maybe because until recently, I thought I *was* human," I said, eliciting some quiet snickers from the back of the room. "I lived the first half of my life in ignorance of my own abilities and of this world we now share. Perhaps that's why I see so clearly the great need for the Council's work. The world is not getting better. It's getting worse. Post-pandemic, our world is more unstable than it's ever been. Draught, serious weather events, inflation, and dramatic changes in work—not to mention the emergence of artificial intelligence—have all contributed to greater uncertainty, hostility, and deep political divisions around the globe. These conditions breed more intolerance, not less, and they create ever more opportunities for extremists to hold office. Only this group can help stop that. I for one am glad to be a part of the Council, to promote stability and peace. I hope you will support my father's vision and stay the course. Thank you."

The rest of the afternoon was a blur. A lot of hand shaking and questions about how I survived the battle with Nikola. There is no polite way to discuss a beheading, so I tried to describe things in general terms, but I sensed that many understood what happened that night in Belgrade. No one mentioned the prophecies or my bloodline, and for that I was relieved. When it was all over, I looked up to find William in the corner with Gabriel, the two of them deep in conversation. I pulled out my phone to check my messages and noticed that Diana Chambers had called several times. I listened to her voicemail.

"Olivia, I understand you're back in the country," she said. "I'm calling to collect my favor. I'd like you to come to Washington to meet with me. I'm pulling together an advance team for my presidential campaign and I need someone with your skills. Call me."

What were the odds? For the second time in one day, I'd been offered a job I hadn't been expecting. I slipped my phone back in my pocket and headed toward my father and William. I was going to have to make some choices shortly, and I knew either way, someone was going to be disappointed.

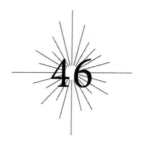

46

THE WORDS WERE SIMPLE: INDIA ROSE SHEPHERD, MOTHER, ARTIST. But they said a lot. The marker, a tall gray marble post, was placed near the edge of her property where it shared a view of the sea and the horizon that she had always held dear. It was near dusk when we gathered at the spot to watch the post being placed into the ground. After the workers departed, my father read "A Clear Midnight," by Walt Whitman.

> This is thy hour O Soul, thy free flight into the wordless,
> Away from books, away from art, the day erased, the lesson
>   done,
> Thee fully forth emerging, silent, gazing, pondering the themes
>   thou lovest best,
> Night, sleep, death, and the stars.

After our brief memorial, we walked back to the house, which temporarily belonged to Elsa and Lily. I wasn't ready to live there, so far from the city and from William's house near Dolores Park. My father had long since vacated, returning to the city himself. As Lily had predicted, his departure sent a few of the more aggressive magical creatures that had been lurking on my mother's property back to points unknown. But Elsa loved the enchanted nature of the land,

and Lily, still on sabbatical, had converted my mother's studio into a
darkroom, taking up photography as a full-time hobby. India's home
was full of life again, and that, I thought, was as fitting a tribute as
anyone could conjure up.

Her exhibit had also been a huge success, the art critic for the
San Francisco Chronicle calling my mother's paintings "as close to
witchcraft as you can get" for their "seemingly supernatural ability
to capture the energy of the land." She would have been happy to
read the review and know that her spring retrospective had been
well-attended. True to his promise, Jason had honored my mother
and ensured that India Rose Shepherd's talent would not be forgotten, at least not for a while. I donated the proceeds from the first
sale of a painting to the Belgrade Zoo—anonymously of course—to
help repair some of the damage.

Later that evening, Gabriel fixed a meal reminiscent of the
dinners he'd made when we first reunited after my mother's death.
There was beef stew and fresh bread, followed by a lovely butter
lettuce salad with a mustard dressing. Wine flowed, and the vampires
joined us at the table while we ate. We fell into our usual routine of
good conversation fueled by strong wit and plentiful alcohol. But I
felt a growing sense of anxiety as we finished the meal. I'd made a pact
with myself that I'd share my news—my decision—before dinner was
over.

After the plates were pushed aside and espresso and whiskey
passed about, I seized on a lull in the conversation and finally spoke
up. "I have something to tell you," I blurted out. "An announcement."

The room went quiet, all eyes on me.

"Diana Chambers is running for president," I said. "She's offered
me a job on her advance team. I'm flying to Washington next week."

Gabriel scowled. "What about your position here? How will you
do both jobs?"

"I won't," I said. "I'd like a year's leave of absence from the Council.

You could appoint Madeline to take my place in the interim. When I return, I'll run operations as you've requested."

"Are you punishing me for Serbia?" Gabriel asked. "Is that why you're leaving?"

"This isn't about you. It's about *me*," I said, taking his hand. "I want to do this. It's the opportunity of a lifetime."

"Congratulations," Elsa said. "You know you'll be facing Stoner Halbert again."

"I know," I said. "It's one of the reasons Diana asked me to join her team. It's odd, but it also feels right, like I'm closing the circle."

"And the rest of us?" William asked brusquely. "Are we coming with you?"

I glanced over at Josef, his eyes focused on William, a concerned look on his face. I knew he was worried I would break his brother's heart to mend mine, but I wasn't seeking revenge. On the contrary, I was hoping to find some peace, some sense of myself so that I could live my life with confidence, certain that my motivations were my own and not engineered by others. Mustering my courage, I faced William directly, knowing he deserved my full attention.

"No," I said. "This first trip, I'll be going alone."

THE END

Turn the page for a sneak preview of *The Campaign*, book three in The Council Trilogy.

THE CAMPAIGN

Chapter I

THE MAN HOLDING THE SIGN WITH MY NAME ON IT inside the arrival lounge at the Friedman Memorial Airport offered little more than a slight nod when I acknowledged him. Silent as the grave, he packed me into an enormous Suburban, its windows tinted the color of midnight, and set off toward the highway. I'd been cooling my heels at an airport bar in Chicago—halfway to Washington, DC, from San Francisco—when a page over the O'Hare public address system directed me to the customer service desk. My ticket had been rerouted to Sun Valley, Idaho. I almost missed the flight. I ran away from home to see a lady about a job and was brooding about the mess I'd left behind. Thanks to a champagne haze, it had taken a few seconds to recognize my name blasting from the airport's speakers.

I shook off a chill as I settled into the backseat of the SUV. According to the captain of my flight, who apologized profusely for the turbulence that rattled our two-engine plane as we threaded our way through the narrow mountain gap that led to the runway, it was the coldest and wettest spring on record in the Mountain West. Through a persistent downpour, the blurred welcome signs for the cities of Hailey and Ketchum whirred past. According to Google, we were headed north toward the Galena Pass.

Forty minutes later, our car pulled up in front of a handsome log cabin-style lodge. I couldn't help but notice the emerald green lake with its swimming beach and boat dock as well as the enormous mountain peaks jutting into the sky in the distance. I stepped onto a thin layer of frost covering the lawn as I exited the car, the frigid air causing my eyes to water. The driver walked ahead of me carrying my duffel bag. I followed him through the doorway, scanning the room to understand my surroundings better. My host sat at a table inside the lodge's dining room, a mug of something warm and steaming in her hands. Her aura was as bright and shiny as it had been the first time we met a few months earlier.

We were both guests at a cocktail party. I was attending as a newly hired campaign monitor for elections in Serbia. Diana Chambers was attending as Secretary of State for the United States. She provided me with crucial documents I needed to help prove that a member of an organization I'm a part of was secretly running a criminal empire. She warned me at the time that her assistance would come with a request for a favor, and now, here I was, on her doorstep.

"Sorry for all the cloak-and-dagger stuff," Diana said. "I thought we could speak more freely here."

"Where's here, exactly?" I asked, still standing with my duffel bag at my side.

"Redfish Lake, Stanley, Idaho," she said. "My uncle owns a ranch a few miles up the road. I spent most of my summers here at Redfish. The owner is a friend. The lodge typically opens on Memorial Day, but it's been delayed because of unseasonably cold weather."

"Why here?" I asked.

"Because, as you know, in addition to being Secretary of State, I'm also a candidate for president. The press is camped outside my office and my home," she said. "Being seen with a political consultant from San Francisco would start tongues wagging about my campaign drifting too far to the left before I've gotten things off the ground."

"Makes sense," I said. "Is that coffee in your hands? Could I have some too?"

Diana's eyes narrowed. "I was warned you were hard to read," she said. "Aren't you angry I changed your itinerary midflight?"

This was a test. Presidential campaigns don't run in straight lines. No one knows where they'll wind up at the end of the day, especially working for a hard-driving candidate used to having her way.

"I was in an airport," I said. "I had to end up somewhere. If you want to see me angry, lie to me during a campaign; then you'll see my temper."

"So, you'll work for me?" Diana asked. "I'll be announcing in a matter of days."

"I haven't decided yet," I said, lying. I'd as much as told my family I was joining her campaign and crossed the country, leaving behind an unhappy father and a furious pair of vampires, one of them my mate. "Why do you want me, anyway? You can have your pick of consultants with much higher profiles than mine."

A Secret Service agent appeared from the kitchen carrying my coffee and set the mug on the table. I walked over, set down my bag and took the chair across from Diana. I wrapped both hands around the warm mug, trying to shake the chill that had settled into my bones. I hoped it was the weather and not something more serious. My empathy skills allowed me to pick up on other people's emotions, but I also had a strong sixth sense for trouble.

"What you say is true, but you have important skills I need," Diana said. "That, and Levi Barnes trusts you. He may be my number two in this race. If that happens, he'll need you by his side."

"Number two? I just got him elected to Congress. That's a bold move, even for someone like you."

"The old rules of campaigns have been shattered. Our last president proved that in spades. Besides, this isn't Levi's first rodeo," Diana said. "He has far more policy experience than many of the senators eyeing the spot. And thanks to his video mishap during his last campaign, he's had a taste of the brutal nature of this volatile digital frontier of ours. Of course, I don't have to tell you that this is all confidential. It's too soon to announce potential running mates."

I snorted into my coffee. "As the frontrunner, you're under a microscope. It won't take long for the press to connect the dots and begin to speculate," I said.

"Let them talk," she said. "To be honest, there are moments when I'm not one hundred percent certain I want the party's nomination. I've traveled around the world and been forced to negotiate with dictators and tyrants, and it's nothing compared to the public circus that comes with running for president."

"It's not for the faint of heart," I said.

"Yes, but what's really got me concerned is your friend Stoner Halbert," Diana said. "The Foxx brothers have hired him as their advisor for this presidential election cycle. He's also a party consultant. As you know, he's considered a lightning rod, willing to say or do anything to win a vote. The primary debates haven't happened yet, and a few of their more moderate candidates have already dropped out. Not only is he without scruples, but the gossip is that Stoner can wilt flowers with his gaze; that he's a real monster with a fierce temper and a taste for revenge."

I tried to keep my facial expression neutral as Diana mentioned the name of a man who had nearly killed me. It wasn't an exaggeration to say that he was one of the main reasons I was sitting in this mountain lodge, having this conversation. If he hadn't gone rogue, turned to black magic, and arranged for a demon to attack me back in San Francisco, I would never have met Elsa, my best friend, as well as a time-walker and spirit guide. Thanks to Elsa, I learned I was the daughter of a powerful witch and became a member of the Council, a secret organization of supernatural beings that dabble in elections and other current affairs to help keep the world's democracies stable. My father, Gabriel Laurent, is the leader of the Council. He's also a powerful witch. I didn't know who my father was for most of my life.

I learned all of this while running a congressional campaign in Silicon Valley. Stoner ran the campaign for the opposing candidate and tried to undermine me at every turn. He secretly filmed my client and posted the video out of context. He also attempted to have an unscrupulous reporter seduce me and blackmail me into dropping out. We battled the negative press, and eventually, I managed to beat Stoner at his own game. My candidate, Levi Barnes, won the race— the same Levi Diana has her eye on for vice president.

I didn't know Diana well enough to know if she exaggerated, but her assessment was spot on in this case. Taking on Stoner meant battling forces far more treacherous than trolls on social media. Diana was right to be concerned, but I worried she didn't fully understand what she was signing up for.

"Stoner is no friend of mine, but I do know him well," I said. "Before we discuss him, tell me what you meant by my 'skills.'" I knew Diana possessed some knowledge of my background. When we'd first met at the diplomatic party in Slovenia, it was clear that she knew about the Council. But what did she know about my world, about my skills as an empath and a witch?

"I know about the Council," she said. "Madeline told me you're a witch."

I wanted to tell her I was a brand-new witch, still learning to use my powers, but instead, I nodded for her to continue.

"I want to become the first female president of the United States," she said, looking around to make sure the dining room was empty. "I'm going to need all the help I can get to make that happen. There are forces at work in this world that I don't fully understand, Olivia, but I want access to them and protection. If I see this campaign through to the end, it will force me to face down demons: my own and others."

"You don't know the half of it," I said, a bit sharper than I intended. "After Madeline Klein introduced us that evening in Ljubljana, I nearly died. The forces you're referring to can be deadly, fight dirty, and have weapons at their disposal you can't begin to imagine."

Diana sat silently, her eyes refusing to reveal her thoughts. I could feel her anxiety; she was trying to decide if she could trust me —a concern that was too late in the process as far as I was concerned since she'd already flown me out to her doorstep.

I leaned in, my patience for her stalling nearing an end. "I'll ask again. What do you know about the Council and me?"

"Meet me at the boat dock in twenty minutes, and I'll tell you," she said, and abruptly left the room.

ABOUT THE AUTHOR

Photo credit: John Cameron Photography

EVETTE DAVIS is the author of *The Others* and *The Gift*, the first two installments of The Council Trilogy, published by Spark Press. The third and final book in the trilogy, *The Campaign*, will be released in September 2025.

She is also the author of *48 States*, which Kirkus named one of the Best Indie Books of 2022. The book was also a quarter-finalist for the BookLife Prize 2023 and longlisted in the 2023 Indie Book Awards.

Davis is a member of the board of directors for Litquake, San Francisco's annual literary festival. She's been twice honored by the Friends of the San Francisco Public Library as a Library Laureate. Her work has also been published in the *San Francisco Chronicle*. When she's not writing novels, Davis advises some of the country's largest corporations, non-profits, and institutions as a consultant and co-owner of BergDavis Public Affairs, an award-winning San Francisco-based consulting firm. Davis splits her time between San Francisco and Sun Valley, Idaho.

Visit www.evettedavis.com for more information or to sign up for her newsletter.

Looking for your next great read?

We can help!

Visit www.gosparkpress.com/next-read or
scan the QR code below for a list
of our recommended titles.

SparkPress is an independent boutique publisher
delivering high-quality, entertaining, and engaging
content that enhances readers' lives, with a special
focus on commercial and genre fiction.